BY JAY CROWNOVER

The Loveless, Texas Series
Justified
Unforgiven
Blacklisted

Blacklisted

JAY CROWNOVER

HEADLINE
ETERNAL

The right of Jay Crownover to be identified as the Author of
the Work has been asserted by her in accordance with the
Copyright, Designs and Patents Act 1988.

Published by arrangement with Forever,
An imprint of Grand Central Publishing.

First published in Great Britain in 2020
by HEADLINE ETERNAL
An imprint of HEADLINE PUBLISHING GROUP

1

Cataloguing in Publication Data is available from the British Library

ISBN 978 1 4722 5429 0

Printed and bound in Great Britain by Clays Ltd, Elcograf S.p.A.

Headline's policy is to use papers that are natural, renewable and recyclable
products and made from wood grown in well-managed forests and other
controlled sources. The logging and manufacturing processes are expected
to conform to the environmental regulations of the country of origin.

HEADLINE PUBLISHING GROUP
An Hachette UK Company
Carmelite House
50 Victoria Embankment
London EC4Y 0DZ

www.headlineeternal.com
www.headline.co.uk
www.hachette.co.uk

Blacklisted

Dedicated to everyone who has learned the hard lesson that it is so much better for your soul to stand out than to fit in. Be noisy. Be loud. Be unapologetic. Be annoying. Be smarter than everyone else. Be kind. But most important, be yourself.

PROLOGUE

∞

My life used to be boring, predictable. I had a job I worked hard to succeed at, an ill mother who I devoted all my free time to taking care of, and one single friend I trusted and relied on. My days tended to bleed together, all of them seemingly the same, and I liked it that way. I liked knowing what to expect. I thrived with a set routine and did not field surprises and unexpected occurrences well. Part of that was because my mother had been sick for so long, and when things stayed the same, it meant she was still with me. Any upset in our day-to-day meant I ran the risk of losing her, and since she was the only family I had, I never adjusted well to even the smallest of inconsistencies in my schedule.

Unfortunately, those boring, dull, and predictable days were long gone. The job I loved and had worked my butt off to advance in was in limbo. My mother was no longer with me. And not only had I lost my only family, but her passing had set off a domino effect of life-changing and suspicious scenarios in my life. On top of losing both my professional reputation and my mother, I'd come to realize my one and only friend, the woman I'd relied on since we were in med school together, the woman who held me, and held me together, when I broke down after finding out my mother had passed, was the person behind my sudden issues at work … and though it wasn't confirmed, and there was no physical proof, I firmly believed she was directly involved with my mother's death.

I'd suffered a horrible loss and faced the ultimate betrayal all at the same time.

After all of my former friend's malicious acts came to light, the Texas Rangers put me in protective custody. She'd threatened to kill me and warned that she planned to take away everything and everyone that mattered to me. Since she had proved to be just unhinged and unpredictable enough to follow through on the threats, I complied with orders from law enforcement and stayed out of sight.

However, I soon realized the only way to ensure the people around me stayed safe was if Ashby Grant, my former friend and current tormentor, could see that I was suffering from the havoc she rained down on my life. She needed to know her efforts weren't in vain.

The first step was to get myself out of protective custody so I could remain her prime target. After that, I retreated into myself, locking the front door to my apartment and shutting out the rest of the world. I was lonely and missing my mother, feeling like my life was a mess. However, I knew I didn't want to die, and more than that, I really didn't want anyone else to die because of me and the choices I made. I couldn't stand the thought of seeing any of the Lawtons, who had suddenly invaded my life at the same time it fell apart, injured or worse, just because we all had the unfortunate luck of having the same father.

If it hadn't been for my newly found half siblings forcibly inserting themselves into my life, I would have effectively disappeared, hiding while I waited anxiously for whatever fate Ashby had planned for the two of us to befall me. They threw an absolute fit when I declared I no longer wanted police protection or a full-fledged security detail. The Lawtons—and more specifically my younger half sister, Kody Lawton—refused to let me sink into my grief and overwhelming anxiety that something would happen to her and her two older brothers because of me. No matter how hard I tried to push her away, she kept dragging me back into the land of the living. She forced me to interact with my new family and stubbornly made me stand face-to-face with all my paralyzing fears.

When she called me in the middle of the night not long after I ditched my protective detail, screaming that she needed my help, my first instinct was to tell her no. I didn't want to leave my house during daylight hours on a good day—no way was I driving out to her dive bar on the outskirts of town while I was both alone and afraid in the dark. Her disappointment was palpable over the phone, and I immediately felt the sting of letting her down under my skin, even though I told myself over and over again I didn't owe her anything. She was the one trying to force a relationship even after I made it clear I wanted to be left alone. The argument sounded petty and weak as my mind went to battle with my conflicted heart.

No matter how hard I tried, I couldn't shake loose the panic in Kody's words. She might be the toughest of the three Lawton siblings, so if she sounded scared, something was really, really wrong. It took five minutes for me to change my mind. It took ten minutes for me to get my on-hand medical gear together and another five to convince my feet to take me out of the front door. I almost turned around twenty times on the way to her bar, but the nagging voice in the back of my head wouldn't let me run away. When push came to shove, I couldn't ignore that I really did owe the Lawtons a lot, regardless of trying to convince myself otherwise. And I knew that given enough time I could grow to love them like they were my own. For someone who'd never had anyone, being part of such a tight-knit, loyal family was too appealing to turn away from.

Kody's big, bearded bouncer was waiting for me outside and whisked me safely into the chaotic scene inside the bar. It was well past business hours, but the bar was packed. I tried to appear outwardly calm as I took in the battered and bloody bikers all hovering over a single, downed body on the floor. Kody caught sight of me and rushed over to where I was standing. She went to reach for me, but hurriedly pulled back when she noticed her hands and the front of her clothes were soaked through with blood. Eyes, the exact same green as mine, widened, and I could see the stark panic clear on every line of her pretty, freckled face.

Before she could thank me for coming or launch into an explanation of how she came to have the entirety of the Sons of Sorrow motorcycle club bleeding in her bar after hours, my medical training kicked in and I found myself pushing past her to tend to the injured man on the floor.

I'd seen many a bullet wound in my time working at the medical examiner's office, but I'd never seen one, well more than one at the moment, that was fresh and still seeping blood. I had a moment of indecision, wondering if I could actually help this man. I had purposely picked a medical field where I didn't have to deal with living and breathing patients. The risk was too high, and the responsibility for their well-being felt suffocating. All of that pressure I had purposely avoided now pushed down on me. I felt all eyes in the room look toward me as I started to assess the damage to the dark-haired man on the floor.

He was losing too much blood. I immediately knew he was going to need a transfusion. He wasn't stable enough to stay where he was, but when I told Kody to call an ambulance I was instantly, and loudly, overruled by the rest of the bikers. The wounded man was the club's president, and they insisted I just needed to keep his vitals strong enough to be moved somewhere else safely. They didn't go into detail, but apparently they had facilities and someone who could take care of him. For whatever reason, they didn't want the bullet wounds reported as would be mandatory if he went to the ER, thus getting the police involved in their business. None of it sounded on the up-and-up, but I had my hands full keeping the man from bleeding out, so I decided not to waste precious time arguing with them.

One biker showed up out of nowhere with a medical-grade bag of donated blood for an on-the-spot transfusion, and again I decided not to ask too many questions. The big, bleeding man also had a collapsed lung and his chest cavity was filling with air, making a dangerous situation even more complicated. It had been years since I'd inserted a chest tube, so there was no stopping the shaking of my hands or the nervous sweating. Kody was right next to me, offering silent encouragement, but I could tell how worried she was.

In all honesty, I was shocked by how well the biker was holding up. If it had been anyone else, I wasn't certain they would've survived this long. After the chest tube was in place, and I had successfully pulled most of the air out of his chest cavity, the man's breathing settled into a still shallow but more even rhythm. Once I had the blood transfusion hooked up in the most rustic manner possible, I declared him safe enough to move. The rest of the bikers immediately jumped into action, setting a plan in place to move their president back to their clubhouse up in the hill country.

Before I could be dismissed and ignored, I told the entire room, "I'm going with him."

I had no idea where the words came from, or where I got the guts to make such a declaration to the room at large, but I knew I couldn't send the man off without medical supervision. I was scared something would happen to him, and I was worried the rest of the bikers would blame me if he didn't make it.

Kody immediately protested. It was clear she didn't want me involved any further. Saving an injured man's life was one thing; knowingly helping that same man evade proper medical and legal channels was another. Even though I was on a hiatus from work, my job was still closely tied to law enforcement, and getting tangled up with an outlaw motor-cycle club was the last thing I needed. But I couldn't turn my back on the scarily still man. Even deathly pale and covered head to toe in blood, I could tell he was someone with a powerful presence. And even though he was uncon-scious, his aura remained intimidating and fierce. He was also incredibly good-looking beneath the gore, something I shouldn't have been noticing considering his current state and the fact that he was the exact opposite of the type who usually caught my eye.

My love life tended to be as staid and dreary as the rest of my life. The men I dated were bland and boring. I'd never had my head turned by tattoos and brawn, which the biker had plenty of. There was nothing about him I should have found intriguing or interesting, but I was unable to deny that I was curious about what he looked like when he wasn't on the brink of death. I also wondered what his voice sounded like, and what color his eyes were. All wayward thoughts that came out of nowhere and took me completely by surprise. I rationalized it as my mind's way of keeping me calm in a crisis. Cataloguing all his attractive points definitely worked as a good distraction.

It took some convincing to get both my half sister and the rest of the club members to let me ride with their injured president. Apparently, outsiders weren't let onto club property...for any reason.

Today they were willing to make an exception for me, but they made it clear things would not end well if I spoke about *any* of the things I witnessed once I was allowed through the gates.

"Are you sure you know what you're doing, Presley?" Kody's tone was full of worry and concern. She looked like she was ready to sit on me to keep me from going with my still-critical patient. I appreciated her apprehension. It'd been a long time since I'd had anyone in my life who actively and visibly cared about me. But I was independent by nature, and having come this far, there was no turning back now. I was determined to keep the biker alive come hell or high water.

"No. I have no clue what I'm doing, but I'm doing it anyway." I decided to embrace the chaos that had overtaken my life lately instead of hiding from it. "Too many things can go wrong between here and there. As soon as I know for certain he's made it back to their compound, I'll breathe easier and head home."

Kody shook her wild tangle of dirty blond curls and gripped my arm hard enough to bruise. "They're all decent guys but they're still an outlaw club. If you want to go back to work anytime in the near future, you can't afford to have your name mixed up with this club—with Shot in particular."

Shot.

It was a fitting name for a biker, and for someone who has just been shot and who was already sporting more than one scar from a bullet.

I shook off my concerned sibling and took a deep breath. It wasn't my fault things with my job were so uncertain. They'd offered me a promotion, which had set in motion my former best friend's break with both sanity and reality. Jealousy over my advancement had pushed her over the edge. After all her evil and illegal misdeeds came to light, the ME's office had apologized for doubting me and assured me the promotion they initially offered was waiting for me. Only I wasn't ready to go back.

After these last few months, I'd had enough of death and destruction to last a lifetime. Which might have been why I was determined to make sure the biker pulled through, regardless of what side of the law he fell on.

After assuring Kody I would be fine and telling her I would call her as soon as I was on my way back home, I let the bikers sweep me out of the bar and into the back of a plain white van with blacked-out windows. I knelt on the floor of the large vehicle, next to the still unconscious biker. Without understanding why, I reached for one of his hands, immediately noticing how rough it was beneath the slippery coating of blood. I also took note of the skull face tattooed across the entire back of it. He was alarmingly cold to the touch, which made me frown and press my hand to his forehead. It wasn't exactly a professionally medical move, but one I was compelled to do as a human hurting for another human.

"He'll pull through."

The rough words were barked by a huge man in a leather vest with patches all over it. He had one that read VICE PRESIDENT on one side, and TOP HAT on the other. He was issuing most of the orders, so I assumed that meant he was in charge while the president was incapacitated.

"He's going to need surgery." I had no idea what kind of damage the bullet had done internally, but he was still bleeding and his breathing still gave me cause for concern.

The second-in-command nodded and dragged a hand over his tired-looking face. "I told you, we have a guy who will take care of it. The prez was in such bad shape we panicked and brought him to Kody's, figuring we'd call him out. But she told us you were closer, and we weren't going to take any chances with Shot's life on the line."

"Top Hat," I tried out the unusual name and cringed when I received a lifted eyebrow and a smirk in return. Regardless, I plowed on with my warning. "He needs to be in an actual medical facility. If you try and do any kind of major surgery in an unsanitary environment, the chances of him getting an infection and dying are higher than him dying from the wound itself." I knew I sounded cool and clinical, but I couldn't help it. I was nervous. Nervous to be heading off into the unknown with a bunch of strangers, with men who very well could be involved in some serious criminal activity. Nervous that my patient would die and I would be blamed. Nervous I would let Kody down and the tentative bond I was building with my new family would be broken.

"I go by Top, Doc." Soft snickers went around the van and I got the distinct impression I was being laughed at. The man who called himself Top gave me a look. I could tell he was tense and worried for his friend, and he wasn't thrilled to have me along for this ride. "Our clubhouse is an old ranch that used to be owned by a vet. The barn is outfitted as a big animal hospital, complete with an operating room. It doesn't see much use for livestock, but we've benefited from having access to it more than once over the years."

He swore and rubbed his eyes. He still had his president's blood smeared on the back of his hands but didn't seem to notice. "If we get Shot to the property, the chances we can save him are pretty high."

I cleared my throat and went to pull my hand away from the injured man's head. I had a lot of questions and a million concerns but decided it was best to keep my mouth shut. I didn't know how to deal with bikers, or really anyone who had need of their own operating room on the regular. I was so far out of my comfort zone, it was going to take a miracle and a detailed map to get me back to where I belonged.

I gasped when fingers suddenly wrapped around my wrist in a weak grasp. My gaze locked on eyes such a deep, dark, and rich brown they appeared black.

"Kody?" The word was rasped out and barely audible. It was a whisper of sound, but filled with emotion.

Before I could explain that I wasn't my half sister, that we just happened to look very much alike, the dark eyes drifted closed and the hold on my hand dropped away.

It was impressive, and a fairly good sign that he'd gained consciousness, even for a second. I could practically feel the relief that flooded through the crowded interior of the van.

Suddenly my hand was grabbed again, this time by the man sitting across from me. He had bright blue eyes, and they were intent and serious as the VP told me, "Whether he makes it or not we owe you. Anytime, anywhere, no matter how big or small, the club owes you a favor. Your call when and how you want us to make good on it, but it's there until you use it."

I frowned and tugged my hand free. "I can't imagine why I'd have anything to do with your club after tonight." My life might not be streamlined and predictable any longer, but I doubted I would ever have the need to be involved with the outlaw club beyond this instance.

The big man snorted but gave me the space I was silently asking for. "Doesn't matter if you have anything to do with us in the future. We owe you, and the Sons of Sorrow always pay their debts."

It sounded more like a threat than a promise, and I had no idea what to do with any of it. So I simply held my breath and reached for the unmoving biker's hand. I knew deep down that this would be the one and only time I was going to be wrapped up in the club's mess, so I planned on seeing it through to the end, no matter what the results were.

I had no idea that fate had other plans for me…and for Shot.

CHAPTER 1

∞

SHOT

Three months later…

I didn't like to be indebted to anyone.

I prided myself on never owing anyone anything. I'd been that way my entire life. My father, one of the founding members of the motorcycle club I was a part of, had taught me early on that it was better to be the one collecting favors rather than being the one doling them out. Better to have others to do your bidding, rather than dangle at the end of someone else's whims.

When I'd left Colorado, and my father's less than legal influence, first to fight for my country, then to start my own chapter of the club I'd grown up in, I'd gone with the promise I would never put myself or any member of the Sons of Sorrow in a position where they owed anyone anything. We weren't going to let anyone pull our strings, my father included. It was a promise I'd managed to keep, up until a few months ago.

I had enemies. A lot of them. Some I'd acquired through business with the club. A few lingered from my time in the military. My day-to-day was never anything close to a walk in the park, but my reputation, along with the club's fierce legacy, generally kept me safe and fairly insulated. Apparently the last few, mostly uneventful, years I'd spent in Loveless, Texas, had lulled me into dropping my guard. I never expected the ambush attack, and my lack of preparedness toward the threat resulted in the loss of two of my brothers, and had left me taking a couple of bullets to the chest. I should have been dead. Very nearly was. If it hadn't been for my quick-thinking vice president and Kody Lawton's relentless friendship, I would be six feet under.

But the real reason I was still alive and kicking, the only reason I survived, was because Kody's half sister, Dr. Presley Baskin, jumped into the fray and stayed by my side until I was out of the woods. I was unconscious for most of the ordeal, but I vaguely remembered concerned green eyes watching me, and incredibly soft hands valiantly trying to keep my heart beating.

The club had a member who was a former field medic. Stitch was a solid doctor, but my injuries had been bad enough he was uncertain if he was going to be able to save me once he got me into our rough but effective operating room. According to Top and a few of the other members, Kody's newfound half sister refused to leave, even though it would have been in her best interest. She scrubbed in and assisted Stitch until everyone was mostly certain I would pull through. She'd broken any number of laws in the process and now the club, and I, owed her more than we would ever be able to repay.

I hated it.

The feeling of being in debt to her, the anticipation of waiting for her to call in her favor, grated on my nerves and made me twitchy and uncomfortable every single day. I wanted the slate cleaned...now. I was going out of my mind waiting for the other shoe to drop.

Considering I literally owed the woman my life, I'd done what any reasonable person would do and had dug up every single thing I could find on her. There wasn't a ton of information on the medical examiner, and what I did find was pretty basic and tedious, right up until her path crossed with the Lawtons. The Lawton family was infamous around this small town in central Texas. The patriarch had left a legacy of corruption and crime, all while wearing a badge and pretending to serve and protect. Not too long ago it was revealed that Conrad Lawton had been a philanderer, on top of his other misdeeds, when it came out that he was being blackmailed by his mistress to keep their daughter's existence quiet. After the mistress passed away, her daughter—who turned out to be Dr. Baskin—found out about her father, the blackmail, and the fact that she suddenly had a whole new family living a few miles away in Loveless.

Presley Baskin's life had been boring, boring, and more boring up until a few months ago. Now she was all tangled up with the Lawtons' constant chaos, and doing her best to hide out from a killer. The same killer who'd tried to run Kody down, and who had burned the Lawtons' family home to the ground. The same killer who had once been Presley's one and only friend. I'd heard about how scary the woman after Presley was from Kody, and through the gossip circulating around town. In fact, it was all anyone was talking about for a while. Considering she had all of that going on, I expected her to put her favor to good use anytime now, but she'd yet to reach out to the club. We'd heard nothing from her since the night she saved my life, and I was getting impatient.

"Are you sure this isn't considered stalking?" Top's sarcastic statement was issued with a slow southern drawl.

We'd been sitting on our motorcycles outside of Presley's apartment since the sun went down. The apartment complex was fairly small, and the parking lot remained mostly empty. It was quiet and dull, so the irritation threaded throughout that drawl was hard to miss.

I cut a look at my VP and shrugged. "I consider it recon."

Top—or Simon Riggs, as he'd been known before starting up the Texas branch of the SoS alongside me—had been my right-hand man, my ride-or-die, and my second-in-command since our military days. We'd done our initial training together at Parris Island and had had each other's backs ever since.

"Consider it whatever you want. Lurking outside of a woman's home is still a little bit creepy and totally out of character for you." A Low Country native, his drawl was slower and deeper than the melodic Texan twang we were typically surrounded by. His voice often sounded soft, which was a total contradiction to the man himself. Top was ruthless. The line between right and wrong tended to be very blurry where my VP was concerned, which made him a perfect balance to me and my typically black-and-white way of thinking. He could see the gray in dicey situations when I was color blind.

He also knew me better than anyone else. So when he said it was out of character for me to be keeping tabs on the lady doctor who saved my life, he was absolutely right. I had enough on my plate, including tracking down the angry redneck who'd filled me full of holes in retaliation for taking his older brother out. There was no way I or the club could let the ambush go unanswered, but I'd been more focused on trying to figure out the woman who jumped in the middle of the club's bloody business like it was nothing.

"Why doesn't she ever leave her apartment?" I asked with a frown. "Doesn't she have a job to go to? Or friends and family to see?" The Lawtons were a tight bunch. One of the reasons I knew a relationship with Kody would never work was because of how close she was to her older brothers. Case Lawton was the town sheriff, and far from being my biggest fan.

I'd nearly convinced myself I was in love with Kody a while back. It hurt when she broke things off, but it wasn't unexpected. What *was* odd was the fact that I hadn't seen any of the Lawtons, or anyone else for that matter, check on the good doctor any of the times I'd lurked outside her building. There was more to the story than I'd gotten secondhand, and I wanted to fill in the blanks.

Top sighed heavily and lifted a hand to stroke his beard. We were the same age, both of us pushing forty, but he'd gone gray before I had. His beard and dark hair were both liberally peppered with white and silver strands, whereas mine was still solid midnight and thick enough that it was a pain in the ass when it got long. Considering the hard and rough way we lived, it was almost a miracle neither of us was sporting a snowy-white head of hair.

"Didn't you say she has someone after her? Maybe she's just lying low because she's scared. Normal people don't know what to do when their lives are in constant danger. She isn't like you, buddy. She's not even like Kody."

While it was true the two women looked startlingly alike, their overall demeanor and attitudes had nothing in common.

I frowned and kept my eyes trained on the front door of her apartment. She'd opened it exactly once in all the days I'd been observing her, and that was for a pizza delivery guy.

"If she's in danger, shouldn't the people who care about her have even more reason to make sure she's okay?" I shook my head slightly. "I don't get it."

Top swore softly and shifted on the seat of his motorcycle. "What you're gonna get is arrested if someone reports us for loitering again. Last time Case showed up he told you point-blank he didn't want you hanging around this apartment or the woman inside. The sheriff already has you in his sights. Stop trying to provoke him."

It was an old warning, one I'd learned to tune out. I wasn't afraid of Case Lawton or the long arm of the law. I wasn't afraid of anything, really, other than the unknown. Which was why I couldn't stand waiting for the lady doctor to make her mind up about how the club could pay her back.

Top shifted on his bike again, his impatience evident. I was getting ready to tell him to leave; after all, we still were trying to track down Jed Coleman, the guy who'd nearly killed me. I thought that Jed was still locked up, so I'd dropped the ball when it came to watching my back and taking precautions. I had no clue he'd been released early on a technicality. I also had no idea he had figured out I was the one who took out his older brother, Jethro. Jed had spent his time in prison plotting to avenge his older brother. He'd nearly succeeded, but now it was our turn to seek out justice... we just had to find the man first. However, my train of thought completely faded away when the door to that silent, seemingly lonely apartment suddenly opened and a woman walked out.

She was on the tall side, and her long legs were encased in tight jeans. She was wearing an oversized hoodie although the temps in Texas were outrageously high, even at night.

She also had on a dark baseball hat and a pair of giant dark sunglasses, as if those two things would make her less conspicuous rather than making her stand out like a sore thumb. Her head rotated as she scanned the parking lot of the apartment complex. She noticeably halted when she caught sight of the out-of-the-way spot where Top and I had been parked for the last couple of hours.

I cocked my head to the side and lifted my eyebrows as the woman visibly pulled herself together and psyched herself up before taking a few tentative steps in the direction of the stairs.

Top also straightened and muttered, "What in the hell?" Both of us watched in surprise as the leggy redhead practically marched across the parking lot toward us.

She stopped directly in front of my bike, anxiety radiating off every line of her lean body. She was incredibly pale, and I could tell she was shaking under the bulky weight of the hoodie. However, I was begrudgingly impressed with her moxie to face off against us when she was obviously terrified.

She didn't say anything for a long moment, eventually squeaking out, "Can you please leave?"

Not one to take to being told what to do in any circumstance, which was probably why he'd been dishonorably discharged right after I was, Top growled, "It's a free country, lady. We'll go when we're ready to go."

The pretty doctor practically jumped out of her skin. She lifted a trembling hand to her throat and tilted her head downward so I knew she was looking at the ground instead of either of us.

"I know that Kody is worried about me and I appreciate her concern, but I've asked her, and now I'm telling you, I'll be fine. I don't need anyone looking out for me. It's better if everyone just lets me handle Ashby on my own. I don't want anyone else to get hurt because of me." She took off her sunglasses and I could see she was fighting back tears in those bright green eyes. She pointed the glasses in my direction and muttered, "You barely survived your last run-in with a lunatic. Why would you risk another one?"

I was confused as hell as to what she was saying. But it was obvious she believed the reason I'd been hanging around her place was because of Kody.

"I have no idea who or what an Ashby is, or why you need to handle her. I also wouldn't be hanging out in this heat as a favor to Kody, or anyone for that matter. I'm not that nice of a guy." I smirked at her and leaned forward on the bike. "Whatever I risk or don't risk is up to me, no one else. If I get hurt, that's on me, not you." I couldn't help but find myself becoming more and more curious about this complicated and confusing woman. The way she spoke to me was an odd mix of overly confident and completely clueless. She looked familiar, but the way she approached me was completely foreign. She was afraid. But not of me, which was entirely foolish on her part.

She shook her head and almost seemed to shrink in on herself. "I don't know why you've been lurking around lately, but I'm sincerely asking you to stop. It's drawing unnecessary attention and it might be keeping away the person I'm trying to lure out into the open." She dropped her gaze and her hands curled into tight fists. "I want my life back. I won't accomplish that goal if Ashby doesn't come out of hiding."

"Ashby the one gunning for you? Is she the one you're worried will hurt someone else because of you?" The typically straightforward way Top blurted out the question made the woman flinch.

Presley took a minute to answer, clearly trying to pick her words with care. "Everyone assumes she went on the run since her plan fell apart, but I was best friends with her for most of my life. I know this isn't the end of things. She failed in framing me for murder, and she threatened to kill me and everyone I care about. Until I draw her out into the open, everything in my life is in limbo. I need you to back off so she will show herself. I left protective custody for the exact same reason."

I stared at the woman and tapped my fingers on the gas tank of the bike. "You want us gone?"

She nodded vigorously. "I do. I would be very grateful if you left and didn't return."

Not an uncommon reaction to having a bunch of bikers loitering around, in all honesty. My expression shifted into a full-blown smile when I realized I could leverage her request into clearing myself and the club from owing her any further.

"I do owe you a solid. It can be anything, no questions asked, and no limitations. Are you telling me you want to use your one and only favor from the Sons of Sorrow, to get us to leave you alone?" Clearing the slate was going to be much easier than I thought. I was gonna kick my own ass for not approaching her sooner.

The lady doctor started to enthusiastically agree. She was opening her mouth to accept the bargain when a window on the late model car I was parked next to suddenly exploded in a shower of glass. A loud *pop* filled the air and Top yelled, "Gun!" at the same time he dove for cover. Another window shattered, and I moved without thinking and with years of training and instinct guiding me.

I grabbed the doctor by the wrist and pulled her to the ground. Immediately covering her smaller frame with my own, I inched us closer to the car, hoping I could use the front end as cover, while Top pulled out his own weapon and returned fire.

I could feel the woman underneath me quivering in fear, but she stayed still and silent, her hands curled around the leather of my cut. It wasn't totally uncommon that I had to dodge bullets, but this was the first time I wasn't sure who the target was, me ... or her.

CHAPTER 2

∞

PRESLEY

I hated hospitals. And most doctors.

They reminded me of all the hours spent by my mother's side while she got sicker and sicker. I hated the defeat and resignation that was always on her face when they told her there was little they could do for her without a transplant. And I equally hated the cold and detached way all her doctors delivered what was basically a death sentence. She was on the donor list, waiting and waiting. Of course, I'd been tested to see if I was a match, but I wasn't. And we didn't have any extended family or close friends who could step up to the plate. Well, we had Ashby, and she'd gotten tested at the same time I had, but she wasn't a match either. Not that I believed she would've gone out of her way to save my mother's life now that I knew what kind of person she really was.

My unease with the entire medical process was one of the main reasons I was more comfortable with the dead than the living. I dealt in hard facts and evidence, not possibility and probability. I'd had enough of hinging all my hopes on the hint of a miracle. None of the patients I had on my table in the morgue were going to break down and fall apart under my care. I was with them at the end of their journey. I did my best to send each and every one of them off with as much respect and reverence as possible. My mother never understood why I worked so hard to get through med school only to end up working with the dead. I never had the heart to tell her she was the main reason behind my decision. Years and years of watching her suffer and not getting anywhere solidified the knowledge that I wasn't cut out for a career filled with heartache and loss. The dead were easier on my heart than the dying.

The tiny emergency room in Loveless was busy, as any ER tended to be. I tried my best to assure the sheriff's deputy who showed up shortly after the shots were fired that I didn't need to see a doctor. I'd hit my head on the ground when Shot pulled me down to the asphalt, and I was pretty sure I had a slight sprain in my wrist from the force he used to pull me to safety, but neither injury was serious. I even pulled the "I'm a doctor" card, but apparently being the sheriff's half sister trumped my medical training. The deputy refused to let me go after a brief questioning as the parking lot was suddenly swarmed by what seemed like the entire Loveless Sheriff Department. No matter how vehemently I insisted that I was fine, the deputy was just as adamant I get both my head and hand checked out. He seemed to believe his job would be on the line if Case found out he didn't go the extra mile in looking after my well-being.

It seemed futile to explain I wasn't actually part of that legendary Lawton bond, so I caved and let them rush me off to the emergency room, all the while fuming that both bikers who'd been caught in the crossfire with me had disappeared before the police arrived. I shouldn't have been surprised. After all, my first encounter with Shot Caldwell had been because his biker buddies didn't want the law involved in his shooting. But for some reason, I felt abandoned when they took off as soon as they determined the coast was clear. To his credit, before vanishing, Shot took a moment to make sure I was okay. He'd probed the knot on the back of my head with his tattooed fingers and asked if things were blurry and if I had black spots in my vision.

Once I assured him it was just a little bump, he'd given me a hard look and declared our conversation far from over. I wanted to protest, to accept his decree that leaving me alone for good would be the perfect favor to collect from the club, but I didn't get the chance. And when the deputies started asking me about enemies and if I had any idea who could be behind the shooting, it all got tangled and messy, because I didn't know for sure if it was Ashby, my former friend, or if it was someone aiming for the bikers. It was convoluted and complicated, like everything in my life currently.

When the curtain surrounding the hospital bed I was perched on finally pulled back, I was expecting to see a harried and hurried ER doctor. I'd been waiting for well over an hour since the deputy rushed me back and left after I answered a long list of questions. To my surprise, it wasn't a doctor storming into the small space, but my half sister.

Kody was a firecracker by nature. Passionate. Wild. Reckless. She was all the things I'd never dared be, and then some. She was also kind, caring, and considerate, and she had the biggest heart I'd ever encountered. While we didn't hit it off at the start of our tenuous relationship, she'd done her best to bridge the gap created by our upbringing and personalities. I'd only ever had my mother, and it hurt like hell to lose her. I couldn't get my head around the idea of being part of a big, boisterous family, and I didn't even want to imagine what it would be like to suddenly be left alone if they decided I didn't fit or that they didn't want me. I tried to keep my distance, but Kody refused to let me push her away.

Kody's green eyes were wide, and she was pale under the freckles that dotted her pert little nose. She always seemed so vibrant and bright, and she practically hummed with life and energy. I flinched when she wrapped her arms around me in a tight hug, not because it hurt but because the affection was so instinctual, like she didn't even have to think about offering solace and comfort to someone who was still mostly a stranger.

"Are you okay?" She pulled back but left her hands on my shoulders so I couldn't pull totally away. "Case told me you were rushed to the ER. He's on a call out in the hill country, so he won't be back in town for an hour or so. I asked what happened, but he wouldn't give me any details other than you were hurt and headed to the hospital. Do you need anything? Was this that crazy woman who's after you?"

The questions were rapid-fire and rushed together. I had to lift a hand to get her to slow down and back up a step. I touched my temple where I felt the start of a headache building and briefly closed my eyes.

"I'm fine. Really. There was no need to rush over here. As soon as I see the doctor and get checked out, I'm headed back home." I forced myself to meet her probing gaze and told her, "Someone took a shot at me while I was standing in the parking lot in front of my apartment. It could have been Ashby, but I'm not sure."

Kody took the hint and put some space between us. She copied my pose, leaning against the side of the bed rather than sprawling across the top of it. She crossed her ankles and her arms over her chest. I could see a muscle twitching in her cheek before she quietly asked, "Do you have someone else trying to kill you that I don't know about, Presley?" Her tone made it clear that if I did, indeed, have a new enemy she wasn't aware of, she wasn't going to be happy about it.

I rotated my sore wrist and let out a heavy sigh. "No, no one else is trying to kill *me*." I put the emphasis on the last word and sighed again. "I wasn't alone in the parking lot. Shot and one of his biker friends have been hanging around my apartment on and off since he recovered from his injuries. Today I finally got up the courage to tell him to leave me alone. I was worried they would scare Ashby off if she was waiting to make a move on me. I told Shot I wanted my life back, but then someone started shooting and everything went to hell and I have no idea if I was the target or if he was."

Kody was silent for a long moment, then she let out a low whistle and turned her head to look at me. "That's gonna make things complicated."

I nodded carefully in agreement. My head was starting to throb, and I couldn't tell if it was from the headache or the knock it'd taken earlier. Either way, I wanted to lie down in a dark room and pretend like none of this happened for at least an hour. "I know it is. Shot and the VP didn't stick around and wait for the police to show up." I was going to remain bitter about that.

Kody snorted. "Of course they didn't. That's going to piss Case off, and now he's going to be thrilled he has a legitimate reason to find Shot and bring him in for questioning. Those two are like oil and water. They never mix well, and Case isn't going to like Shot having anything to do with you and your situation."

Having anyone invested in me was a strange feeling, but the idea of suddenly having a big-brother figure in my life was completely foreign.

Reiterating my original statement, I whispered, "I can take care of myself, really." But it didn't sound nearly as convincing as I wanted it to.

Fortunately, the ER doctor finally made an appearance. He looked at me, then at Kody, and did a double take. The locals in Loveless were still adjusting to the fact that Conrad Lawton had another child floating around no one knew about. It was particularly startling when Kody and I were next to one another and the resemblance couldn't be ignored. The older man quickly recovered his composure and gave the blond woman next to me a friendly grin.

"Kody. I thought I told you I didn't want to see you here for the rest of the year. The Lawtons and their associates are getting too comfortable in this ER." He clicked his pen and gave me a curious look, clearly trying to connect the dots as to how I suddenly fit into the Lawton family circle.

Kody scoffed and pushed off the side of the bed. "You know how hard it is to keep the Lawtons and the like out of trouble." She grabbed her purse and gave me a narrow-eyed look of warning. "I'm gonna step outside while you look my sister over. I'll be back to take her home once you give her a clean bill of health." She switched the sharp look to the doctor. "Don't let her convince you she's fine if she's not."

The doctor chuckled and nodded. I could see him puzzling over the word *sister*, but he was too polite to say anything. Once Kody cleared out of the small space, the doctor turned kind eyes in my direction and took note of the way I was holding my sore wrist.

"Got a little banged up, did ya?" He pulled a pair of reading glasses from his pocket and looked over the chart in his hand.

"I'm fine. It's just a sprain, and a bump on my head. I don't have any symptoms of a concussion, and my wrist will be fine if I ice it and wrap it up for a few days." I gave the self-diagnosis with quiet confidence, which made the older man's eyebrows lift.

"Have you been to medical school, young lady?" There was a hint of condescension in his tone, and if my head hadn't been killing me I would've rolled my eyes hard enough to see into the future.

"Yes, I'm a medical examiner. Same training, different title." I wasn't just a medical examiner either. Before my life had imploded, I'd been in line to become the chief medical examiner for the entire county. It was a huge honor, one I'd worked diligently toward. It was also the breaking point for my former best friend's sanity. When the promotion had been offered to me instead of her, Ashby decided to frame me for murder. I'd never seen it coming.

The doctor didn't seem impressed by my career choice, but that wasn't anything new. When your patients weren't breathing, those in the medical field typically tended to look down on you and your work.

The man didn't say much else. He gave my head a brief look and tried to rotate and flex my wrist until I protested in pain. It took him less than ten minutes to repeat back my original diagnosis. He asked me if I wanted a prescription for pain meds and told me he would send in a nurse to wrap up my wrist. I declined both, not wanting the drugs or to wait around for another hour when I could wrap my wrist on my own. After he shrugged and told me I was good to go, I maneuvered out of the room. I gave a brief thought to trying to give Kody the slip, but I knew that if I did she would just show up at my apartment, more riled up than she already was.

Normally, aggravating Kody wouldn't bother me, but I hated the idea of something happening to her because I was being stubborn and foolish. I couldn't risk her safety. The guilt I felt over taking the Lawtons' father away, even indirectly, was crippling. It was the Lawtons themselves who'd forced me to accept that Conrad was gone because of his own misdeeds and bad choices. Ashby was certifiable, and that had nothing to do with me. On bad days I still struggled to believe both of these things, but my new siblings were unshakable in their emotional support.

Kody caught sight of me as soon as I cleared the noise and chaotic energy of the emergency room. She gave me a critical look since I was still holding my injured wrist tightly and asked, "Why didn't they take care of that for you?"

I tilted my chin in the direction of the desk used for check-in and out. I told her I needed to take care of whatever I owed and then I would explain why I was leaving seemingly untreated. She didn't seem too happy with the curt answer, but she didn't hound me with questions or try and manhandle me with aggressive affection like she normally did until we were in the parking lot and headed toward her unmissable lime-green Jeep.

Once we reached the neon vehicle she turned to face me. "Why didn't you let them help you? I know you think you can handle everything on your own, but isn't this taking things a little too far?"

"I didn't want to wait around for someone else to wrap up my wrist when I can do it myself. I just want to go home and take a nap." I fought back a tired and slightly frustrated sigh. I was navigating the ups and downs of our newly formed relationship. The boundaries between friend and family were still new to me, and I kept tripping over them. "But I honestly appreciate your concern and how you rushed to the hospital to check on me."

Kody sighed dramatically and tossed her fall of curly hair

over her shoulder. "You can't seriously think I'm going to leave you on your own after someone took a shot at you today. You're not going back to your apartment until Case gives the all clear. You're coming home with me. There's an armed Texas Ranger there. That should be enough to make anyone think twice about shooting at you again. You can nap better knowing that you're absolutely safe under my roof."

Her words were fierce and so was the expression on her face. This was exactly what I meant by her aggressive affection. She cared so much, almost to the point of it being painful to someone very unused to being the center of all that concern. She looked like she was going to take no arguments from me, but I had a few.

"Kody," I started, and she immediately held up her hand to get me to stop talking.

"You're going to say that you're fine on your own and you've been trying for months to draw Ashby Grant out of hiding. I know you think if you come home with me it will ruin all of that and you might miss your shot at drawing her out, but I don't care. I care about you. I'm worried about you. And I'm telling you it won't matter if you go back to that crappy apartment or not because even if you do, Case is going to surround the place with his deputies. If Shot lurking about was really enough to keep her away, what do you think the entire Loveless Sheriff Department is going to do?" She paused in her tirade long enough to blow out a breath. "I know the whole 'family' thing is new to you and you're trying to adjust to having all of us all up in your life. So, I'm asking—no, I'm pleading with you to do this for me, Presley. Come home with me, for a few days at least. Let me take care of you. Let me help you."

It was on the tip of my tongue to tell her no, but I couldn't do it. No matter how independent and solitary I was, there was no looking into those big, green eyes so like mine and denying her. It was a strange sensation, putting Kody's wants and needs before my own survival instincts. I'd lived so much of my life as the primary caregiver for my mother, it was nearly impossible to switch gears and accept being the person who was being cared for. I'd never had to worry about hurting anyone before, and the weight of that responsibility was honestly alarming.

I slowly nodded my agreement to her demand and told her softly, "I'll come, but only for a day or two. I don't want to impose on you and Hill."

They were a new couple, both with busy schedules. They didn't need a third party lingering around during their honeymoon phase, and I didn't know how long I could tolerate being in the middle of Kody's constant bedlam. But I was going to try to acquiesce because she was family, and because she was important to me. I didn't want to give her more reasons to worry about me, as much as I didn't want to worry about something happening to her because of me. It was exhausting, and again I longed for the days that all passed in one beige blur.

Plus, Kody was right. I needed to figure out what family meant to me now, and it was up to me to learn to function as part of one.

CHAPTER 3

❦

SHOT

"Stay away from my sister, Caldwell."

I lifted my eyebrows and looked at the sheriff of Loveless over the rim of the coffee mug I had pressed to my lips. I'd done my best to avoid Case Lawton for the last few days. I knew he was going to have questions I didn't have answers for, and I knew he was going to get cranky when I stone-walled him. It wasn't that I had anything against the stern and stoic lawman. I actually respected him and appreciated his no-nonsense approach to keeping the peace. However, we were never going to see eye to eye when it came to my view-ing certain laws and regulations as suggestions rather than absolutes. We were also never going to be on the same page about me being an acceptable partner for his sister…either one of them.

Pushing his buttons, mostly because I could, I set the coffee cup down and asked dryly, "Which one?"

Case's low growl rumbled from the other side of the table and his big hands curled into fists. I grinned when a muscle ticked in his cheek. I could practically hear his back teeth grinding together in frustration.

"Stay away from both of them. I'm sure you know that most places have some kind of surveillance equipment installed, even crappy apartment buildings in small towns. I don't know why you're suddenly interested in Presley, but I don't like it. If I have to, I'll push her to get a restraining order, and if you break it, it'll be my pleasure to lock your ass up for stalking." He leaned his big body back in the booth and narrowed his sharp, observant gaze in my direction. "Kody went and found herself the right kind of forever, and I'm sure that had to sting your pride. But I'll be damned if you're trying to replace her with Presley since they just happen to look so much alike."

I blinked in surprise, honestly taken aback at the accusation. Sure, the women bore an uncanny resemblance to one another other than the difference in their hair color, but they couldn't be more different. Kody was as unpredictable as the day was long. No one ever knew what kind of crazy scheme she was going to come up with, or how much trouble she was going to bring to the table. As far as I could tell, Presley was the opposite. She seemed methodical and as calm and cool in a crisis as they came. If Kody was a tornado, Presley was like a cool summer breeze. Kody's chaos could be fun in small doses, but I found the good doctor's unflappable and quiet reserve when all hell was breaking loose to be oddly reassuring. I had enough noise and pandemonium in my life. It was often too loud to even hear myself think. In the short moments I spent around Presley, things seemed to be much quieter, even with a lunatic in the mix. I liked the serenity that seemed to surround her, and I wondered if that was one of the reasons I'd been unable to just walk away when she made it clear she wanted nothing to do with me or my crew.

"Don't be ridiculous. Kody is a friend, first and foremost. I'm glad she's happy. You think I would've let that Ranger have her if I didn't honestly believe he was better for her?" I winged up an eyebrow and reached out to tap a tattooed finger on the table between us. "As for the doctor, I have unfinished business with her. It doesn't concern you."

I'd yet to figure out why she hadn't told the sheriff she saved my life and that I'd been littered with bullet holes...which I guess meant I technically owed her more than one favor. The thought had me clenching my teeth in annoyance.

Case curled his hand into a fist where it rested on top of the table and shifted uneasily across from me. We both had our limits, and it wasn't uncommon for either of us to push right up against the other's. I could tell he was trying his best to tamp down the desire to reach across the table and choke me. Instead, he focused on doing his job.

"Why were you at Presley's apartment that day? Did you see who fired the shots? Were you the target or was it my sister?" He bit off the questions angrily, his scowl darkening with each one. "Why didn't you stick around and wait for the police so we could question you along with the other witnesses? I know you aren't stupid, Shot. You know leaving makes it look like you're involved in what went down at Presley's place."

I sighed and dragged a hand down my face. "Someone takes a shot at me, you think I just sit on my ass and let that go?"

The man opposite me stared at me without blinking, and I could practically see the wheels turning in his head. "You saying you were the target?" There was no missing the hopeful note in his deep voice. He really wanted me to assure him that someone was gunning for me and not his half sister.

I gave my head a little shake. "What I'm saying is someone who took a shot that could have easily hit me or my VP doesn't do so without repercussions. That doesn't fly in my world. I made sure the pretty doctor was all right, then Top and I left to try and find whoever was firing at us." I gave a careless shrug and told him honestly, "Most people who shoot at me don't miss. So if you're asking me for a guess, I would say I wasn't the one they had in their sights. But who knows for sure? We both know that I have a handful of enemies who wouldn't be above taking a random shot if the situation presented itself."

Case growled again and I could feel the tension radiating off him in waves. I had to give him credit. If I was in his position and being purposefully provoked, I probably would've pulled my gun on them.

"Don't suppose you'd be willing to hand over a list of those enemies so we can narrow the field for possible suspects?" He knew the answer before he asked it. The last thing I was going to do was start cooperating with the police. I had way too many secrets and skeletons in my closet for that. I also had my own agenda when it came to payback. Not to mention the rest of the club to look out for as well.

"It won't make any difference. Most of the people looking for me aren't the type who want to be found. Even if you did run across them, I'm not sure it would end well for you. As I said, Kody is a friend. I can't knowingly put her older brother in the line of fire." I gave him a wink. "Besides, it's not like you're great at keeping the bad guys behind bars anyways."

Case's eyes narrowed even more until he appeared to be practically squinting. "Are you talking about yourself, or someone else?"

A low chuckle escaped because he had a point. "I'm

saying you might want to start by looking at those who have slipped through the legal system's cracks. The woman who killed your father and burned down your family home is still missing—after how many months? The man who almost got your woman killed gets bounced because of a paperwork error, and who's keeping an eye on him?" I lifted my hands and let them fall. "Lots of dangerous people on the streets, Sheriff, and it's not my job to regulate them." I winked at him again. "Until it is."

Case blew out a deep breath and leaned forward, hands on the table. His intensity was palpable and so was his simmering anger. "Not your job to regulate? Then what would you call what happened with Jethro Coleman and the school shooting?"

The reason I'd been shot and two of my brothers had died was because Jed's older brother had set his sights on punishing Case in the most effective way possible. He'd taken aim at the sheriff's teenage son and the rest of the kids who attended Loveless's only high school. Case had been literally caught in the crossfire, so I'd stepped in to handle the problem...permanently.

Knowing I'd pushed my luck as far as I could for one day with the big man, I settled back in my seat and offered up my honest opinion. "I'd call that particular incident justice." We both knew he had no proof that I was the one who took the older Coleman out, and I wasn't about to implicate myself. "If you have any other questions, send them through my lawyer, Sheriff. I'm going back to my breakfast if you don't mind."

Case swore, long and loud, smacking his palm on the table and making the diners around us jump. "I still want to talk to your VP. He was with you that day at the apartment. Maybe he saw something you didn't. I want an official witness statement. Have him come to me, or I'll show up at your clubhouse when you least expect it."

I nodded and reached for my abandoned and now cooled coffee. "I'll pass the request along."

Case grunted his response and went to slide out of the booth, but I stopped him by asking, "How is the good doctor? She took a pretty good knock on the head."

For once, I wasn't asking the question to get under his skin. I was genuinely curious about how Presley was doing. Her apartment appeared abandoned, and the parking lot still had police tape around it. She'd seemed so frightened that day but was also totally determined to face on her own whatever was hunting and haunting her. I was admittedly impressed. Plus, I was still indebted to her, and I needed to get that damn noose off of my neck.

Case turned to give me one last warning. "I told you to keep your distance, and I meant it, Shot. Presley has a lot going on in her life right now. The last thing she needs is you stirring the pot and leading her astray. Leave her the hell alone and don't make me find a reason to arrest you."

I took the threat in stride. It wasn't the first time he'd issued it. When Kody and I had casually dated, I'd found myself hauled into the sheriff's office on trumped-up charges more than once. However, I got the distinct feeling Case felt like he had to go above and beyond to protect his new sister because he didn't think she could protect herself. Which was definitely not the case with Kody.

After the sheriff left, I finished my breakfast and left the waitress a hefty tip to make up for disturbing the other diners. The club had a pretty decent relationship with the locals, but that was mostly because we kept our business outside of the city limits. When my uncle offered to sell me his failing ranch after I was kicked out of the military, he'd

given me the rundown on all the small-town intricacies. I
knew what I was getting into when I moved down to Texas
to start up a new chapter of my father's club. However, it
was an opportunity I couldn't turn my back on, and I'd yet
to regret the decision, even if it came with more prying eyes
and idle gossip than I preferred.

I was tossing a leg over my bike when my cell phone
rang. Seeing that it was Top, I settled on the seat and
answered the call.

"What's up?"

"You having breakfast with the law now?" The sarcasm
was thick and so was the censure.

"Didn't have a choice. Neither do you. He wants to
know about the shooting the other day." I rested an elbow
on the gas tank and let my gaze wander over the sleepy
Main Street. It honestly looked like one of those postcards
sold in every tourist shop everywhere. All the storefronts
were purposely kept cute and charming, giving everything
a throwback-to-another-time kind of vibe. And even though
it was called Main Street, there wasn't a lot of pedestrian
traffic. Loveless wasn't the kind of place vacationers flocked
to, so it was mostly locals whose families had been in the
area for generations. It was honestly the last place on Earth
I'd ever thought I'd end up, but here I was and I had to
admit I liked it. Being here helped quiet down some of that
noise that was constantly screaming through my hectic and
dangerous life.

I suddenly sat up straight when I caught sight of a flash
of red hair and superlong legs. It would be hard to miss the
elegant way Presley Baskin carried herself. With that bright
hair she stood out like a beacon and I knew I would have
zero trouble spotting her even in a crowd.

Keeping my eyes on the woman as she hurried along

the street, I muttered to Top, "He wants to get a witness statement from you as well. Your call if you go down to the station or if you have our lawyer handle it. Don't need him showing up at the ranch."

Top grunted his agreement and said something else, but I completely missed whatever it was. My attention was fully focused on the woman walking on the opposite side of the street. She had those giant sunglasses on her face, but now it was daytime so she didn't look as ridiculous as the last time I'd seen her in them. I noticed that she kept turning her head as if she was looking for someone. Her pace quickened until she was almost jogging. The entire scene would have been comical if fear hadn't been evident in every one of her actions. She ducked into the only drugstore in town, and before I knew what I was doing, I found myself climbing off my bike and walking in the direction she disappeared.

"Have you heard a damn word I've said?" Top's sharp reprimand brought me back to reality but didn't stop the forward motion of my feet.

"Nope. Not a single one."

My longtime friend swore loudly into my ear. "I was telling you that we might have a lead on Jed Coleman. Someone saw him in Austin. It seems like he's trying to hook up with a well-known extremist group based there. May be looking for a place to hide out, or for some kind of backup."

I gritted my teeth in irritation, pausing before I walked into the drugstore. "If you can lock down an exact location, let me know."

"Are you still thinking someone else took the shot outside the apartment?" Top hadn't originally agreed with my assessment until I pointed out that the last time I went against Jed Coleman, he'd managed to nearly kill me.

"I don't think he's the type to miss when he lines up a

shot. We won't really know either way until we pin Coleman down." Huffing out an annoyed breath at being delayed in the pursuit of my current prey, I snapped at my VP, "I got something to take care of. I'll check in on my way back to the ranch." I hung up before he could question me further. I wasn't sure how to explain my overwhelming need to see what the doctor was up to, or why I continually found myself unable to leave her alone.

I was irritated that even though the slate between us was technically wiped clean since she'd saved my life and then I'd saved hers, I still felt a twinge of responsibility toward keeping her safe. After all, that bullet might have been meant for me. She adamantly insisted I didn't owe her anything more, but if she wasn't going to look out for herself, maybe she needed someone else to do it for her.

I wasn't sure why I believed that the someone else looking out for her had to be me, but I couldn't fight back the urge to follow her and see what she was up to.

The bell over the door dinged when I entered, drawing curious looks from the young man behind the counter and the elderly woman checking out. I nodded in greeting and started to make my way up and down the different aisles in search of that red hair.

At first, I didn't see Presley anywhere. It was like she'd disappeared into thin air, even though I knew for certain she hadn't left through the front door. I was about to go ask the cashier if she'd maybe gone out the back when I was suddenly hit in the face with a blinding spray of something chemical and potent. My eyes immediately started to burn, and I began hacking like my lungs were trying to climb out of my throat. I couldn't see anything through the water flooding my eyes, and I could hardly breathe.

"Oh!" The soft exclamation was followed by gentle hands

grabbing my face. "It's you. Why are you following me?" Presley's voice was equally concerned and condemning.

"What did you spray me with?" I wanted to gag and couldn't get the truly awful taste out of my mouth.

Since I couldn't see, I let Presley drag me toward the front of the store, where she demanded to know where an eye-flushing kit might be located.

Once we were situated in another aisle, I asked again what she got me with through fits of hacking.

"Umm...bug spray. Why are you following me?" She pushed my head back and I felt her body lean into mine as she reached up to dump the eyewash solution into my burning eyes. "Don't blink until I tell you."

I had to fight the urge to squeeze my eyes shut, but her fingers pressed my cheeks and held my face still.

"I wasn't following you. I saw you running down the sidewalk and got curious. You looked like you were running from someone...or something."

Slowly, the sting in my eyes lessened and my blurry vision started to come back into focus. My mouth still felt like I'd just drunk a gallon of diesel fuel, and my throat felt raw, but the cough subsided as Presley quietly asked, "Did you swallow any of it? If so you need to go to the ER and get your stomach pumped. That stuff is highly poisonous."

Her touch was incredibly tender, and so was her voice as it wrapped around me.

I caught one of her wrists in my hand and pulled her fingers away from my face. "I'm fine. Tell me why you were running and why you looked so afraid."

She tried to tug free, but I tightened my hold, not letting her go. We stared at each other for a long moment, then she relented.

"I've been staying with Kody and her boyfriend since

the shooting. She finally went back to work today, and Hill got called out on a new assignment. I was getting stir-crazy and I thought a quick run into town wouldn't hurt anything. I also planned on stopping by my apartment to grab a few things. As soon as I left Kody's I got this feeling like I was being watched. The sensation got worse when I got into town. I'm probably just being paranoid, but I was convinced that someone was following me. Then you appeared out of nowhere and"—she shrugged sort of helplessly—"I'm sorry I overreacted."

This time when she tugged on her wrist, I let her go. I went to rub my eyes and got my hands smacked away.

"Don't touch. It'll make it worse."

I sighed and let my arms drop to my sides. "You were in the line of fire not too long ago. Seems to me like it's a good thing you're on high alert. If I had been following you, your reaction was on point. I think you're better at taking care of yourself than anyone believes."

She heaved a sigh and crossed her arms over her chest in a protective movement. "I took some self-defense training when my life went sideways. I can't believe I might actually have to use it." She sounded utterly defeated and resigned.

I grunted and tilted my chin up a little. "Gonna be a minute before I can see well enough to get on the bike. How did you get into town? Grab the stuff you came for and I'll go to your apartment with you so you get what you need."

She blinked up at me, eyes wide and surprised. "Excuse me?"

I narrowed my eyes at her. "Get your shit and let's go."

She balked a little, telling me, "I took a cab. My car is still at the apartment."

I shrugged. "Doesn't matter. The apartment is a short enough walk away. You can get another cab once you're situated or take your car back to Kody's. If someone is actually following you, you don't need to be out there wandering around alone."

I could see she was going to argue so I bent down and put my red, irritated face close to hers and told her through gritted teeth, "You practically blinded me. Can you stop arguing for five minutes and just make one of our interactions easy?"

Who knew being a nice guy was so damn hard?

It took another long moment before she relented, and I could tell she only gave in out of guilt, but I didn't mind. There was something about the pretty medical examiner that kept pulling me in, and it'd been a very long time since I'd been this interested in someone outside of my world.

Sure, I'd had it pretty bad for Kody Lawton, but I'd gone into that knowing it would never work out. The doctor was a mystery and full of surprises. I had no idea what our next encounter was going to bring, and for the first time in forever, I found I didn't mind being surprised.

CHAPTER 4

❦

PRESLEY

I glanced at the man walking next to me out of the corner of my eye.

I didn't know much about bikers or the outlaw lifestyle, other than what I'd seen on television and in the movies. So far, all my interactions with Shot Caldwell and his club led me to believe some of the outrageous scenarios presented for entertainment weren't actually that far off base. There was an intensity about the man, a rebellious quality that practically oozed from his pores. It was easy to tell he wasn't one for convention and standards, just by looking at the ink that covered most of his visible skin. While tattoos were more and more common on every kind of person, the heavy, dark images scrawled over the biker's arms and up the side of his neck made a bold statement. He was a grown man, living life on his own terms, and to hell with conformity. It was unsettling how intrigued I was by the dangerous and mysterious aura that surrounded him, just as I had been when he'd been clinging to life while my hands were covered in his blood. It was an unexpected fascination, one I had no time for, and it was completely out of character for me.

I was even intrigued by the way he smelled, like leather and sunshine, mixed with a hint of something that had to be gasoline or motor oil. It was an unmistakably masculine smell, and I was surprised by how much I liked it. It made me want to lean in closer and bury my nose in the crook of his neck so I could fully take it in and memorize it.

At the moment the skin around his dark eyes was red and irritated, and he kept clearing his throat. He also repeatedly rubbed his nose, which made the tip of it bright pink. I felt terrible for catching him dead in the face with the Raid, but my survival instincts were at an all-time high and would more than likely remain that way until Ashby Grant was behind bars. He caught me by surprise when I'd already been questioning my trip into town for Cheetos and a Red Bull. I really was feeling a little hemmed in at Kody and Hill's place, mostly because I couldn't breathe without Kody asking me if I was okay. I appreciated her concern, but the way she watched me, both with confusion and concern, made me feel like my skin was paper-thin and too much of myself was being exposed. My emotions were already stretched to their breaking point, and I simply needed a breather to get my head together.

Shot dug a knuckle into his eye, and I reached up to knock it away without thinking about the familiarity of the gesture. "Stop touching it. I told you that you'll just make it worse."

Black eyebrows lifted in amusement and his mouth twisted into a grin. Belatedly, I realized that maybe it wasn't the best idea to act so forward with the president of a biker gang. I'd already watched the man face down a barrage of bullets without being fazed, so there was no telling what he was capable of.

"You said you started to take self-defense classes when your life went sideways. What exactly happened that made you think you have to be able to take someone out with whatever weapon you can find?" His voice was deep and smooth. The low rumble didn't have any trace of an accent or a twang, letting me know he wasn't a Texas native. In fact, I couldn't pinpoint what his origins were.

I sighed and pulled open my bag of cheesy puffs. "It's a long story."

One strong shoulder lifted and fell as he slowed his pace to stay next to me. "We got time."

The walk wasn't the longest, and the need to rush wasn't as pressing as it had been when I got dropped off in town. That eerie feeling of being followed and watched was no longer making the tiny hairs on the back of my neck stand on end, but I wasn't sure if that was because the threat was gone, or because of the man walking next to me. He was big and intimidating; however, his presence was surprisingly comforting. I felt safe when I was around him.

I sighed again and licked the tip of my finger. "I like routine and predictability. I was always focused on school and then on work, so I never had time for friends or things that are frivolous and fun."

I gave him another look out of the corner of my eye to see what his reaction was. His expression didn't change much, but it was hard to tell if he didn't have a reaction or if he was just in pain from the bug spray.

I squeezed the bag of snacks in my hand and heard the remaining few crunch into dust as I thought about how things had gone sideways so fast.

"My best friend and I were both candidates for the chief

ME position of our county. It was a huge opportunity, and it was unprecedented to have two female candidates for the job. A few months before they officially decided to offer either of us the job, strange things started happening with the cases I was assigned. The evidence went missing and turned up mislabeled. Some of my rulings surrounding cause of death came into question, and more than one court case relying on my testimony was suddenly dismissed. It was a huge deal, caused a media circus and a whole internal investigation, because my record was pristine. I wasn't ready to walk away from my career and all I'd worked for just yet. But then on top of the trouble at work, someone started stalking me and making me think I was losing my mind. I really began to wonder if I'd actually made those kinds of mistakes and risked setting criminals and killers free."

I took a shaky breath and let it out very slowly as all the missteps and mysterious mishaps replayed in my mind.

"I went to stay with my friend, the one who I was going up against for the promotion, because I didn't feel safe alone. While I was at her place she kept mentioning to me that maybe now wasn't the best time to advance my career if I was the one offered it."

I shook my head at my own cluelessness. "I should've realized how badly she wanted the job then, but I didn't. I was naive and too trusting."

A bitter, broken laugh escaped, and I missed a step as Shot turned his head to look at me with obvious concern.

It took a minute for me to get my head around the rest of the words because they hurt to say. "While I stayed with her, she also kept mentioning my mother's health, which wasn't good. I didn't realize it at the time, but she was warning me what would happen if I got the job over her."

I released the bag of puffs when Shot pulled the mangled

mess from my hands. I didn't even realize I'd crushed the contents and crinkled the bag between my hands. I looked down at my orangey fingers and wiped them absently on my jeans.

"My mother died shortly after I told Ashby that I was going to take the promotion."

I'd said the same thing to the Texas Rangers, and the FBI who investigated the case, but for some reason telling Shot on the simple walk to my apartment was harder. Grief clogged my throat and I felt the burn of tears at the back of my eyes. My fingers quivered, so I curled them into fists at my sides.

"There were things about my mother suddenly passing that never made sense, but it wasn't until it became clear that Ashby was trying to frame me for Conrad's murder that I realized she more than likely had something to do with my mother's death."

It still made my stomach turn when I thought about just how cold and inhumane the person I considered myself closest to ended up being. I would never forget how gleeful and deranged she sounded when she explained she was not only responsible for Conrad's murder, but also the one behind everything that happened leading up to it. She couldn't wait to gloat, and she'd made sure I felt the weight of her actions, all while the Lawtons stood by and watched their childhood home burn to the ground. It was just one more catastrophe she was responsible for. I wondered what it said about me that I became friends with Ashby in the first place. I hated that I'd been too blind to see who she really was and ultimately lost so much because of my own ignorance.

Clearing my throat so I didn't break down in front of Shot, I changed the subject and concentrated on moving forward instead of getting stuck in grief and regret. Each step I took was heavy, but I somehow managed to keep pace with the tall man moving next to me.

"In the middle of dealing with my career crashing and burning and losing my mother, I learned who my father was and that I had several half siblings, all with their own ideas about how I should be handling things now."

I lifted my hands and let them fall dramatically to indicate how overwhelming it felt to suddenly be caught up in all of the Lawtons' concern and care. I appreciated them, but I also felt helpless to give them what they wanted.

"Case still wants me in protective custody, but it's been months and Ashby is still on the loose, and I can't just be under lock and key for my whole life. Kody acts like she wants to be my human shield, which is super sweet, but I don't want anything to happen to her if Ashby decides she's not done taking away the things that matter most to me. I know their intentions are good, but it's overwhelming. And Crew, well, he's honestly the only one of the Lawtons who still treats me like he's not sure if I'm friend or foe. I honestly appreciate his caution. His reaction makes the most sense to me. He's supposed to be planning a wedding, not burying his father and learning how to deal with a new sister."

Shot blew out another low whistle. "That's some story."

I nodded silently in agreement, feeling like a balloon that had lost all its air. It was the first time I'd laid all the heartbreaking details out for someone who wasn't in law enforcement. It was the first time I'd let the exhaustion, fear, and frustration slip through instead of simply reiterating the facts. I tried my best to handle everything stoically, but inside I was anything but. I was feeling everything all at once and had no idea how to get a handle on so much emotion. Being honest with Shot about how hard it had been on me lately was as close as I'd come to some kind of catharsis since this whole thing began. I couldn't put my finger on why he was so easy to talk to or why I hadn't glossed things over the way I did with everyone else, but I was glad he let me get rid of some of the emotional weight I'd been carrying. He didn't seem to be burdened by my baggage at all. As my apartment complex came into view, I responded to his wry statement: "I wish it was just a story. I hate that I had to live any of it."

The large man in leather and denim next to me offered a soft chuckle. "The key is the *living* part. As long as you're living your life, she hasn't won."

I faltered a step and blinked for a moment. "What do you mean?"

Shot stopped walking and gave me a sharp look with his swollen eyes. "You mentioned more than once that you're worried she is going to keep taking what's most important away from you, but that's exactly what you've let her do. You're avoiding your new family. You haven't gone back to work and cleared your name. You haven't done anything to find closure where your mother is concerned. You are letting this woman control your life. She's living in your head rent free and I bet she knows it."

I let out a startled sound because of his brutally honest words—and because he reached out and tapped the tip of my nose with one of his fingers. The move was playful and surprisingly sweet. He was touching me in the same familiar way I'd touched him to keep him from rubbing his eyes. I was never that comfortable with a stranger, or even someone I knew casually. I had no clue what to make of it.

"If you really want to draw this woman out into the open, go back to your life. Go back to work. Get to know the Lawtons better. Get out of that shithole apartment. Take. Control. Of. Your. Life." Shot bit out the words, and I felt the impact reverberate all the way down to my bones.

Collecting my composure I took a step away from him and started to head for the apartment building. "Easy for you to say. You have an entire gang of guys ready to lay their lives down for you. You aren't out there facing the world and your enemies on your own."

He growled low under his breath and reached out to catch my shoulder. "We're a club, not a gang. And you don't know me well enough to know what kinds of things I've had to face on my own." There was a dangerous thread through his voice which made me instinctively want to put some serious space between us.

I cleared my throat nervously. "You're right. I don't know, and I have no reason to. Getting involved in one of your club's messes was enough for me." I made sure to emphasize the word *club* to avoid poking at an obvious sore spot.

I yelped when he used his hold on me to spin me around so we were fully facing one another. His impossibly dark eyes were intent and probing even with the whites being more of a rosy pink color.

"Since you brought it up, why did you jump into the fray that night? From what you've told me you're a straight shooter and a rule follower. Why do something that might endanger your medical license?"

He sounded genuinely curious about my decision to get involved and I couldn't blame him. My actions that night had been very out of character.

I shook loose of his hold and cleared my throat again. "I couldn't tell Kody no when she begged for my help. And once I got there, I couldn't let you die. I was admittedly in way over my head with you guys, but once I was in, I was all in."

Shot chuckled at my response. "Guess it was my lucky day. But why didn't you report the gunshot wound?"

I froze and tried to recall why I'd talked myself out of following protocol that night. When I couldn't come up with a valid reason for acting so out of character, I muttered, "Well, I wasn't currently working in the ME's office, so I wasn't on duty of any kind. So it wasn't really required or a breech of policy or ethics." Which was true, but the real reason I didn't report the wound was because I didn't want to make things more difficult for him when he was already fighting so hard for his life. I was also slightly terrified that his club would do something horrible to me if I had reported it like I was supposed to.

Before he could grill me any further, I turned to head toward my apartment, telling him, "You didn't hesitate to pull me to safety when someone started shooting that day in the parking lot. I saved you. You saved me. That makes us even. The favor from the club is cleared. The slate is wiped clean as far as I'm concerned."

I wanted to make sure he knew we didn't have any kind of realistic reason to interact in the future.

I hitched a thumb in the direction of my place and pushed back the sudden rise of something that felt like sadness at saying a final goodbye to this man. My words were quiet when I told him, "I'm gonna run in, grab some stuff, and drive myself back to Kody's. You don't have to stick around anymore. I'm sure your vision is okay now. You should be able to ride your motorcycle with no issue. Once again, I apologize for overreacting." I fought the urge to stick my hand out for him to shake. It seemed overly formal and silly, and I already felt clumsy and awkward around him. It wasn't like I was trying to impress the biker, but it irked me that I always ended up making some kind of scene or needed rescuing when we were together.

Shot's dark eyebrows quirked and his lips followed. He

was an outrageously good-looking guy, one who clearly knew his own appeal. The men I normally spent time around were confident in their abilities and skills. They used titles and bank accounts to brag. Shot needed none of that. He knew when he did something as simple as smile it made hearts foolishly start to race. He was cocky and self-assured, without that practiced charm and charisma so often found in men with high-powered and well-paying jobs, but the sexy swagger he had to spare was too potent to ignore and far more appealing.

When I realized I was staring—because he had really pretty lips for such a rough and rugged man—I jolted and hoped I wasn't blushing. I also hoped it wasn't obvious that I couldn't quit looking at his mouth.

"Have you ever heard, 'When you save a life, you're responsible for that life until the favor is returned'?"

I shifted my weight nervously from one foot to another and dragged my gaze away from the magnetic pull of his. "Of course, I've heard that. Everyone has."

He bent at the waist slightly, which brought us nearly eye to eye. My breath caught and I lifted a hand to my chest where my heart was pounding underneath my palm.

"As of now, I'm responsible for you, Dr. Baskin." It took me a second to realize he was referring to when he pulled me out of the line of fire in the parking lot. One of his dark eyes closed in a flirty wink as he straightened while I struggled to form an argument against his words. "Gonna be interesting to see how that plays out, isn't it?" Before I could say anything, his hands landed on my shoulders and turned me around to face the apartment. "Go get your stuff. I'll hang out here until you get into your car, just in case."

I started to protest, but I could tell he wasn't going to listen to anything I had to say. Swearing softly under my breath I asked, "You're just going to do whatever the hell you want regardless of what I say or do, aren't you?"

"Pretty much." His grin turned into a full-fledged smile, and I swore I forgot how to breathe for a moment. It was unfair that a badass biker was blessed such a pretty, persuasive smile. How was that fair to innocent hearts everywhere?

Huffing in frustration, I let myself into my apartment.

I'd only ever been responsible for myself, and for my mother. Shot telling me he intended to be responsible for my well-being in any way made me dizzy and made me feel off-center.

I also couldn't shake Shot's theory that running away from my life was giving Ashby exactly what she wanted. I'd given up everything to try and play her game and didn't have anything to show for it.

Something needed to change, and it was slightly disconcerting that the revelation came from the last place I would've expected it to. Taking life advice from a guy I'd had to dig a bullet out of not too long ago probably wasn't the brightest idea I'd ever had, but for some inexplicable reason, listening to Shot didn't seem as scary as everything else happening in my life.

CHAPTER 5

∞

SHOT

So this is the place, huh?" It didn't look like anything special, and there was no effort to hide the Confederate flags that decorated the exterior. They weren't being subtle, that was for damn sure.

I pulled down the black face mask I'd worn on the ride from Loveless. It was a pretty drive out to the small town located near Lake Travis, but oddly desolate and empty once you got through all the subdivisions. It was a good place for both a clubhouse and a dive bar catering to a group of less than desirable individuals to set up shop.

When we got word from another club that Jed Coleman was hiding out in the bar, I'd gathered a handful of my most trustworthy and lethal guys and hit the road. We didn't really have a plan in place, other than to grab Jed Coleman and make him pay for what he'd done to me and the club. It still burned deep down in my gut that we'd lost two of our brothers because of Coleman. Once we had our hands on Jed, I'd figure out a proper punishment.

"You can count on pretty much everyone inside the bar being armed, and a lot of them know how to fight. Last time my club clashed with them, a couple of my guys ended up in the ER. One lost an eye, and another lost a couple fingers on his hand. They play dirty."

The youngish Hispanic man who called himself Rocker and who was the president of the other club sounded rightly furious over the previous encounters.

Heavy is the head that wears the crown, or in this case the PRESIDENT patch on the front of his cut. I sympathized with the man's ire. It was hard enough to worry about your own well-being and if the decisions you were making were the right ones. That weight was exponentially more when you have twenty to thirty guys willing to follow you to hell and back. Guys who trusted you implicitly and who were willing to risk it all just because you asked them to. It was our job to keep everyone as safe as possible, and when we failed, the loss was crushing and often impossible to shake off.

I grunted and narrowed my eyes as a young man with a shaved head, complete with a swastika tattooed on the back, came out the front door and lit up a cigarette.

"We play dirtier. You sure the guy I'm looking for went in there?" So far, I hadn't laid eyes on Coleman, and I wasn't about to force my way in without verified information. As much as I'd taken away growing up at my father's side, I'd also learned many valuable lessons while I was in the military. It was a combination of both brutal educations that made me great at what I did, and it was the main reason I had so many willing to follow my lead.

"I've had eyes on this place since I first contacted you to verify your guy has been hiding out here. He's definitely in there." The younger guy rubbed his fingers over his goatee and frowned. "We've tried to figure out another way besides the front door, but we haven't come up with anything. Even though the bar is supposed to be open to the public, they keep the place as secure as Fort Knox. My guess is they run meth through there."

I made a disgusted noise low in my throat. I wasn't what anyone would consider a good guy, but I had a deeply ingrained sense of what was and wasn't an acceptable way to make a living on the wrong side of the law. Drugs were a hard no when it came to my club and the people I did business with. I hated how dependent and unpredictable they made people. I also didn't like the chain of command involved when it came to narcotics. If you cut off one head, it was likely three more dangerous versions would grow back in its place.

Turning my head, I looked at Top, who still had a bandana with a skull wrapped around the lower part of his face. He held a pair of very expensive, very high-tech infrared binoculars to his eyes as he intently watched the bar down at the bottom of the hill where we were parked.

"How many people are inside?" I kept my voice low as I started to ponder the best way to gain entrance to the bar while ensuring the least number of casualties. I wanted Coleman no matter the cost, but I was never one for unnecessary carnage. I wanted to extract the man from his hiding place with a scalpel, not a chainsaw.

"About fifty. And there is an unidentifiable heat source coming from the basement, so the theory about them cooking meth is probably accurate." Top sounded disgusted and I didn't blame him.

"That means we have to be careful when we go in. I don't want our guys exposed to those chemicals." It was too soon to lose anyone else. I wasn't sure I had the mental capacity to bounce back from another failure. It'd taken a lot longer to get to a good place following the loss of my brothers than it had to heal from my actual, physical injuries. "You see another way in, Top?"

My VP swore softly and pulled the expensive goggles away from his face. "The roof. Let's pull it off the damn building and make them come to us. Why give them home field advantage?"

The building was mostly comprised of tin siding and big sheets of tin on the roof. It resembled some of the temporary outbuildings on our ranch, or a really big shed. It wasn't an uncommon structure out in the hill country since the material was durable and the weather was unpredictable. Top's wild plan was a possibility.

The young biker next to me balked. "How are you going to pull the roof off with no one noticing? That sounds insane." He looked between me and my VP with huge eyes and a face full of confusion.

Top snorted. "We want them to notice. If we pull the roof off the building, most of the people inside will come running out to see what the commotion is all about. The less people inside, means less risk of injury if that meth lab goes up, and less places for our side to get cornered and taken unaware. It'll also make it easier for us to spot Coleman. If he comes out in the fray, we snatch him up. If he doesn't, we go in after him and he has nowhere to hide. He's who we're after. We don't need to start a war with strangers over one man."

Rocker blew out a whistle and rubbed a hand over his face. "You guys are nuts."

It wasn't the first time I'd heard that. One of the reasons I'd left my father's branch of the SoS was because he often opposed my more logical and less destructive way of going about things. It took a while for me to realize that my dad's moral compass pointed a different direction from mine. He played fast and loose with his own life, which I'd always understood as being part of his character. My friends thought he was cool. I thought he was foolish. What I couldn't take was him being so indifferent toward the lives of his members, and toward mine. My father was ruthless. I was rational. Those two things did not mix well when it came to making big calls for the well-being of the club and its members.

"Rave." I called for our club secretary. He was also our youngest member. A computer hacker with a lime-green mohawk I'd recruited as soon as I got out of the military. The kid was in deep trouble with Homeland Security, so I pulled in a few favors when he was still a teenager. He was a valuable asset to my team and the closest thing I had to a younger brother.

"We need tow chains with hooks on the end. Get the twins up on the roof and tell them to find the best place to hook on." The young man nodded enthusiastically and immediately started tapping out messages on his phone. "We need a distraction so they don't hear us pounding around on the roof when the twins hook up the chains." I cut a look in Top's direction. "You got something in mind?"

The other man scoffed as if insulted. "Of course I do. Chaos is my middle name."

He lifted a gloved hand and we bumped fists. A moment later a shrill whistle split the air as he lifted a hand and indicated for the guys wearing our patches to follow him as he fired up his bike and raced down the hill in front of us.

I turned to look at my fellow president and ordered, "You take your guys and keep the local law off our backs while this goes down. We don't need them tangled up in this."

Rocker growled low in his throat and offered a nod. "Our history with the deputies around here isn't very good."

I flashed a grin. "We have a good lawyer if things go south. Don't worry too much about it."

He left, still grumbling about getting involved with a crazy person, but he obeyed my orders. We might have the same rank, but my reputation and lineage preceded me. Even if I wasn't exactly close to my father, Torch's history of violence and disregard for law and order was legendary, and I was often found guilty by association. Very few members or clubs wanted to be put on my old man's radar for any reason. Even if folks knew nothing about me and how I led my own crew, they knew I was Torch's one and only son, and that was enough to gain me respect and blind compliance.

A moment later it was almost too loud to think, and definitely too loud to have any kind of conversation. The bar was suddenly surrounded in a wide circle by guys revving their engines and sending clouds of dust and dirt in the direction of the tin-covered building. The noise on the inside had to be deafening as the debris ricocheted off the exterior. Dressed head to toe in black, a couple of our members who we simply referred to as "the twins" blended in well with the night sky as they scurried across the thin road, heavy chains rattling in their hands.

As expected, a flood of people came storming out the front door. Most of the men held metal baseball bats as they started to scream obscenities and threats while the women scattered. If there were fifty people inside the building, approximately half had come out to see what the commotion was all about or to take cover. Top continued to rev his engine, spraying the gathered group and covering them in a cloud of dust and exhaust fumes. Angry yelling did its best to rise above the noise, but it was no match for the powerful motorcycle engines.

As soon as the twins were off the roof, I got a text from

Rave that the tow chains were hooked up. The crowd was now gathered around the disruptive bikers. After scanning it and not seeing Coleman, I gave the order for the roof to be removed.

It was an ear-splitting sound as the metal was violently ripped away from the underlying structure. The bending and buckling tin shrieked loudly as more and more people came running out of the bar. I imagined it was similar to how folks in these parts would react to a tornado ripping through the building. A gunshot sounded, and voices rose. Off in the distance I heard sirens start to wail, but amid all the noise and confusion, there was still no sign of Coleman.

Heaving a deep sigh and pulling my mask back up over the lower half of my face, I sent a brief message to Top to let him know I was going inside to try and find him. I didn't get a response, or expect one, because by now a full-on brawl had erupted in front of the club. It was bikers versus the bargoers, and the fight was evenly matched. I knew my guys could hold their own, so I circled the building, dodging a flying two-by-four on the way. Once I was around back where the mangled, crumpled roof had been discarded, I searched for a way to get over the wreckage and inside the building as unobtrusively as possible.

Unhooking one of the tow chains, I climbed up on top of a propane tank that luckily hadn't been crushed under the weight of the flying roof, and hooked the end onto the top of the exposed frame of the building. It took a few tries to get a solid grasp, but once I had it hooked on, I hauled myself up the side of the building and dropped down on the other side. Luckily it was a short distance to fall, and the interior of the building was mostly emptied out.

An older man was standing behind the bar, looking like he was in shock. A few women were huddled together in the corner, clearly questioning their life decisions. A young guy across the room shouted at me and sent a worried look toward a door partially hidden behind the bar. Still not seeing Coleman anywhere, I made the decision to see what was behind the door.

I was grabbed from behind as I made my way toward the bar. I shook off the hold and put the kid on the ground with a single punch. I ordered the women to stay where they were, and easily knocked the knife out of the bartender's hand when he suddenly lunged at me. I didn't want to hurt him, just get him out of my way, so I knocked him to the ground and ordered him to stay there unless he wanted to bleed. He stayed still and lifted his hands up in surrender. As expected, the men who knew how to fight were all outside engaged with the rest of my club, leaving an opening for me to find Coleman with little fuss.

Still, as I shouldered the heavy door open, I pulled my weapon. I wanted to be prepared for anything. Coleman and his older brother had both proven to be unpredictable and wily. They were also both master marksmen, something I'd failed to consider previously. I wasn't going to make that same mistake again.

My boots banged heavily on the rickety steps, which led down into what was effectively a root cellar. It was dark, dank, and smelled bad. Mostly because of the heavy chemicals used in the manufacturing of methamphetamine. I was glad I'd pulled my mask back up around my face, though it only offered a modicum of protection. Noise from the outside situation rang against the hollow walls. The sounds took me back to any number of bunkers I'd had to hunker down in while in an active combat zone. Blinking back against more than one unpleasant memory, and the dim darkness, I scanned the underground meth lab for any sign of movement.

It didn't take long for my prey to show himself.

From underneath a long table covered in drug para-phernalia, including all kinds of beakers and unidentifiable chemicals, I caught sight of twin barrels aiming right for me. I dove off the stairs and hit the hard, cold ground before the first shot fired in my direction made my ears ring. Rolling to get behind an old beer cooler for protection, I returned fire, hearing glass shatter as a result.

Exactly what I'd been trying to avoid was now happening. All those chemicals were going to be volatile and loose in the air, making the situation even more dangerous than it already was. They were highly flammable, and the slightest spark could turn the entire bar into a fireball.

"Coleman. I don't know what you're thinking, but it's best if you just come out. There is no scenario in which this ends well for you." I tried to keep my voice calm, but the bastard had killed two of my brothers and nearly killed me. The score I had to settle with him was huge.

"You killed my brother, Caldwell. What makes you think this will end well for you either?" The thick Texas twang didn't have a hint of fear in it. Coleman was just as set on revenge as I was.

I swore loudly as another shot echoed through the space. "You want to blow us both up? Idiot."

"As long as I take you with me, I don't give a shit!" The words sounded unhinged, and the man wasn't making any sense. The situation was getting more and more dangerous by the minute, and as much as I wanted Coleman in my hands, my conscience couldn't bear the idea of the women and other innocent people upstairs getting caught in the crossfire. I couldn't abide unnecessary casualties.

The sound of the shotgun being reloaded had the hairs on the back of my neck lifting up. Also, the commotion from

outside the bar had grown to deafening levels and I was sure
bloodshed had started. This whole thing had turned into a
mess, and I was reminded why revenge wasn't always the
best answer. Sadly, I'd never been able to walk away from
the search for retribution. My soul was restless until the
proper price was paid.

The cooler I was hiding behind shifted as Coleman's
shot blasted into the side. I jumped a little, more because
the sulfur smell of smoke and burning chemicals started to
fill the air, making it increasingly hard to breathe. My eyes
started to burn, and my exposed skin started to feel itchy and
too tight. Things were going bad, quicker than I expected,
and my options were limited.

Swearing loudly, I shoved the cooler out of the way
and took a shot at all the beakers on the now-littered table,
sending a shower of glass over the spot where Jed had
taken cover, as well as spilling the unknown contents all
over his hiding place. I knew he would have no choice but
to abandon his cover and reveal himself once his protection
was compromised. The toxic smell was overwhelming and
it became nearly impossible to breathe, even though I had
protective fabric covering the lower half of my face. Knowing Coleman was going to try and take a shot as soon as he
got to his feet, I gave him my back as I turned to run back
up the stairs. I decided the chemicals clogging the air were
more dangerous than the bullets that were bound to start
flying between us.

I tried to crouch down and make myself as small as
possible as I dashed back up toward the main bar, tripping
over my own feet because it was so hard to see through the
tears rushing out of my eyes. A gunshot sounded behind me
and I went down to one knee as the back of my thigh exploded into a riot of painful spots. Loud pops and a sizzling

sound followed the sound of the gun going off, and an acrid, noxious smell instantly wafted up from the cellar.

I groaned and touched the back of my bloody thigh, looking at the stunned older man who was still standing behind the bar as I practically crawled through the opening.

I met his gaze with a watery one of my own and choked out, "If you don't want to die in a chemical explosion, help me move something heavy in front of that door, and get everyone else out of here. We have less than five minutes before this place goes up like a bomb."

The older man looked shocked, but when thick black smoke started to seep around the bottom and sides of the door, he finally moved. He yelled at the few people still seeking refuge in the bar to leave and helped me muscle a heavy fridge in front of the doorway to stop it from opening. He didn't ask about the man still in the basement, and I didn't offer any explanation. Coleman had made his choice, and now he was going to have to live with the outcome.

The old man gave me a once-over as I stumbled and tripped my way toward the exit, before hauling himself over the bar and darting toward the door. Of course he didn't bother to help me. I would've done the same thing in his shoes.

Coughing and trying to peer through watery, burning eyes, I dragged myself across the bar. My leg was killing me, but I knew the injury wasn't fatal. The thing that was going to get me in trouble was inhaling the poison that was steadily filling the room. The blast of Raid from Presley the other day didn't have anything on the toxic fog I was currently trying to fight my way through. I was about ten feet away from the front door, could see outside, when I suddenly couldn't make my feet move any further. I hit the floor, my knees jarring against the wood hard enough to click my back teeth together. I was wheezing behind the mask, choking and trying not to vomit.

Gasping, I tried to push myself back to my feet so I could muscle through the last few steps to fresh air, only to collapse in a gagging heap as toxic smoke continued to roll through the room.

Right before I stopped breathing altogether and everything around me went black, I vaguely felt hands reach around my torso and pull me up. My head lolled lifelessly forward as I was dragged out of the smoldering, dangerous bar.

"Sometimes you're more trouble than you're worth, Caldwell." Top's familiar drawl sounded a million miles away, but the frustration that filled it was music to my ears. This was far from the first time my VP had pulled my ass out of the fire, literally. And we both knew it wouldn't be the last.

CHAPTER 6

❧

PRESLEY

Keep the key, Presley."

Kody deliberately slid a copy of her house key back across the scarred wood of the bar top and gave me a hard look. "I want you to know there is always a safe place for you. I want you to know that you are always welcome in my home. I need you to understand that only family gets keys to the front door, and you are part of my family." She huffed a little bit and picked up a towel to wipe down a nonexistent spot on the bar in front of where I was sitting. "I don't want you to leave in the first place. It's nice having someone around while Hill is away on assignment." She pouted and it made her look adorable. It was a look I could never pull off, no matter how similar our faces were.

I'd purposely waited until she was busy at work to drop by and tell her I was going back to my apartment. There'd been no progress on finding whoever took the shots outside my building, and I was sick and tired of living in constant fear and hiding from everything and everyone who might cause me harm. Shot's words about me giving my life up wouldn't stop echoing inside my head. Over the last few days I'd come to the conclusion he was right, and it was time to stop living in stasis and regain control of my life and my future. Not only was I going back to my apartment temporarily, I was also going back to work.

I was done being a sitting duck.

"Okay, I'll keep it." I picked up the key and twirled the ring holder around my finger. Kody lifted her head and a smile broke through the grim look on her face. I smiled back and told her, "And once I find a place of my own, a permanent place, I promise I will get you your very own copy of my front door key, because I want to be a safe place for you as well."

She blinked in surprise and abandoned pretending like she was cleaning. "Wait. You're going to look for a new place? Here in Loveless, right?" She didn't bother to cover the slight panic in the last question.

I reached out and patted the back of her hand, instinctively trying to ease her sudden fear. "I'm going back to work, so that means I need to find a place closer to Ivy." Ivy, Texas, was a suburb outside of Austin and only an hour or so away from Loveless. "I was thinking I'd look for something in between here and there."

I also wanted to find somewhere that was my idea of perfect. All my life I'd bounced between apartments, condos, and town houses because it was just me while my mom was in and out of the hospital. I was too busy taking care of her and working to worry about the upkeep of any kind of property, so temporary and tiny worked. Now my outlook on everything was different. I wanted somewhere lasting, some-place that required me to care for it and put my mark on it. I also had a family to think of now, as Kody was so fond of reminding me. I might need more space in the future, since they'd made it clear they weren't going anywhere anytime soon. And maybe, once I was settled, I could even get a dog. I'd always wanted one, but there had never been time or enough emotional availability.

I squeezed Kody's hand and tilted my head to the side to consider her carefully. She'd gotten past all my defenses without me even being aware they had been breached. I'd stopped fighting her when she insisted that I join girls' night along with Case's and Crew's significant others. I'd also stopped feeling like a total outsider when I was with them. It was starting to feel like maybe I had a place where I really belonged.

Kody and I even spent late nights chatting when she came home from the bar while I was camped out at her place. We talked about everything from the serious threat still hanging over my head to the differences in our upbringings. She answered questions about our father, even though I knew it was painful for her, and I tried to explain what it was like growing up being smarter than everyone around me. Over the last few weeks I found myself actually wanting to spend time with her. As over the top and noisy as she was, there was something about being in her company that soothed all the frayed edges of my nerves. It was similar to how I felt when I was around Shot. There was just something about their larger-than-life personalities that helped me forget to be afraid and lonely.

"You know you can always call me if you're lonely while Hill is gone." I knew how dark and heavy loneliness could be. The weight of it could be crushing.

Kody gave me a grin that was unmistakably grateful as she moved away to help a customer tapping on an empty glass a few seats down. After she poured the beer and took another order, she moved back to where I was sitting. "Hill says we spend a lot of time alone together. We were both independent, driven people before we got together. Each of us had our own plans and ideas about what the future should look like. I was worried when we made things official and moved in with one another it'd get annoying being constantly in each other's space. Shockingly, we ended up fitting together seamlessly. It's like we already knew how to move around one another, and move with each other. I do really miss him when he's gone, but I try not to tell him that too often. I don't want him to worry. There are times that I've felt like I've had to relearn how to be by myself."

I took the glass of water she set in front of me. I didn't want to make light of the fact that she was showing a shockingly vulnerable part of herself. She was prickly and thorny, but underneath that armor she had a very soft center. "Well, we can be alone together as well. I spent most of my life alone, so I'm the opposite of you. I'm having to relearn how to be around others and not take for granted the fact that people actually want my company."

Kody let out a boisterous laugh like I was joking and asked me if I wanted to order something to eat, since it was dinnertime. It was an obvious tactic to change the subject, so I told her I'd already grabbed something with one of my former colleagues when I'd gone to tell my old boss I was ready to accept the promotion they'd been holding for me.

"You're really going back to work?" She seemed surprised by my decision but not discouraging.

Then Kody motioned for one of her staff to come behind the bar so she could take a seat next to me on one of the vintage bar stools. The Barn, her honky-tonk bar on the outside of Loveless's city limits, was an old horse barn she had refurbished from the ground up. The place was a mix of country-western and boho chic. It had its own vibe that was totally Kody, and lately business had been booming. When I first met her, she admitted she was struggling and the only reason the bar stayed afloat was because she had a business agreement with the Sons of Sorrow. When Hill reentered her life, she'd cut those ties and had to figure out how to survive on her own. Step-by-step she was making it, and even though our relationship was new, I felt incredibly proud of her.

I traced a finger down the wet side of the glass in front of me and responded, "Someone told me if I really wanted to push Ashby to make a move, I needed to live my life as if she was inconsequential. Her ultimate goal was to take everything away from me, and that's exactly what I let her do by hiding out and pushing everyone away. What I ultimately want is justice. I want justice for Conrad, for my mother, and for myself. I worked my ass off for that promotion. I deserved it, then and now. Why should I let her win?"

Kody nodded aggressively in agreement. "It's brave to go back knowing it might trigger retribution and put you in danger."

I sighed and turned my head to look at her. "I told them that I couldn't be directly involved in handling any evidence or official rulings until Ashby is behind bars. I want her convicted of tampering with my previous cases so there is zero question as to whether or not I'm qualified to handle any case that comes my way. For now, I'm going to supervise the existing staff, handle some consulting for the bigger offices that are understaffed around the state, and do some guest lecture spots at different universities." I was also going to dig deeper into my mother's murder. I was still the only one who questioned the how and the why of it all. I was the only one convinced beyond a shadow of a doubt that her death, while imminent because of her illness, had been helped along and hurried. The questions I harbored felt like they were growing to the point I could barely think of anything else. I needed closure in more ways than one, just like Shot had so bluntly pointed out.

Kody turned to look at the door to the bar when an audible murmur worked through the patrons at the sight of a new arrival. "It sounds like you've thought this all through. When you're ready to start house hunting, let me know. I'd love to tag along." She hopped off her stool as her bouncer put a hand on Shot's chest to stop the biker from stepping around him.

Harris, the big, bearded, redheaded bouncer who was a former rodeo clown and a friend of Crew's, was super thankful to the Lawtons for landing him the gig at the bar when he was in a tough spot. It was no secret he was extra protective of Kody and the bar, and now that she'd claimed me as her sister, that watchful eye fell on me as well. It appeared he hadn't yet forgiven Shot and his boys for bursting in and bleeding all over the floor a couple of months ago. But as tough and burly as Harris was, he was no match for Shot.

Kody yelped in alarm and quickened her pace, scurrying across the bar to put out the potential fire. I decided to make my exit as quickly as possible because I was trying to stick to my conviction that we didn't really have any reason to be around one another. I hadn't seen him in several days, and I figured my lingering fascination with him would die a natural death given enough space. Unfortunately, that didn't seem to be the case. When I was alone at night I wondered about both the man and the biker. I wondered how different the two were, or if there was any difference at all. So far I'd only ever dealt with Shot, and I wondered what the man underneath the leather and badass bravado was actually like.

And even though I'd never admit it to another living soul,

there was more than one night when I'd woken up short of breath and tangled in the covers because my dreams had taken on a life of their own, with Shot as the star. I wasn't used to having a man make my heart race, especially when he wasn't even in the same room as I was. I was avoiding all of it—the feelings, the reactions, and most importantly the man. Only, Shot didn't look like he intended to keep being ignored.

As I walked toward where Kody was determinedly putting herself between the two large men, I felt his dark gaze settle on me and stay there. The intensity of it made my skin prickle and warm. I gulped in response and shifted my eyes to the floor. I swore the man could see right through me, including my unexpected reaction to him. I hated feeling like there was no way to hide anything from him.

"I don't want him in here, Kody. He's nothing but trouble, and your brothers don't like him." Harris had a thick drawl and deep voice. Sometimes he sounded like the character Boomhauer from the old cartoon *King of the Hill*. His words blended together and became indecipherable when he was excited about something.

Kody put her hands on the bouncer's barrel chest and nudged him backward. "I like him. My brothers don't get a vote about anything that happens in this bar. Back off, Harry."

I cleared my throat and nodded in greeting when Shot lifted an eyebrow in my direction, carefully watching as I tried to skirt about where they were all gathered. "I'm going to get going. It was a long day. I'll see you later, Kody."

She bobbed her head distractedly and gave a half-hearted wave, still trying to keep the bouncer from rushing at the biker. "I'll give you a call later. Be safe, Presley."

I went to step around the melee when a rough hand

wrapped around my arm right above my elbow, stopping my detour. I couldn't stop the chills that followed Shot's deep and authoritative "I'll walk you out."

The bickering bar workers both stopped and fell silent as they watched me work on prying Shot's fingers off my arm. I didn't want to cause another scene by trying to escape, but the need to get away from him and how he made me feel was burning through my veins. "No. It's fine. It's a quick walk and I parked under one of the lights in the parking lot and Case still has his deputies patrolling the area. I'll be fine on my own."

"Stop being stubborn. Remember what happened last time you were in a parking lot at night?" He tugged on my arm, making me fall into line next to him. When I was practically plastered to his side, I noticed that his movements seemed stiff and that he was favoring one of his legs.

Before I could comment on his condition, Kody was bending down, looking at the back of Shot's leg, her face alarmingly close to his backside.

"What's wrong with you? Why are you favoring one side? Are you hurt?" She reached out to touch a dark spot on the denim covering his strong-looking thigh, only to have Shot try to knock her hand away. "What happened to you, Shot?"

He didn't have the mobility to shoo Kody off because he refused to loosen the hold he had on my arm and his other hand was too far away to reach her. "It's nothing. I already had Stitch take care of it."

Kody reached for the spot on his pants again, only to have him clumsily evade her probing hands by lurching in my direction and nearly falling over. Bewildered by his suspicious behavior, she snapped, "Stop being shy. It's not like I haven't seen it all before."

That exclamation had all of us pausing and going awkwardly still. I knew Kody was close to Shot prior to her relationship with Hill, but I hadn't realized exactly how *close* they were. It never occurred to me they might be former lovers, though given their similar personalities, and stubbornness, it made a lot of sense.

Shot cleared his throat and started to pull me out the front door. "I'm gonna walk your sister out to her car. You can give me the third degree some other time."

Finding myself more irritated than the situation called for, I forcibly pried my arm free from the almost-punishing hold Shot had on it and marched out of the bar, failing to call out a final parting to my sister on the way. Shot followed at a slower pace, his gait uneven and his face set in hard lines as I turned to confront him.

I took a deep breath, shoved my noticeably shaking hands through my hair and ordered him, "Stop. Stop ignoring me when I tell you something. Stop pulling me around after you. Stop inserting yourself into situations where you weren't invited."

I blinked in surprise at my own reaction and at the stunned expression on his face. I didn't get vocal and forceful like this and wasn't sure how to handle the response, mine or his.

His dark eyes narrowed slightly and a furrow pulled at his brows. The corners of his mouth tilted down in a slight frown, and a muscle in his tanned cheek started to twitch. Maybe I should have been concerned that I was obviously making him angry. But I couldn't put the brakes on now that I was speaking my mind and trying to shove him into the safe and secure box I'd designated for him.

"I keep telling you that we don't owe each other anything. I know you're used to getting your own way, but not with me. If you can't respect the boundaries I've made very clear,

I'd rather you pretend we're strangers, just like I'm trying to do. I'm fighting to take my life back while not losing it, or myself, in the process. I really don't have the time or energy to fight you as well."

Shot stared at me in silence for a long, drawn-out moment. The tension between us was suffocating. I knew he probably wasn't used to having someone talk back to him the way I just had, but I'd had it with everyone trying to steamroll over me in the guise of it being for my own good. I'd had to make difficult choices and stand on my own through the consequences since I was little. I didn't need someone to hold my hand through every mistake I was bound to make, even if I appreciated the effort.

"I know you can do it on your own. I've never questioned how capable you are." Shot took a step toward me, driving me backward into the shadow cast by the bar behind me. "Did it occur to you that you don't *have* to do things on your own? You don't have to walk through town to the drugstore on your own. You don't have to walk to your car in a dark parking lot alone. You have plenty of people around you willing to be there for you while your neck is on the line." I shook my head and gasped as my back hit the wood of the old barn as he pressed even closer. I put my hands up in front of me as Shot deliberately stepped into my space and growled, "Would it kill you to accept help when it's offered, regardless of where it's coming from?"

"I've been on my own my entire life. I never needed anyone to help me." The argument sounded weak, and we both knew it.

Even injured, he was still the most intimidating man I'd ever met. I put my hands on his chest to hold him back when he leaned into me so that our chests were touching. I could feel his breath on the side of my face, and the controlled fury radiating off his strong body where it pressed against mine.

"Do you know how many people Kody has looking out for her each and every day?" He growled the words into my ear as the fingers of one of his hands gently wrapped around my jaw and held my head still. "Her brothers. Their women. Her staff. That Texas Ranger. She's a tough cookie, but she's always been protected and had someone at her back. She knows she can't do everything on her own. She knows it's okay to rely on people she can trust, on people who care about her. She's stubborn, but she isn't stupid."

He moved my face so we were nearly eye to eye. "Eventually, you're going to have to recognize that you have a crowd around you just like Kody does. There is no reason for you to keep on thinking you are fighting this fight alone."

I made a strangled noise and lifted a hand to wrap around his wide, tattooed wrist. I intended to pull his hand away from my face but got thoroughly distracted when I could feel his pulse racing under my fingertips.

His voice dropped to a low, intimate whisper as his words caressed my skin. "I'm the one who is going to purposely cross your path. I'm never going to walk the other way when I see you coming. I'm going to head right toward you." He chuckled and rubbed his thumb along the line of my jaw. Goose bumps immediately broke out all over my skin, and I wondered if he could hear my heart pounding inside my chest because it sounded super loud to my own ears.

"The only reason I stopped in the bar tonight was because I saw your car in the parking lot." His dark eyebrows winged upward, and the smirk that crossed his face should have been illegal in all fifty states. "My leg is killing me and I have other things I should be doing, but I couldn't convince myself to keep going on my way when I knew you were close

by. I wanted to see you. I wanted to make sure you were safe
and sound. The need was too big to fight, so I'm going to
stop trying."

His face moved even closer to mine and I stopped func-
tioning. I couldn't breathe. Couldn't see straight. Couldn't
hear anything other than my heart pounding. I couldn't feel
anything other than the heat of his body against mine.

He kept talking and I was ready to beg him to stop. Every
time he opened his mouth, he said something else that was
absolutely confusing and a total turn-on. My entire system
was ready to short-circuit at his proximity and his softly
worded warning.

"As for boundaries, I approve of you having them and
knowing what they are. As long as they're in your best
interest I'll respect the hell out of them. But if it's something
stupid, like you proving you don't need anyone or anything
by walking to your car in a dark parking lot, I'm gonna go
ahead and ignore that shit because I'd rather have you mad
at me and offended than dead."

The tip of his nose dragged across my cheekbone, and I
swore he flicked the tip of his tongue against the shell of my
ear. I'd never shivered so hard in my life. This guy had the
uncanny ability to turn me inside out, and it baffled me. I
kept reminding myself he wasn't my type, but my body and
my hormones weren't listening... at all.

I thought he was going to kiss me.

I prepared for it.

I told myself I would stop him, that I would scream my
fool head off if he made an inappropriate move.

So, it made absolutely no sense that the disappointment
I felt when instead he pushed away from me was heavy
enough it nearly flattened me. I jolted when Shot grabbed
my hand and muttered, "I'm taking you to your car, not

because you need me to, but because I *want* to. I don't want to see anything happen to you, and regardless of how you feel about me, I know you can understand that."

I had no idea what I was going to do with him, or how to keep him from interfering in my life anymore. The truth was that there was no place in the life I was preparing to go back to for someone like Shot Caldwell. It was boring, predictable, and staid...well, it would be once no one was trying to kill me. And who was I to expect someone who lived their life full tilt, full speed, and out of control to try and understand that? To try and find their space inside the stillness?

Not me. I would never. Could never, which was why it was better to walk away.

CHAPTER 7

∞

SHOT

W hat happened to your leg?"

The soft question came after Presley noticeably slowed down her hurried pace across the parking lot to match mine. The slight limp I had, due to the buckshot that'd been recently picked out of my leg, was impossible to hide. I hadn't planned on making a stop at the bar because I didn't want to get the third degree from Kody. But as soon as I caught sight of Presley's car in the parking lot my plans changed. It wasn't like we had a lot of reason to run into one another regularly as it was, and now that it seemed like she was actively avoiding me, I felt like I hadn't seen her in weeks. I was compelled to stop so I could see her. So I could hear her voice. So I could see for myself that she was safe and still in one piece. She'd been on my mind a lot, which was a new experience for me. I hadn't lied when I told her I was done fighting myself and the logic that screamed it would be better for both of us to keep some distance.

I grunted as I gave her the CliffsNotes version of how I

got injured. "Ran into a situation with the club and ended up taking some buckshot in the back of my thigh. Hurts like a son of a bitch, but it's not too serious."

"You always seem to have someone shooting at you. I'd say that's pretty serious." Presley shifted her gaze away from mine and frowned out into the darkness around us. "It seems like an exhausting way to live. Don't you get tired of always being injured and barely surviving dangerous situations?" A slight frown crossed her delicate features and her words dropped to a whisper I could barely hear. "I'd hate it if you ended up the victim in one of my murder cases. That would be devastating."

She didn't want me to end up dead.

The thought made the area around my heart tingle just a little bit. It wasn't a feeling I'd ever really experienced before. Not even with Kody. I was pretty good at keeping my emotions and expectations in check. I was realistic when it came to knowing what I did and didn't have to offer someone else. I wasn't a good bet when it came to starting anything serious with a woman, and there had yet to be one who made me want to change that. However, I was starting to wonder if the pretty doctor was going to be the one who inspired me to look at my life and my choices in a new way.

"I grew up in a motorcycle club. My mom took off before I could walk, and my old man lived and breathed the Sons of Sorrow. He was one of the founding members of the club." I grinned reflexively, burying old pain behind false bravado. "I was practically feral as a kid, and not much changed when I joined the military. The Marines said they saw potential in me, but what they really saw was a kid who had already experienced his fair share of violence and wasn't one to shy away from doing the dirty work. They took a wild teenager and molded him into a ruthless killer."

I paused when Presley let out a small gasp. Her eyes were big as she watched me carefully. I was pretty sure she didn't realize we'd both stopped walking as I started telling her about my past.

"I've seen the worst the world has to offer, and I'm not only talking about war. Even now, one of the main reasons my branch of the club survives and funds itself without being involved in drugs and prostitution is because we go into the places in the world other people are afraid of. We provide protection. We bring the lost back home. We use the training the government gave most of us to keep alive people that others want dead."

I lifted my eyebrows at her and shifted my weight off of my injured leg. It was starting to burn, but I was going to power through the pain as long as Presley wasn't running away from me. I wasn't used to being the one who did the chasing. It was far more common that I was the one running because the person trying to catch me wanted more than I was willing to give.

"Death isn't something I'm afraid of. It's been a constant in my life since before I fully understood the permanence of it. I don't think you can live life fully and appreciate the important memories and moments unless you recognize everything we have and everyone we love will eventually be gone."

When I was done talking, Presley vibrated with a whole-body shiver, as if she could easily imagine pulling back the sheet and seeing my lifeless body in her morgue. I figured it wasn't a good move to tell her I was more likely to put some-one else there than I was to end up on the slab. She already had enough reasons, many of them valid, for running away from me. I wasn't about to give her another one. Almost as if she could sense the morbid and dark turn of my thoughts, she shook off the stillness and resumed her steady march toward her car.

I couldn't tell if she was talking to me or herself when she stated, "Death has been a constant in my life as well. I think I respect it more than you do, though."

"What do you mean?" I was seriously annoyed that my injured leg kept me a few steps behind her. I really was chasing after her in more ways than one. I was also irritated at how casually she dismissed my complicated relationship with life and death. I profoundly respected the power of both love and loss in someone's life. I didn't know much about love, but I was pretty much an expert when it came to all the different kinds of loss a person could go through. I kept my emotions in check because it was expected of me as the leader of my club. But I wasn't a heartless monster, even if being one, the way my father had wanted, would make my life and my lifestyle easier.

"My mother was sick my whole childhood. I never knew how long I was going to have with her. There were as many bad days as good. I lived every single day knowing her death was inevitable. I tried not to be scared, since I knew it was coming and there was no stopping it. No matter how rich you are, how well you lived, what kind of deal you made with the devil, death is one thing all humans have in common. It's one thing that ties us all together."

We were almost to her car, so her pace slowed a little and she turned her head so I could see her profile. I felt like I'd learned more about her in these last five minutes than in any of our other encounters. I wanted to believe she was getting more comfortable around me, but that could just be wishful thinking. Selfishly wanting a few more moments with her, I asked, "Is that why you became a medical examiner? To prove to yourself that you weren't afraid?"

She nodded as I moved closer. "Partly. I chose to be a medical examiner because I couldn't handle the thought of being the person trying to delay the inevitable. I'm not strong enough to fight the battle for life and losing it. The idea of not being able to save someone..." She trailed off and I saw her shoulders slump. "It's too much. I remember how my mother cried when she was told she was going to die no matter what the doctor did. I will never forget how helpless and hopeless I felt when we got the news. I never wanted to be in a position to bring that disappointment into someone's life. Instead, I picked a field where I get to tell people that I'll make sure their loved one didn't die in vain. I don't go up against death, I make sense of it for those who are left behind because I understand it so well."

She stopped at her car. As she beeped the door open, she asked, "Did the situation you ran into recently have anything to do with the shooting in the parking lot in front of my apartment?"

I wasn't shocked at the subject change, since things were getting pretty intense for such a short walk in the dark. "More than likely."

I still wasn't a hundred percent certain Jed Coleman was behind that incident. Regardless, he was no longer a threat to either of us, which meant anything that occurred in the future was undoubtedly because of her friend turned enemy. It would make keeping her safe a tad bit easier. "But that doesn't mean you can be any less vigilant. Your plan is to purposely trigger a psychopath. You have to take extra precautions when it comes to safety now that you've decided it's time to take your life back." Which I assumed meant she was going back to her apartment and work.

She lifted her chin in a sign of agreement. "I feel like I haven't been able to breathe since my mother died and

I found out who my father was and the Lawtons all came charging into my life with guns blazing. The walls have been closing in, and sometimes I feel like I can't move."

I glanced over my shoulder into the darkness around the parking lot to make sure nothing seemed out of place. The only thing that didn't fit was the elegant woman in front of me. She wasn't the usual type to frequent Kody's rowdy bar. I knew instinctively that Presley Baskin wasn't a jeans-and-cowboy-boots kind of woman. I doubt she knew how to two-step or the words to "Cotton-Eyed Joe." She tended to dress in all black, and she always seemed to be more covered up than the Texas heat called for. The mystery of what she looked like underneath all the fabric was one I dreamed about solving. Her tendency toward darker clothes also made her pale skin and coppery hair seem brighter and more vibrant than they actually were. I felt like I could find her in the darkest corner of the world without even trying. She was pretty in a different way than I was normally attracted to. She wasn't about flash, but when I looked at her, it seemed like she was lit from within.

I reached out and brushed a piece of coppery hair away from her pale cheek. It was a silk ribbon wrapping around my fingers, and I knew if there was enough light to see her clearly, she would be blushing. I grinned as she practically jumped out of her skin. One of these days she was going to stop starting like a frightened doe when I got close enough to touch her. Even if she wanted to pretend that the chemistry that sparked to life whenever we were together didn't exist, her body and addictive reactions couldn't help but betray her. I bent my head so I could put my lips next to her ear, grinning as she jolted when I spoke softly.

"The walls haven't been closing in, they've been knocked down, and you can see far and wide. Your world is so much bigger now that it's a lot to take in. That's why you can't breathe. It's all a matter of perspective."

She blinked up at me and I could almost see her searching for the right words, or any words, really. She said I was walking all over her boundaries, and maybe I was a little bit. But from what I saw so far, she could do with pushing a few of those lines she'd drawn so clearly for herself. She was used to living carefully and by the book. Even though I didn't know her well, I could tell she was stronger than she seemed to believe. She wouldn't have been able to save my life if she didn't have a spine made of steel hidden away in that graceful line of her back.

Being this close to her, and having her warm, soft skin so close to my mouth was torture. I really wanted to kiss her. I almost did earlier when I had her backed against the building, but I also wanted her to know I heard her when she said I couldn't just do whatever I wanted. Even with her staring at my lips like she was starving and they were the first meal she'd seen in months, I made myself be respectful. Instead of making the move I desperately wanted to, I took a step back and followed her to her car like I originally intended. I could be a good guy when I needed to be. However, I questioned if I was going to have the willpower to do it again.

I reached past her, bringing our bodies closer together so I could knock my knuckles on the roof of her car.

"Get in and go home." I didn't tell her I planned on following her to make sure nothing happened on the way. She wouldn't like it, but it wasn't for her peace of mind. It was for mine.

She was turning to pull the door open when a sudden, deafening *bang* rang through the parking lot. It was loud enough to make my ears ring, but I knew immediately it was nothing to worry about. It was just a car backfiring.

In the dark and already on high alert, Presley obviously assumed the sound was something else. She shrieked, which made my ears ring even more. She also jumped a foot in the air and threw herself into my arms, hitting my chest hard enough to make me grunt in surprise. Her arms locked around my neck and she buried her face into my shoulder. I reflexively put a hand on the back of her head, my fingers threading through her feather-soft hair.

"Shhhh...it was just a car backfiring. You're fine. Everything is okay." I didn't have a lot of experience with soothing someone else, but I was willing to try and wing some compassion for her. I kept muttering soft reassurances until I felt her body stop shaking. "I'm not going to let anything happen to you, Presley."

It was a bold declaration, one I was determined to follow through on.

She knocked her forehead against my collarbone, and I felt her fingers curl around the back of my neck. Her breathing remained rapid, but it no longer seemed rough with fear.

"When I'm around you, I can't decide if I'm the safest I've ever been, or in more danger than ever." The words whispered against my skin, and I felt a slight tremor where her hands were clutching at me. "It doesn't make any sense."

I chuckled as I put my free hand on the base of her spine. I liked the way we fit together. I knew we shouldn't. All the parts and pieces we were made of didn't match, yet somehow and someway we clicked. "I am dangerous." No use in lying about it, not with the way we'd first met. "Right now, maybe you need someone dangerous in your life." And maybe I'd finally reached the point in my life where I was ready for someone who balanced out all the rough and ragged edges. When I was around her, the raging river of my life felt like it slowed to a trickle. Some days it was hard to keep my head above water, but when I was around Presley, I felt like I finally had my feet firmly on the ground.

When she pulled back to look at me, with worried eyes, I couldn't resist lowering my head so I could seal my mouth over hers. The temptation was too much. She was too close, and her racing heartbeat was too compelling. I didn't know when I was going to be this close to her, or if she was going to be caught off guard like this again. She gasped against my lips and her nails dug into my scalp. There was surprise in her actions, but not protest. I expected hesitation or even a small amount of reserve and shyness, so I was stunned when she lifted up on her toes and pulled my head closer. Once I realized what I was doing, I assumed she was going to make me work for the smallest reaction. Instead, I ended up with an armful of highly responsive woman who was setting my insides on fire with a simple kiss.

For someone who was cool and collected on the outside, Presley Baskin burned hot and fast as soon as our lips locked. She kissed me back with a kind of quiet desperation, almost as if she was afraid she would never be kissed again.

I'd kissed a lot of women in my day. A kiss was always a pretty pleasant experience. However, this particular kiss was on another level. There was nothing simply pleasant about it. It was better than good. It was as close to perfect as I'd ever come. It was the kind of kiss that made the earth shift beneath my feet and had my head spinning in circles. It was a kiss that made me question everything I'd ever done in order to be lucky enough to be on the receiving end of such passion and promise. It was the kind of kiss I instantly knew I would never get enough of.

I lowered my hand to the soft curve of her backside and tugged her even closer until there was barely any space between her pounding heart and mine. Everywhere we touched she was soft and malleable. She molded to me, following the guide of my hands as my mouth did its best to devour hers. She opened up obediently when my tongue teased the silky seam between her lips. The tip of my tongue flicked against hers, and I heard her breath catch. Her lips slid against mine as the kiss went wet and a little wild. It was like making out when I was a teenager, trying to get as much as possible as fast as possible. The finesse was lacking, but not the enthusiasm from either one of us. I was worried she was going to come to her senses and remember all the reasons she thought having anything to do with me was a bad idea, so I needed to keep her focused on how good I could make her feel instead.

Our tongues tangled together. Our teeth clicked clumsily. Neither one of us could catch a breath, but none of it mattered. The rest of the world seemed to slip away as this moment expanded and became the center of my entire universe. I couldn't recall anyone ever feeling this right in my arms. I felt like if I let her go, I might never get her back, and that made me kiss her deeper, longer, harder. If we were anywhere else, I would've pushed my luck and started removing clothes and trying to get my hands on her delectable curves. She went to my head quickly, and all of my common sense disappeared when the throbbing flesh trapped behind the zipper of my jeans took precedence. She made me hard as a rock without even trying.

I nipped at the plump curve of her lower lip and slowly pulled back because we were in a parking lot, and she didn't need the entire town of Loveless to know I was ready to strip her naked and bend her over the hood of her car. Not only would the locals have something to say about her getting mixed up with me, but the Lawtons would have my head if they found out I was messing with their newest family

member. Kody was crazy protective of her sister, and Case
had already warned me to keep my distance. I wasn't scared
of her siblings, but I didn't want to give her something else
to worry about when she already had a target on her back. I
told her I would protect her and that meant I would do my
best to keep her from getting caught up in the small-town
gossip mill, which I knew could grind someone down to
nothing if left unchecked.

I was near panting when I pulled away to catch my
breath. I pressed my lips to her forehead and put some
much-needed space between us. She was tying me in knots
with no effort.

"Go home, Presley."

I was dangerous, but as it turned out, so was she, given
the right circumstances. I was going to keep that knowledge
to myself so no one else could come along and snatch her
away before I had the opportunity to convince her we were a
better fit than anyone could imagine.

CHAPTER 8

∞

PRESLEY

Are you certain you're ready to go back to work, Presley? You look terrible."

I didn't bother to hide my eye roll as I looked at my mother's long-term nephrologist, Dr. Kemper. My mother had been under his care since my senior year in college. The man had watched me grow up. He was the one who broke the news to us that there was no hope. He was also the one who told me my mother had passed away. For a long time, he felt like an extension of my very small family. Then Hill Gamble and his partner confirmed that he'd helped Ashby fool me into thinking she'd been injured by whoever was stalking me. Now I realized he didn't care about me or my mother in the slightest. I'd avoided this confrontation since her passing, because even though I'd gained the Lawtons, it was hard to lose the last person who knew me before my life had been flipped upside down. It was an impossibly bitter pill to swallow to know that the two people I'd trusted so completely when I was at my lowest had conspired against me.

I was here today because I was convinced this man had helped my former friend orchestrate my mother's death. Part of me taking my life back was answering any lingering questions about the events that forced me into hiding in the first place. I'd never been the type to wade into a fight on purpose. I didn't like to make waves. Now I wasn't going to rest until I knew the truth. Now I was angry in a way I'd never felt before. I'd spent so long being calm and serene for the comfort of others, I'd forgotten how cathartic anger could be when it was called for.

I forced a fake smile and felt my fingers curl into fists where they were resting on my lap. My nails dug painfully into my palms, but the tiny sting kept me focused on the reason I was here at the hospital in Austin.

"I'm fine. I didn't sleep well last night."

That wasn't a lie. I'd been uneasy being back at the apartment by myself. Every little noise and flickering shadow on the wall had me ready to climb out of my skin. On top of that, I couldn't stop replaying the kiss with Shot over and over again in my mind. Every time I closed my eyes, the image of the two of us entwined would dance across the backs of my eyelids.

It was almost like it was my very first kiss. I didn't lose my head over a romantic move like that. I didn't lose control of my emotions or my body like that. I didn't forget who and where I was because of a man. Not ever. None of the men I'd kissed before had ever made me tingle from head to toe by simply touching their lips to mine. No kiss had ever had me envisioning silk sheets and naked bodies writhing together. No kiss had ever had me ready to risk it all for a man who was so absolutely wrong for me. I always knew when to walk away, but last night, I knew I would've blindly followed Shot wherever he chose to lead me.

I knew Shot followed me home. I knew he waited outside my apartment until the sun came up because I was still awake in bed, tossing and turning, wondering what in the hell I was doing and when exactly I had lost my mind when I heard the thunderous sound of his motorcycle pulling away. I couldn't deny that I wanted him, which was problematic in more ways than one. The existing relationships in my life often felt tenuous at best. I didn't need the kind of emotional earthquake Shot brought with him to disrupt the uneven landscape I was already having trouble navigating.

Blinking back into focus, I watched the older doctor seated across from me in his pristine office. When I was younger I looked up to him so much. Now, I resented him, and his lies, with every fiber of my being.

"It's been a long time since you've come to visit. I would've reached out after everything happened, but you know how busy I am, and frankly, I didn't want my name tied up in the mess Ashby created. It was humiliating to have the FBI and the Texas Rangers lurking around the halls of the hospital."

I had to bite the tip of my tongue to stop myself from screaming at him. He sounded so pompous, so removed. He also sounded like he hadn't played a part in the events that unfolded, as if he hadn't taken advantage of the fact I admired him and would never think to question him. Old me was an idiot, but I was learning.

Swallowing back the bitter words burning across my tongue, I kept the painfully plastic smile in place as I told him, "Law enforcement wouldn't have been here if you didn't give them a reason to suspect that you helped Ashby evade capture. You shouldn't have covered for Ashby when she lied and said she was hurt by whoever was stalking me." I lifted my eyebrows and my fingernails dug even deeper into my palms. "I wasn't aware the two of you had gotten so close. I sincerely hope you didn't know she was the one terrorizing me all along. Not when you knew how hard dealing with my mother's illness and my job already was."

Ashby would come and visit with me and my mother on dialysis days. Back then, I honestly believed she was a welcome distraction, even as self-centered as she tended to be. She would frequently keep me company when my mother was particularly ill and I was too afraid to leave her bedside. Before her plan was uncovered, I thought my former friend and my mother's physician were nothing more than passing acquaintances. Little did I know the two had been engaged in a torrid affair. Throughout our friendship Ashby had a history of getting close to the people in my life, regardless if they were a love interest, an acquaintance, or someone I admired. I didn't realize she was coming between me and anyone who might care about me, who might want to protect me, until it was too late.

"I know I shouldn't have covered for her when she lied about being pushed in front of a car, but at the time it seemed like a harmless favor for a close friend." He shrugged as if that lie hadn't allowed Ashby time to plant the murder weapon used to kill Conrad Lawton in my car, making me the number one suspect in his homicide. "It's a shame the police still haven't found her. She has a lot to answer for."

He spoke almost as if he was talking about a stranger and not a woman he'd helped to convince me I was losing my mind.

I blew out a frustrated breath as I struggled to keep my composure. "She does, and since she hasn't been found yet, I have a lot of questions—some of which I'm hoping you can help me clear up."

The doctor sat up straighter in his leather wingback chair

and narrowed his eyes at me. His bushy, silvery eyebrows dipped into a fierce frown and his expression pulled tight and rigid. "I don't see how I could possibly help you here, Presley. I admitted to the affair. I admitted I lied about her being injured the day you went on the run. There's nothing more to tell."

Leaning forward, I pressed, "What about access to my mother's room? Did you notice if Ashby came to visit my mother when I wasn't there?" It wouldn't be totally out of the question. We were close. She was my only friend, so my mother treated her like a surrogate daughter. She was also in the medical field, so her frequent comings and goings wouldn't raise any questions. "Is that how the two of you got close?" Because I hadn't noticed any overt flirting or chemistry when I saw the two of them together.

Dr. Kemper sighed as he laced his fingers together and looked at me with a hard stare. "Again, I'm busy. I have no idea if she visited when you weren't around. I'm sure the people investigating have already checked with the nurses and looked at our surveillance footage to see when she came and went."

I gritted my teeth and ordered myself to remain calm. "I want to know about the day my mother died. Was she here the day my mother passed away?" If she was, he never reported it, which I found highly suspicious.

The older man leaned forward as well, and I could feel the way the tension ratcheted up in the room. I was uncomfortable with this kind of confrontation, but I was unwilling to walk away because ultimately he was the one who should have felt uneasy. He was the one who'd done something questionable and possibly lethal. He was the one who should have been worried about the truth coming out, even though I was the one who had the cold sweats and was feeling slightly nauseous.

"I don't recall if she was here that day or not." I watched as he reached up to tug at the knot of his tie. It was the first outwardly anxious sign he'd exhibited. "I was focused on trying to save your mother."

I scowled at him as I reached out to grab the edge of his desk. I held on to the wood so tightly that my knuckles turned white.

"Tried to save her? You told me she died before you made it to her room, that she passed so suddenly there was nothing that could be done. What exactly did you do to try and save her?" My voice rose to a practically hysterical level. I would never forget the heartbreak and crushing disappointment of that day or the absolute devastation that followed. "She was always so closely monitored, it always seemed off that she would've suddenly crashed with no warning."

"Presley," he sighed heavily. "You should know better than anyone that sometimes people die without warning. Your entire career is based around that fact. What happened with your mother was tragic, but not uncommon. Again, I wonder if you are really ready to return to work. You don't sound like yourself right now. You were always such a reasonable young woman."

The fact that he sounded disappointed in me made me see red. I jumped to my feet and slammed my palms down on the desktop, making the older man jump in his chair.

"I think my mother was murdered, and I think you are complicit in it. Even if you weren't directly involved, you didn't do anything to stop it. You should, at the very least, lose your medical license."

The physician had the audacity to smirk. "Where's your proof? You work with law enforcement every single day. You know wild accusations don't mean anything. I'm sorry for your loss, but that's where it ends. Any medical professional who might review your mother's case would find I did my due diligence where her rapidly declining condition was concerned."

"Leaving her alone with a murderer who you just happen to be sleeping with is not due diligence." I bit off each word and I could feel furious heat rising in my face. I didn't lose my temper often, but if ever there was a time for it, now was it.

Only Dr. Kemper remained unfazed by my outburst. He even smirked at me again as I started to breathe hard. If I were a cartoon character, steam would be coming out of my ears.

"If you have proof that Ashby was here that day, if there is a scrap of evidence she was alone with your mother, or that I was aware of either of those things, this might be a very different conversation. As it is, your reputation is still in limbo and you should be focused on making sure your superiors don't regret choosing you for that promotion you fought so hard for. I've said all I have to say to you, Presley. Maybe you should consider getting some counseling. It doesn't seem like you've been dealing with your grief in a healthy manner."

I pushed off the desk and narrowed my eyes at his smug face. "I'm not going to let this go."

"You should. What's the use of lingering in the past? You can't bring your mother back."

I grabbed my purse and turned toward the door. "No, I can't. But I can make sure the questions surrounding her death are answered. *That* is actually what my entire career is based around." I flipped my hair over my shoulder, pausing at the door. I gave the doctor a frigid look and told him pointedly, "Oh, in case you didn't hear, my new half brother is the sheriff in Loveless, and my half sister's boyfriend is the Texas Ranger who initially questioned you. I'm sure if I need to get my hands on any of the surveillance from the hospital, or if I need to question the rest of the staff who looked after my mother, they would be more than willing to help me dig for the proof you're so keen on me acquiring."

I pulled open the door, muttering, "I can't believe I ever looked up to you," as I marched out of his office.

I nodded stiffly at a couple of familiar faces, determined to keep up my bravado until I was alone. As soon as I reached my car, I lost every ounce of composure I had.

I threw my purse in the passenger seat, not even caring when half the contents fell out. I pounded the steering wheel with the side of my fist and let loose a yell that felt like it turned my lungs inside out. I could feel the hot burn of tears at the back of my eyes, but I refused to let them fall. I was done crying and being afraid. Neither of those things had gotten me anywhere. It was time for action.

Unfortunately, Dr. Kemper was right. There was no evidence he had done anything wrong the day my mother died. There was also no proof Ashby had been at the hospital that day. Hill and his partner had questioned the entire hospital staff, and they'd already gone over hundreds of hours of surveillance. There was nothing, but I couldn't let go of the feeling there was more to my mother's death than a sudden turn for the worse. She'd been the same, sick but holding on, right up until I was offered the promotion. That was the turning point in a lot of things.

According to Hill and the FBI, Ashby had long been unhinged. When they interviewed Ashby's family after she disappeared, they disclosed that their youngest had been in and out of mental institutions for the entirety of her youth.

The family was wealthy and had gone out of their way to keep her issues under wraps. Which was in a way another betrayal. I'd met the Grants several times. I always envied the tight-knit unit they presented and appreciated how they seemed to warmly welcome me into the fold. They invited me over on holidays. They got me a graduation gift when Ashby and I finished college. They constantly offered their sympathy when it came to my mother, but I had no clue the reason they did all of that was because with Ashby focused on me, on competing with me, on being better than me, on taking everything away from me, she was harmless to the rest of the world. I was the sacrificial lamb they offered up without qualms, and I had no clue until Ashby lost total control of herself. One-upping me suddenly wasn't enough. She wanted me out of the way so she could effectively live my life. She wanted the rewards I'd earned, and she lost touch with reality when she couldn't cheat her way into my position.

One of these days I needed to have a conversation with the Grants as well, but first I had to figure out a way to get Dr. Kemper to come clean about what really happened the day my mother died. I wasn't lying when I said I knew both Case and Hill would go to the mat for me if I asked. They were chivalrous, honest lawmen who pursued justice with a straightforward determination. However, this time, the good guy wasn't going to get things done.

With my hands trembling I patted the seat next to me in search of my cell phone.

When Shot suggested we exchange numbers I'd been tempted to give him a fake one but didn't want to be immature. I kept telling myself to avoid him, but around every corner there he was.

I hesitated before pressing the call button, trying to

remember I was a good, solid, and upstanding citizen. I was a woman who didn't walk on the wild side. So far the biggest risk I'd taken in my life was saving Shot, then I'd kissed him last night in the bar parking lot and realized there were far more dangerous ways to get involved with him. Maybe he wasn't good news, but I knew he was exactly what I needed right now.

Shot answered after the second ring, his voice deep and gruff in my ear. "Didn't think I'd hear from you so soon after last night." He chuckled. "Or ever, if I'm being honest."

"I need a favor." My voice was unsteady and my breathing was choppy. I lowered my head until my forehead was resting on the steering wheel. I felt like I was about to open Pandora's box, and it was terrifying and thrilling at the same time.

Shot chuckled again, but this time it was sultry and sexy sounding. "If I give a favor, I expect one in return, Pres."

No one ever shortened my name. Mostly because I was never casual or the kind of close with anyone for them to be comfortable enough to give me any kind of nickname. And Ashby always said it was lowbrow to shorten our unique names. Shot calling me "Pres" was one more way he was breaking through the walls I'd isolated myself behind for all these years. I didn't hate it, but I didn't like that I didn't hate it.

"If you do this for me, I'll owe you one." It was like I was signing a deal with the devil. Even though I'd considered it silly that he ever felt like he owed me in the first place, or that he was responsible for me because he'd saved my life once. I knew he was big on give-and-take. There was no asking him for something without him expecting something in return.

"We've been here before, haven't we? One of us owing the other seems to be our thing." He sounded amused.

I sighed. "I really need your help, Shot."

"What do you need?"

Closing my eyes and putting a hand to my chest where my heart felt like it was tied in knots, I responded with a whisper I wasn't even sure he could hear, "The truth. I need the truth."

No matter how high the price I had to pay.

CHAPTER 9

∞

SHOT

P icked a weird place for our first date, didn't you, Pres?"

I asked the question as I took a seat in a rickety plastic chair at an equally rickety table located in the back of a busy truck stop halfway between Ivy and Loveless.

Presley lifted her head from whatever she was looking at on her phone and blinked her emerald-colored eyes at me in surprise. "This is a date?"

She sounded so genuinely baffled that I couldn't hold back a slight chuckle. I really did find her innocence charming and refreshing.

"You asked me to meet you somewhere out of the way and offered to buy me coffee. It's not the best date idea I've heard, but it's also not the worst."

She blushed a pretty shade of pink and nervously fiddled with her phone. "I've never really been much of a dater, so I probably wouldn't be able to tell the difference between a good one and a bad one." She lifted her gaze back to mine. "Thank you for agreeing to meet me."

Like I had a choice. As soon as she called and asked for a favor, I knew there was no way I could turn her down. Same as when she asked to meet in this out-of-the-way spot so she could tell me exactly what she wanted from me. The word *no* never even crossed my mind, even though my sudden availability for this woman and this woman alone had my club questioning my sanity.

"Don't thank me until I come through on the favor." I waved her off when asked if I wanted her to grab the coffee she promised to provide. I didn't want to spend any more time at this truck stop than necessary. The rough crowd didn't bother me much, but I didn't like the way the men looked at Presley on their way to the bathroom or how their eyes tracked her as they lingered at the counter of the small concessions stand. She was dressed in a pinstripe blazer with some kind of silky shirt underneath. She also had on a pair of tight white pants, paired with shiny black heels. She was by far the best dressed in the room, making me think she'd come from work. "Talk to me. Tell me who you need me to get the truth from."

She turned her phone so the screen was facedown and folded her hands together on the table. I could see she was struggling to keep her emotions in check, and I barely stopped myself from putting my hand over hers as her knuckles turned white. Normally when I promised someone everything would be okay, it was because they were paying me a hefty sum to make sure things went in their favor. For the woman seated across from me, I wanted to make the promise free of charge. I wanted her to know she could rely on me and trust me. Which was a first. I'd only felt that way about my brothers in the club before she came along.

"The doctor who cared for my mother while she was ill was sleeping with Ashby. He lied to the police to cover for her. He helped her when she tried to make me think I was losing my mind." She shook her head, a deep frown pulling her reddish eyebrows down low on her forehead. "I had questions I wanted him to answer, but he talked around me. He won't tell me if Ashby was at the hospital the day my mother died. He won't give anything away that might implicate her and thus himself. I don't think my mother took a sudden turn for the worse. I think Ashby killed her. He won't tell me the truth about that day, so I want you to *make* him tell it to you."

I let out a low whistle and leaned back in the cheap chair making it creak under my weight. "You're a little more ruthless than I expected."

Her frown deepened and so did her blush. "I tried to be civil. I tried to get the information through traditional methods, and it didn't work." She cocked her head to the side a little, sending her hair cascading across her shoulder. Someone else whistled, causing me to whip my head around so I could glare at whoever was creeping on her.

"To be clear," Presley was saying, "I don't want him to die or anything that extreme. I just want him persuaded to tell what he knows, and if that persuasion gets a little more forceful than he is accustomed to, so be it. He made his choice when he decided to protect Ashby even after he knew she killed Conrad Lawton."

The guy with the beer belly and trucker cap scurried away after I stared him down. I focused my attention back on the woman who didn't even realize the buzz she was creating around herself.

"If he admits he knows that Ashby killed your mom, if he says he played a part in her death, what then?" I was honestly curious about her answer. If it was one of my guys, they would want immediate revenge. Hell, even Kody would want the man to pay something fierce. But I couldn't see Presley being that bloodthirsty. Her response didn't disappoint.

"I want him to get the punishment he deserves. He should lose his medical license at the very least, and she should be charged with my mother's murder. They need to be held accountable." She gave me a wry grin and pried her hands apart. "However, I won't be heartbroken if either of them ends up a little banged up and bruised on the way to answering for what they did."

I chuckled at her sweet honesty and stopped resisting the urge to reach for her hand. Her fingers were long and grace-ful looking. They also twitched uncontrollably as I wrapped mine around them. The skull tattooed on the back of my hand looked like it was grinning up at me in approval when she didn't pull away.

"You're a nice woman, Presley Baskin." Niceness wasn't something that had particularly attracted me to women in the past, but I really liked it when it was coming from her. "I don't like it when other people hurt you." There was no doubt about it, I was going to make this doctor tell me what he knew.

She cleared her throat before she muttered, "I'm surprised at how kind you can be, Shot. When you're kind, you're even scarier than when you're being all fierce and biker-like."

I tossed my head back and let out a real laugh. I brushed my thumb over the back of her hand and watched as the small touch made her shiver in her seat. "I'm never not biker-like. But there is something about being around you that reminds me there are people and things in the world that need to be handled with a slightly more delicate touch."

She audibly gulped and finally pulled her hand free. She reached up to push some of her hair back behind her ear as she watched me shyly. "Like I mentioned, I don't really know the difference between a good and bad date, but this oddly enough feels like a pretty great one."

I laughed again. "Are you going to let me kiss you good-bye when I walk you back to your car?"

I was only halfway joking. I hadn't been able to get the kiss from the parking lot out of my mind. The fact that I couldn't close my eyes without seeing her clinging to me and kissing me back told me I'd better pay attention to this woman and my response to her.

She picked her phone up and looked at the time before shaking her head. "No. I'm running a little late to meet Kody and the other girls for Della's wedding dress fitting. The last time we kissed it felt like time stood still, and if that happens again and I don't tell Kody why I'm late, she'll lose her mind."

I grinned when she suddenly slapped a hand over her mouth at her admission about that kiss. I decided to let her off easy...this time.

"All right. We'll make sure the next date doesn't include a truck stop but does involve a kiss. Text me the doctor's info and I'll check in when I have something to share."

She looked relieved, but I couldn't tell if it was because I was going to follow through on the favor she asked for, or if it was because I mentioned a second date.

* * *

"What is it about Dr. Death that has you suddenly willing to jump through hoops?" The irritation in Top's voice was evident. "Never thought I'd see you so sprung on a woman. Especially not one like her."

It was a few days after I'd met up with Presley. I'd needed the time to get a plan together and to do basic recon on the doctor. Now, Top and I were across from a McMansion in an affluent suburb of Austin. It was a gated community, so getting in took some work, and it was impossible for us to blend in, even without the motorcycles we'd left parked outside the fancy subdivision. Every single house seemed to have those video doorbells, or an even more high-tech security system, which made our simple task far trickier. We were likely to get popped for trespassing before this Dr. Kemper made an appearance. In order to buy some time, Top messed around with the transformer that supplied power to the entire neighborhood. Once all the lights went out, a slew of repair trucks and city workers showed up, helping us move unnoticed with the other visitors.

"What exactly is Presley like?" I lifted an eyebrow in my friend's direction, unable to deny that the pretty doctor did have me acting in ways that weren't typical.

Top sighed and shifted uncomfortably. We were crouched down behind a row of artfully trimmed hedges that lined the long driveway leading up to the huge house. The sun had gone down not too long ago, allowing us to blend into the shadows.

"I dunno exactly, but I don't think you and her make much sense." He shook his head and gave me a look out of the corner of his eye. "Kody Lawton, I understood. She's a handful and her temper is almost as bad as yours. I saw the attraction there, even though her brother is a cop, but this lady doctor"—he made a face of confusion—"she's cold as ice. She obviously isn't much of a rule breaker in her day-to-day. And she seems a little odd. I mean, who purposely picks a career where they're around dead bodies all the time? Have you considered what's going to happen if she comes across someone you or the club is responsible for putting in the morgue? That's not going to end well for either of you.

Sure Dr. Death has a killer pair of legs, and she's beautiful, but I still don't understand why you're willing to help her out for free. You normally charge a small fortune for this kind of thing."

"I don't plan on putting anyone in the morgue today." I reached out and punched him lightly in the arm. "And stop calling her Dr. Death."

Top snorted and rubbed the spot where I hit him. "You might not plan on it, but it happens. Can't get around it with the kind of lifestyle we live."

He wasn't wrong. Everything in life and with the club always seemed to be all or nothing. "That's a bridge I'll cross when the time comes, I guess. And I'm not doing this for free. We're exchanging favors, just like we did when she saved my life. What does it hurt to have her indebted to the club for this or that?"

Top snorted again and gave me a look. It felt like he saw clear into the center of my soul. "Indebted to the club, or to you? I'm not an idiot, Shot. We've been friends for a long time and I can tell when something is different. You're sprung on this woman, and I just know it's going to bite you in the ass eventually."

Something was different about Presley. "When I'm with her, things get quiet. I can hear myself think." And all I could focus on was her.

My life was so loud. The club was noisy, and all the choices and trappings that went along with being a member were blaring and booming. There was never a moment that felt serene and still. My previous encounters with women were the same. I was typically after a good time, not a long time. My life was unpredictable and dangerous. I didn't live in an ideal environment for romance and commitment. There was very little softness and tenderness in my existence. The idea of being involved with a real-life outlaw tended to be far sexier and more seductive to women than the reality.

Kody was honestly the first woman who I was involved with on any level that I wanted to stick around longer than a few weeks and for more than a few stolen moments. But even as tough and resilient as she was, the harsh landscape that made up the hills and valleys of my life proved to be too much for her. She was annoyed with me more often than she was infatuated with me. And it became blisteringly obvious after we started spending more time together that Kody's heart wasn't even up for grabs. That bossy, uptight Texas Ranger was the owner, even if Kody was oblivious to the fact that she'd given her heart away.

It caught me totally off guard that I was now actively looking for reasons to keep Presley around. Top was right. She wasn't a woman who chose to live her life on the edge the way Kody was, but I think that was what I liked most about her. She didn't fit into my way of life, but she did take me out of it, giving me a reprieve I hadn't been aware I needed.

I grinned in Top's direction as a black Rolls-Royce pulled into the driveway. "Stop worrying about my love life and focus on the task at hand."

He growled and lifted his chin as a well-dressed older man climbed out of the luxury car. He was obviously confused as to why his garage door didn't open, clearly not knowing the power in the neighborhood was out. He had a cell phone pressed to his ear and seemed completely distracted as he reached into the back seat and pulled out some dry cleaning. He was swearing loudly and definitely not paying attention to his surroundings.

"You sure Rave killed the feed to his cameras?" Top asked in a low tone, as we slowly moved toward the garage.

The idea was to simply wait until the doctor opened the

front door, then bum-rush him. Once we forced him inside, I was going to make him talk. I figured it would be a piece of cake. Guys like the shady, wealthy physician didn't tend to hold up well when pressed by guys like me.

It was my turn to snort. "Has that kid ever not come through?"

Patching a hacker into the club was one of the best decisions I ever made. Some fights weren't destined for the streets, like they had been back in the old days. Now you needed to be as digitally savvy as you were street savvy. Having Rave on our team often gave us access to places and people others could never reach.

"If you're sure your ugly mug won't end up on the nine o'clock news, then let's roll."

Because the garage wouldn't open due to the power outage, the doctor had no choice but to use his front door. Top and I broke free of the hedges, creeping up on either side of the doctor just as he was pushing the door open. He made a startled sound and dropped the plastic-wrapped dry cleaning.

"What? Who are you? How did you get into this neighborhood? It's gated!" The questions came fast and furious as we strong-armed the man into his home. Top kicked the door closed and gave the physician a shove. The older man spun around and waved his phone in our direction. "I'm calling the police!"

I reached out, snatched the phone, and slid it into the back pocket of my jeans. I was going to pass the device off to Rave on the off chance the doctor had been in touch with his former lover. I had told Top I didn't plan on putting anyone in the morgue, but if I had a list of people who should be there, Ashby Grant's name would be at the top of it. The woman needed to be stopped, and I didn't have much faith that traditional law enforcement tactics were going to work. She'd been on the run too long and gotten away with too many atrocities.

"The louder you are, the harder I'm going to make this." I put a hand on the doctor's chest and pushed, driving him backward and off balance. He tripped over his own feet and landed with a thump on his backside. "Answer my questions and we're out. Play games, and we've got all night to make it as horrible as possible."

He gulped and shook his head in disbelief. "My family will be home any minute. Whatever you think you're doing, you aren't going to get away with it."

Top snickered and crouched down so he was eye level with the doctor. "Your wife took the kids and left you when she found out you were banging a psychopath behind her back. No one's coming to save you, old man." My VP reached out and pushed against the center of the other man's forehead with his index finger, shoving his head back. "I'm the impatient sort. If you draw this out unnecessarily, I'm gonna get pissed. Trust me, you want to avoid making me angry."

The doctor's eyes slid to me so I crossed my arms over my chest and asked, "What really happened the day Samantha Baskin died?"

The older man's eyes widened to comical proportions and all the color drained from his face. His breathing became rushed and he scrambled backward across the entryway floor. "Why would you ask me that? Ms. Baskin passed away from kidney failure. She was sick for many, many years. Did Presley Baskin send you? That girl has gone off the deep end."

Top shot out a hand and grasped the man's dress shirt. He pulled him back across the hardwood floor, tightening his hold on the fabric until the doctor was obviously struggling to breathe. "We're asking the questions. All you have to do is answer. If you lie, I'll make you regret the decision immediately. Are we clear?"

The doctor turned a shade close to purple as Top continued to twist the material of the collar in his hand, effectively blocking his airway. The older man scratched at my VP's tattooed wrist to no avail.

"Again, what happened that day? Was Ashby Grant there? And if she was, why is there no record of her being at the hospital to see Presley's mother?" I lifted my eyebrows. "If you don't give me an answer I like, he's going to break all of your fingers. One by one. On both hands. It might be hard to do your job in double casts, Doc."

Top let the doctor go with a little shove and cracked his knuckles loudly for effect. The older man cleared his throat nervously and looked up at me with wide, frightened eyes.

"Do you really want the truth, or just what you want to hear? If you're here because Presley sent you, you've already got an idea of what happened that day, regardless of the truth." He huffed a little and wiped his dirty hands off on the thighs of his khaki pants. "I'm not going to change my story to fit Dr. Baskin's paranoid theory."

Sighing heavily, I nodded at Top who reached for the doctor's hand. The older man yelled for help and tried to scramble away, but Top was faster. The *pop* of his pinky finger snapping was loud but drowned out as the man screamed in pain and watched us in horror.

"You're monsters." Tears were running down his face, and he'd gone extremely pale. "Get out of my house."

I dropped my arms and leaned forward. "I told you, it's up to you how easy or how hard this is. When you decide to cooperate, we'll get out of your hair."

He scowled and cradled his hand protectively against his

wrinkled shirt. "I'll see to it you're locked away for an eternity."

I chuckled. "Better men have tried." I nodded at Top again, but this time when he went for the doctor's hand, the older man shrieked at him to stop and scooted away. "The day Samantha Baskin died, Ashby was at the hospital. She told me she needed a couple of minutes to talk to her about the promotion. She said she wanted to ask Sam to help her convince Presley to walk away from the job offer. She asked me to make sure no one came into the room while she visited because she didn't want anyone else to know Presley was screwing up at work. Ashby often came to visit Sam, so I didn't think anything of it. None of the alarms or monitors alerted to a problem. None of the nurses were called. But when I went to check on Sam after Ashby left, she was no longer with us."

Top growled at the confession and I sighed. "So you knew she did something while she was in the room with a helpless patient, and you went out of your way to cover it up. Why is there no evidence she was there that day? No video? No witnesses?"

The doctor shook his head violently from side to side. "She was dressed in scrubs like she was going into autopsy. I thought it was odd, but she said she was heading to work and just had time for a quick visit. She had her hair covered and a surgical mask in her hand. She honestly looked like any other doctor making rounds, and it wasn't the first time she'd stopped by before her shift. No one would've paid her special notice. As for the video footage..." He trailed off and gave Top a worried look. "After I found Sam, I knew something bad had happened. I was already in deep since I was having an affair with Ashby, but I didn't want to lose my medical license. Do you have any idea how much my wife is asking for monthly in the divorce?" He shook his head rapidly. "I didn't know how involved and twisted Ashby's whole plan was. I didn't know she was after Presley or the lengths she was willing to go to. I knew the police would show up eventually, so I made sure the recordings from that day were switched out with another day when Ashby wasn't in the nephron unit. I admit I was trying to cover my own ass. I figured Presley would be too caught up in trying to save her job to really dig into what happened to her mother. I should've known better. That young woman is relentless when she sets her mind to something."

I swore under my breath. "You helped your lover murder her only parent. I don't think you're in any position to complain about Dr. Baskin's personality."

The doctor sighed dejectedly. "Presley's mother was sick for a long, long time. The woman suffered endlessly but hung on because she didn't want Presley to be alone. She was going to die sooner or later. Everyone accepted that but Presley."

I was disgusted by his cavalier attitude. Here was someone who really had no respect for life and death. To him, when your time was limited, you ran out of usefulness. He didn't even comprehend that he'd stolen the most precious thing Presley's mother had to give her: her final moments. The last chance to make memories that would last a lifetime. He took their goodbye away, and it made me want to break all his teeth.

"She knew her mother was going to die. She braced for it and prepared herself for it. What she didn't know was that the people closest to her, the ones she trusted most, were going to rob her of her last few minutes with her mother while she was still here. You took something from her she's never going to get back, and I'm going to do the same to you."

I knew Rave could recover the lost footage now that I knew it existed. So this corrupt physician was undoubtedly going to lose his license for his irresponsible behavior. However, that wasn't good enough. Presley's mother was the most important person in her life; she meant everything to her. This guy only cared about himself. His arrogance was toxic and he didn't need to be around any other helpless patient.

I nudged Top with my elbow. "Make sure he can't use his hands on anyone ever again."

The doctor screamed and got to his feet to try and run away. He was screaming about calling the police and making sure we rotted in jail, but when Top dragged him to a stop he looked at my VP and sobbed, "I told you the truth. I gave you what you wanted. Don't do this to me, please." The plea would've been more effective if he hadn't admitted to turning a blind eye while one of his long-term patients had been killed.

"You should count your blessings, Doc. If I was the one who had this kind of beef with you, I'd dump you naked across the border in cartel country just for shits and giggles. You're getting off easy, at least until the police come for you. Gotta say, finding out she's got a cop in the family is gonna work out well for Presley. Her older brother might be even scarier than me when he finds out this garbage you pulled with her and the investigation." I wasn't overly worried about the doctor trying to come for me and the club after Top was done with him. My VP had a particular way of getting his point across, and the doctor was about to be neck deep in hot water when it was disclosed he'd tampered with vital evidence.

Turning toward the door, I walked away from the sound of the doctor screaming as I pulled my phone out of my pocket so I could call Presley. It took her a minute to answer the call, and when she did, I could barely hear her over the loud country music in the background. It didn't take too much brainpower to figure out she was at Kody's bar and no longer dress shopping.

"Hello? Shot, is that you?" She sounded funny and not just because I could hardly hear her.

"Are you at the Barn?" I was already moving toward the golf course in the subdivision and the unsecured maintenance gate where we'd snuck in.

She said something I couldn't quite make out, but a second later my heart dropped into my boots when she whispered, "I don't feel well."

"What's wrong with you?" I barked the question as the line went dead. I shouldn't be too worried. Kody protected her new sister like a mama bear, but something wasn't right. I was on my bike and headed toward the bar like it was the most natural thing in the world to ride to her rescue, even if she didn't end up needing me to.

CHAPTER 10

∞

PRESLEY

Thank you so much for including me today. It was really special."

I smiled shyly at Della Deveaux, soon to be Della Lawton. She was Crew's fiancée, and while the middle Lawton had been cautious about welcoming me into the family, the gorgeous blonde he was getting ready to spend the rest of his life with had been much more accepting. She fully embraced bringing me into the girls-only club that consisted of Aspen Barlow, Case's live-in girlfriend; Kody; and herself. They were all strong and successful in their own unique ways, but what tied them together was family and the fact that they all had stubborn, complex men they loved unconditionally. I was the odd one out on that front, but it didn't stop them from including me in their girls' nights, and none of them ever hesitated to invite me along when they all got together like they did today for Della's final wedding dress fitting.

Della was going to be a stunning bride. She had an ethereal, unreal kind of beauty that made her stand out in a crowd. Especially in a crowd like the one that filled Kody's bar on a busy Friday night. She seemed so very different from Crew, who was a rough-and-tumble professional rodeo star. Crew made his money getting tossed off horses and bulls. He wore cowboy boots and competed to win giant belt buckles. Della was the CEO of one of the world's premier cosmetic companies. She'd grown up in France, was multi-lingual and elegant to a fault. I had no idea what the two of them had in common, or how they made their relationship work considering both were on the road all the time, but they seemed deliriously happy and were obviously deeply in love with one another.

The blond woman tilted her wineglass in my direction and lifted a perfectly arched brow. "Are you sure you won't reconsider being in the wedding party? You're family. You should be up there with the rest of us."

It wasn't the first time she'd asked or brought forth that argument. She was an inherently kind person, but I couldn't imagine how uncomfortable Crew would be if I was suddenly such an integral part of his big day. I reached out so I could pat her hand.

"I'm touched to be invited. I don't need more than that. You and Crew deserve to have the whole day be about the two of you. If you add my sudden appearance to the mix, all people will be talking about is why I'm there and who I am to the Lawtons. It'll shine a light on Conrad not being there and the fact he had an affair with my mother." I shook my head. "It should be a day of celebration, not speculation."

Della grumbled but didn't disagree with me. Instead, she added more wine to her glass and pouted prettily. We'd been at the bar since happy hour. Kody insisted on drinks and appetizers after the fitting, since the four of us were already together. Aspen had offered a half-hearted protest, saying she had court in the morning, but eventually, she relented. And even though this impromptu get-together was Kody's idea, she'd been missing on and off throughout the evening. I figured she kept getting pulled away to work, since the Barn was packed, but I didn't see her behind the bar, and when I asked our server if she'd seen her, she mentioned she'd bumped into her going into the bathroom. Apparently, my spunky half sister wasn't feeling too well but was too stubborn to mention it. When she came back to the table I noticed she was a little green around the gills and was drinking only water.

When I asked what was wrong, she waved me off, mumbling that she must've picked up a bug. I wanted to press her, but she cleverly changed the subject by asking Della, "You really aren't concerned that Crew and Case might show up to the wedding in old boots and faded Levi's? Your dress costs more than this entire bar is worth. You should at least ask him to wear a suit and tie so he doesn't embarrass you."

Both Della and Crew had some notoriety. Crew was the model and inspiration behind her company's first-ever line of men's products. His pictures had gone viral, and so had their relationship. They were kind of the Blake Shelton and Gwen Stefani of the cosmetics world. People were fascinated by their romance, so even though the wedding was here in Loveless and minimal details had been released, the expectation of there being a media circus around the event was high.

Della lifted a shoulder and let it fall in a careless shrug. "Crew looks good no matter what he wears. He told me he didn't care how much my dress cost, and he let me have my way when it came to most of the wedding details. He hasn't complained once, even though I know he would've been happy eloping to Vegas. As long as he shows up and says, 'I do,' I don't care what he's wearing."

Her words were slightly slurred and her eyes were overly glassy and bright. I realized the bottle of wine on the table was gone, and so was the one that had arrived before it. Aspen was also extra giggly, seeming to think Della's declaration was the funniest thing she'd ever heard.

"Don't worry, I won't let Case show up in boots and jeans. He won't tell me what Crew is planning, but it's something better than what they usually wear. I overheard him talking to Hayes on the phone and he was asking for measurements."

Hayes, Case's son, was currently away at college. The two were close, and according to both Aspen and Kody, Hayes was considerably more fashionable than both his uncle and father. It was a good thing he was part of the wedding party, since the men were in charge of their own outfits. Della wanted Crew to have a part in the wedding, to make his own mark on their special day, so aside from making sure he matched her colors, she gave him free rein to wear what he wanted. Again, they were so different, I couldn't get my head around how she could trust him so implicitly with something that was so important.

Della ordered another bottle of wine from the waitress, who looked in my direction and asked if I wanted anything. I wasn't a big drinker and wine wasn't my favorite, so I stuck with a dirty martini. The one I'd been nursing was gone, and I figured one more wouldn't hurt.

"How do you and Crew agree on anything? You have such different backgrounds and come from such different experiences. How did you start to find common ground?" As I asked, I couldn't help but think about Shot, and the way

I couldn't stop thinking about him. He was different from anyone and anything I'd ever known, and I couldn't decide if that was the reason why I couldn't stay away from him.

Sure I liked the way he looked and the way he moved. I liked that he was confident in himself to the point of being cocky about it. I liked the way he smelled like leather and sunshine, and the way his deep voice softened just slightly when he talked to me. I really, really liked the way he kissed, and I was getting used to the playful way he teased me. I could tell he was different with me than he was around anyone else—maybe that was what drew me to him so inexplicably. I'd been treated differently because of my job and because I was smart, but Shot was the first man who treated me like I was someone special, like I was a woman he was attracted to, regardless of how impossible that attraction might seem.

"God, why would I want to spend the rest of my life with someone just like me?" Della snorted in an adorable way, her cheeks flushed. "I'm a workaholic. I have daddy issues. I can be self-absorbed and insensitive. He forces me to think outside of myself, and he makes me take care of myself. Before Crew, I only dated men who moved in the same circles as I did. They were more interested in my earning potential than my heart. It was boring and bland. When you have white and you add more white to it, nothing changes— you just get more of the same. But if someone comes in and dumps red, or blue, or green into that white base, you end up with a whole new color. Something vibrant and beautiful. Crew balances out all my bad traits, and I like to think I tamed some of his. We're better people when we're together, and that's the common ground. I don't want to change him, because I love who he is and who he influences me to be. I hope it's the same for him."

Aspen sighed sweetly and plopped a hand on Della's shoulder. "I'm so glad you found each other."

Della nodded a little sloppily and placed her palm over the back of Aspen's hand. "You and Case, too. You're very different. You're so warm and caring, and Case is so cold and closed off, but you bring out the best in each other. He's so much more approachable now that he has you, and you're nowhere near as naive as you used to be."

Kody made a gagging sound and rolled her eyes. "You guys are being gross right now."

I giggled and thanked the waitress, who had appeared at my elbow with a fresh martini.

"Oh, stop." Aspen turned her head, dark hair swinging. "You're no different. You were living each and every day like it was your last until you admitted how you truly felt about Hill. He's the eye of your constant storm, Kody, and you know it."

Kody opened her mouth to argue, but before she could get any words out, she slapped a hand over her mouth and jumped to her feet. She made a panicked face and bolted toward the bathroom, practically knocking over a couple two-stepping on the dance floor in her haste.

I took a sip of my drink and asked of no one in particular, "Should I go check on her, or will it just make her mad?"

Aspen grabbed for the last jalapeño popper and told me, "Give her a minute. I'm not sure what's going on with her, but she'll tell us when she's ready."

I frowned. "What do you mean? You don't think she's got a stomach bug or something along those lines?"

Both Aspen and Della shook their heads, dark and light in total agreement. "No, I don't think she's sick." Aspen gave a small smile that was tinted with a shadow of sadness I didn't understand. "I'm not going to say anything until Kody figures it out, and decides she wants to share, but I'm pretty sure what's going on with her is eventually going to be a reason to celebrate."

I was new to all this girl talk, but it seemed like Aspen was hinting at a major life change for Kody, which meant something along the lines of marriage or starting a family. Since Kody hadn't mentioned either of those things, and she wasn't one to keep her opinions and thoughts on pretty much anything to herself, both seemed unlikely.

But as I watched as Della hugged the other woman comfortingly, I felt like I was missing something big. I shook my head, realizing my thoughts were a little foggy and I was having a hard time putting the pieces of the conversation together. I bypassed the martini and reached for a glass of water, but my depth perception was off, and I ended up knocking over both drinks in front of me.

I gasped and got to my feet, nearly tripping over my chair. Aspen and Della both jumped up and scrambled to help clean the mess, but they were blurring together, and the bar was suddenly too loud. I put a hand to my forehead and rubbed the sweaty surface. I could feel my fingers trembling, but when I pulled my hand away, it felt like it belonged to someone else. Almost as if it wasn't attached to my body.

"Are you okay, Presley? You got really pale all of a sudden." I saw Della put her hand out in my direction, but I jerked away. I felt like I wasn't in control of my actions as the world start to swirl alarmingly around me.

"I...uh...I'm going to check on Kody." I needed to get away from the crowd. I needed to splash some water on my face and try and catch my breath. I had no clue what was going on with me, but I felt very, very off.

As I was lurching and stumbling toward the bathroom,

bumping into everyone in my path along the way, I felt my phone vibrate in my back pocket. Everything around me felt like it was closing in, and I struggled to breathe. I could barely see the face of my phone, but I managed to answer without dropping it.

Shot's deep voice in my ear brought my racing heart rate down a bit, but I hardly managed to mumble any words when he asked what was wrong with me.

"I don't feel well." The words were nothing more than a pained rasp, then my phone fell from my frozen fingers and hit the floor. Vaguely, like he was yelling from the far end of a tunnel, I could hear Shot calling my name. I wanted to reply, but all I was capable of doing was slumping against the closest wall.

Slowly, with my back against the wall, I slid down to the floor. My head was spinning, and my stomach started to turn upside down. I blinked rapidly, trying to keep the world in focus, but nothing worked. It felt like an alien had invaded my body and there was no way to get control back.

I muttered a weak complaint as I was suddenly hauled to my feet. The motion was enough to make me lose all the bar goodies I'd indulged in during the last hour. I heard a deep voice swear loudly somewhere outside of my hazy bubble, but I couldn't respond. I felt like a rag doll that was getting roughly jerked around. I feebly tried to push away the hand pulling at me and dragging me, but none of my limbs were responding to any of my commands. I was so frustrated; however, I couldn't scream or cry.

I was hanging like a limp noodle in the hands of a stranger, I couldn't see clearly, and my phone was abandoned on the floor. Even though my mind was fuzzy and I didn't feel at all like myself, I knew this situation was bad, and going to get worse.

"Hey, where are you trying to take my boss's sister?" The question was barked in a no-nonsense tone. Kody's big, bearded bouncer suddenly appeared out of nowhere, and I was dropped on the floor in response.

I could hear the muffled sounds of a scuffle happening around me, and Kody's shrill voice added into the mix. Soft hands touched my face and stroked my hair. I could tell it was Kody, even though I couldn't bring her face into focus.

"It's okay. I've got you. I'm not going to let anything happen to you, Presley." She sounded both comforting and pissed as hell.

I heard the sound of fists hitting flesh but it was all too much and all I was capable of doing was closing my eyes and melting into Kody's embrace.

"Thank God Shot called me." Her voice was sharp. "He knew something was wrong right away and demanded I have Harris check on you. He's going to be here any minute." She sighed. "Case is also on his way. It'll be interesting to see which one gets here first." She tightened her hold on my limp body and squeezed. "I'm so sorry this happened to you in my bar." She sounded like she was on the verge of tears. "I think someone slipped something into your drink."

It was the only reasonable explanation. I was the only one who wasn't drinking wine at the table, and there were plenty of odorless, tasteless drugs that could easily be added to a drink to disable someone.

There was a loud thump, the sound of angry male voices, and the tinkling of glass breaking. I wanted to see what was going on, but I felt like I was in a pool of dark water and each second that passed I was getting pulled deeper and deeper down. I let my eyes close, since I couldn't bring anything into focus anyway. My mind started to drift, and my limbs went heavy and limp.

"Give her to me, Kody." It was a demand, flat-out. Even with my senses dull and my entire being out of sorts, I recognized the command and authority in Shot's voice.

I didn't hear a response before I was suddenly lifted by a pair of strong arms. I felt like I was floating.

"Where are you taking her?" Kody sounded worried, but she surrendered me to the biker with little fuss.

"To the hospital. Tell your brother if he lets that guy go tonight, there won't be anything left of him in the morning. You better find out who drugged her, Kody, or I will take this bar apart piece by piece." I felt the leather of his vest against my cheek and the warmth from his chest beginning to seep into my lethargic body. I sighed heavily and finally allowed myself to give up the fight against whatever was swimming in my veins. Even in my compromised state, my body—and my soul—seemed to implicitly trust Shot. When I could think straight I was going to have to give some serious thought as to what that meant. For now, I let the darkness pull me under and sank into a blissful, peaceful kind of silence.

But not before I felt the soft press of warm lips against my forehead.

CHAPTER 11

❦

SHOT

"**I**s everything okay in there?" I waited a second for a response, and when one wasn't immediately forthcoming, I pushed my way into Presley's bathroom while calling her name. "Presley, I asked if you were okay."

I was trying to keep my frustration and worry in check, since she'd had such a rough night, but my emotions were starting to bubble out of control.

Luckily the door, like everything else in the apartment, was flimsy and popped open without too much of a fight. The water was on in the shower, so the room was steamy and warm. Presley was standing at the small vanity, her hands on the sink as she stared at herself in the fogged-over mirror. Her hair was pulled up in a messy tangle on top of her head, and all she was wearing was a baby pink towel wrapped around her body. If the circumstances were different, I would've taken a minute to appreciate the view. There was an awful lot of naked leg and gentle yet significant curves on display, but it wasn't her phenomenal figure I was focused on. It was the tear streaks on her cheeks and the tremor in her hands. She was scary pale, and her bottom lip looked swollen and sore from where she'd been worriedly chewing on it since coming home from the emergency room.

Presley looked over in my direction, but I could tell her gaze wasn't focused on me. It felt like she was looking right through me. She'd been staring at me the same way since the doctors cleared her and told her she would be fine after she got some rest. Before she was allowed to go home, she'd had to suffer through having her stomach pumped and getting what seemed like a gallon of blood drawn. Case also showed up to question her, but she was too out of it to give a coherent account of what happened. Luckily, Kody had a top-of-the-line surveillance system set up in her bar, and everything had been caught on camera.

The big guy entering the bar shortly after the girls showed up for happy hour.
Him speaking with one of Kody's cocktail servers.
Him handing her something and motioning toward the table.
The cocktail server adamantly refusing and shaking her head.
The man then showing her something on his phone.
The cocktail server then reluctantly taking whatever it was he shoved in her direction.

The video also showed the server pouring the contents of the small vial into a martini glass, then looking directly at the camera behind the bar and mouthing an apology.

Later, when Case arrived at the hospital to speak with his sister about the incident, he would reveal the man had pictures of the server's kids on his phone and had threatened the woman to get her cooperation. So far, the attacker was cooling his heels behind bars and not saying a word. He'd lawyered up, which tied Case's hands. Silently, I made the promise to myself that if the guy who drugged and terrorized Presley walked out of the sheriff's office, he wasn't going to make it very far. I didn't have the same red tape to wade through in order to get the information I wanted, and I wasn't as worried about playing fair and keeping things clean and legal as Case was. I lived my life getting my hands dirty, usually for a good cause, but sometimes for my own personal reasons. I rarely regretted when it was time to climb into the mud.

It was easy enough to wash the filth off the outside. It was the way it stained the inside that always kept me from getting too close to anyone outside of the club. Except for the woman who was currently falling apart in front of my eyes. For whatever reason, I wanted to get as close to her as possible. It was making me angry in a way I couldn't put into words to see someone who was strong, and typically so pulled together, wilting and crumbling to pieces. I hated feeling helpless and ineffective while Presley suffered in a pain-filled silence. Like I told her before, I didn't like it one bit when other people hurt her.

She inhaled sharply and lifted a trembling hand to her wet face. "I'm fine. I just dropped my moisturizer in the sink." She rubbed the back of her hand across her cheek and kept her gaze locked firmly on the ground. "I told you, I'm going to be okay. You don't need to hang around and keep an eye on me. I'm sure you have other things you can be doing with your time." Her words trailed off and her eyes drifted closed. She really seemed to be on the edge of shattering into a million fragile pieces.

Case and I had almost come to blows when it was time for

Presley to leave the hospital. He wanted to take her home, and I knew if he did, he was going to lecture her about her safety and warn her to keep her distance from me. If he took her home, I wasn't going to be able to check up on her and take care of her, and both those things felt as essential as breathing. Fortunately, Presley had enough of her faculties gathered to tell her domineering older brother she wanted me to take her to her apartment. Case looked ready to kill both of us but didn't argue, because it was obvious Presley wasn't up to a fight.

I took her home and put her to bed. She slept for nearly ten hours and woke up still shaken and scared. She was surprised I was still there, and I told her repeatedly I wasn't going anywhere until I was sure she was okay. She kept insisting she was fine, but her actions, and the look in her eyes, told me otherwise. She was having a hard time once again being a victim and the target of such malicious behavior.

"Sure there are other things I *could* be doing, but what I *want* to do is take care of you." I lifted a hand toward her face, biting back a slew of swear words when she flinched. I used my thumb to wipe away a rolling tear and told her, "I need you to let me take care of you right now."

She was quiet for a heartbeat, then one of her hands wrapped around my wrist as I continued to stroke her soft cheek. "I feel like an idiot." She let out an unsteady breath and her bright green gaze finally met mine. "All my life I've been the smartest person in the room. It's the one thing that has always set me apart. I'm not good with people, or social interactions. I'm not warm and friendly like Kody is. I'm not outgoing and fun to be around. But I am smart. So why did I do something so stupid like let my guard down while I was out in public? I knew I was provoking Ashby. I knew I was purposely trying to force her to make a move, and yet I got caught up in being with friends and family. And look what happened." Her grip tightened on my wrist and her eyes once again got glassy and sad looking, which made my heart twist painfully inside my chest. "When I try to live my life, I almost lose it."

"Stop it. That's not fair to you or anyone else. No one was acting stupid—you were all acting how you should act when you're together in a place that feels safe and surrounded by friends and family. Being smart has nothing to do with it. There was a deputy parked in the parking lot and he didn't notice anything amiss. Harris was watching the door and he didn't pick up on a threat. Kody, Aspen, and Della all know what's going on with you and Ashby, and none of them were on alert because they were enjoying your company and not thinking about there still being a threat. You are allowed to have a good time, Presley. You are allowed to build relationships with people. Don't let this woman who's after you be the most important person in your life anymore."

She shook her head slightly, and I slid my hand to the side of her neck. I could feel her pulse fluttering delicately under my fingers. She let go of my wrist and shifted her grip to the front of my faded black T-shirt. I don't know if she meant to, but she pulled me closer, which made ignoring her state of undress nearly impossible. The gentle swell of her breasts above the knot of her towel might've been the most tempting sight I'd ever encountered. I wasn't exactly known for controlling my baser impulses, but I would try...for her.

She didn't need me lusting after her while she was vulnerable and uncertain. She needed me to remind her even the darkest of nights gave into the dawn, that no matter how bleak things seemed, they wouldn't always remain that way. Thinking that way had gotten me through some of the worst deployments any man could imagine. It was also the mind-set that helped me survive my childhood. I knew growing up under my old man's thumb wouldn't be forever, and eventually I could break free, go out, and be a better man than he was.

"What if it had been Kody who ended up with her drink drugged? What if that man had succeeded in getting one of us out of the bar? Any one of us could have ended up kidnapped, assaulted, or worse. None of that would be a possibility if I hadn't come crashing into the Lawtons' lives. How can they be so nice and supportive when all I've brought them is trouble? I would hate me if I was in their shoes."

I chuckled and palmed the back of her head, pulling her forward so she could bury her tear-stained face in the center of my chest.

"No, you wouldn't. You don't have it in you to hate. And the Lawtons know good from bad. Their old man made sure of it. They aren't the type to turn their backs on some-one who clearly needs the love and protection of a family. And neither are you. Which is why you're so damn worried about something happening to someone else because of you. None of this is your fault, Presley." I felt like I'd said it a thousand times in a hundred different ways, but she still refused to believe me. She was going to let guilt crush her and use it to push everyone who wanted to get close to her away.

That would happen over my dead body.

I threaded my fingers through her silky hair and pulled her head back so she had no choice but to look up at me. I lowered my head slightly so we were eye to eye and told her, "You are not alone. Not anymore. You don't have to bear the weight of everything that's happening by yourself anymore. The reason I'm not as worried about your friends and family as you are is because I can see how much stronger you all are together. That guy wasn't going to get you out of the bar, no matter what. Kody would've noticed you were missing in a second. If they hadn't been drinking, Aspen and Della would've picked up on something being off within a heartbeat. Case would travel to the ends of the Earth to find you if you vanish. And the same goes for you. If Kody was the one who suddenly disappeared, I know you wouldn't let it go. You're all looking out for one another, but you still have blinders on and can't see it."

She exhaled slowly, making that towel dip and dance precariously. I gulped audibly and ordered my eyes to stay locked onto hers. I kept most of my reactions in check, but there was no stopping the swell of my cock behind my zipper. That part of my body couldn't ignore her, or all her exposed skin, no matter how hard I tried.

"What about you?" Her voice was so quiet I almost didn't hear her question.

I felt my eyebrows shoot upward as I asked, "What about me?"

"Would you notice if I suddenly disappeared?" She asked it in such an earnest tone I realized she honestly doubted that I was feeling something significant for her.

Normally that kind of obliviousness would enrage me, but she'd been alone for so long, I had to remember she wasn't used to having anyone looking for her when she wasn't around.

I gently tugged her closer so our lips were barely a millimeter away from touching. "I don't plan on letting you out of my sight anytime soon. And if you decide to make me the most important person in your life right now, I won't complain."

Her long eyelashes fluttered and her hold on me shifted

from my shirt to my neck. Her hands curled around the
back of my neck, the edge of her fingernails scraping across
sensitive skin.

"I've never had anyone to lean on before. I'm not sure I
know how to do it." Her breath was warm against my mouth,
and her skin was super soft underneath my hands as I backed
her toward the edge of the vanity. I had a hand on the back
of her bare thigh right where the towel ended. If my fingers
moved just an inch, they would be touching all the places I
shouldn't be thinking about but was.

"I have an entire club of brothers who help me hold on
when the weight of the world gets too heavy. Stick with me,
and I'll teach you how to lean and let go."

Lean she did. Right into me so that our lips touched.

I let her kiss me, slow and sweet, until I couldn't take it
anymore. She was half naked and as close to me as she'd
ever been. My self-control had already been put to the test
and had reached the end of the line. My palm slid up the
back of her thigh, and I heard her gasp over the sound of
the water running in the shower. I put a hand on the slight
curve of her backside, using my hold on her to lift her up
onto the edge of the vanity. I stepped between her long legs,
watching as the fabric of the towel shifted and parted in the
most enticing way.

I stared at her, maybe asking for permission for the first
time in my life instead of assuming she was offering up
something she might not be in the right headspace to give.

"Do you want me to kiss you, Pres?" It was the second
time I'd asked her if I could kiss her, and instead of feeling
burdened by it, I felt like I was stepping foot on new and
unexplored ground. There was a level of respect between us
that was shockingly poignant and powerful. Even if she said
no, I wasn't going to stop her, if she was the one who kept

on kissing me. I would help her work through whatever was going on in her head but keep my cool.

Maybe.

I didn't move any farther until she nodded slowly and said, "I want you to kiss me."

Once I had the words and permission, my self-control snapped.

My tongue twisted around hers, taking the kiss deeper, letting her know my intent. I knew she was still sad and wrapped up in a bunch of different emotions, and all I could hope was that passion and desire were caught up in the mix. I tried to use words to make her feel better and let her know I wasn't planning on going anywhere, but I was better at proving my point with my actions.

I took the hand holding her head and moved my fingers across the line of her exposed collarbone. I traced a line from the base of her throat to the knot of the towel between her breasts. Her emerald-colored eyes widened, and her tongue darted out to flick across her lower lip. I grinned and bent my head so I could chase after the moisture left behind. She said my name on a gasp but didn't protest when I tugged on the knot.

It gave easily, the short towel pooling around her hips.

She was so pretty, all over. Pale and pink, which made sense with her red hair. She didn't have freckles; her skin was flawless and unmarred from head to toe. She was slightly curved in all the right places but ran more along lean, elegant lines. The longer I stared at her, the higher the flush crossing her chest climbed. She wasn't exactly uncomfortable in her skin, but having someone else take in every single inch of it obviously made her a little uneasy. She was far from brazen, and that made her all the more endearing. There weren't a lot of women like her in my world, so I appreciated the charm of her sudden shyness.

I dragged the back of my fingers across the upper curve of her breast. Her breath caught in appreciation, as her nipples tightened into tight points at the contact. I liked the way my decorated skin looked against the alabaster purity of hers. It was a stark contrast, one that turned me on and made my dick even harder than it already was.

"You're stunning, do you know that?" I asked the question, not expecting an answer. I got one in the form of a kiss. This time she didn't bother to start out soft and sweet. She went right for tangled tongues and the nip of teeth.

The kiss deepened, getting wetter and wilder when I cupped the weight of one breast. It was the perfect handful, and the way her nipple tightened even more underneath the pressure of my thumb was enough to make me want to eat her alive. I stepped further into her space, making sure she could feel how hard I was behind my zipper as her thighs tightened around the outside of my legs. One of her hands slid from around my neck and landed on the center of my chest, where I was sure she could feel my heart pounding. It was good she could tell she wasn't alone in this crazy, overwhelming attraction that tended to blaze to life and was impossible to ignore when we were together.

I moved my hand to her other breast, treating it to the same tender torment. She pulled her mouth away, gasping long and loud in pleasure. If just my touch could garner such a strong reaction, I was dying to know what my mouth could do.

I kissed her hard, almost bruisingly so, until she pulled away to catch her breath. While she was distracted dragging much-needed air into her lungs, I kissed my way down the long line of her neck and across her collarbone. When my mouth sealed over the pert tip of one breast, she arched backward, and I put a hand on the small of her back to help her keep her balance. The little peak poked eagerly against my tongue, and Presley made a breathy sound that had my cock pulsing happily in my jeans. Her legs tightened even more, and her hand moved to the back of my head to hold me in place as I alternated between a fast flick of my tongue and the soft scrape of my teeth on each nipple. She was shifting anxiously against the edge of the vanity, as if she couldn't decide if she wanted to get closer or pull away.

I was going to do my best to convince her that closer to me was always the better option.

I moved the hand that wasn't holding her in place to the inside of one of her velvety soft thighs. I brushed my thumb along the surface, watching her eyes for any sign she wanted me to stop or back off. Her teeth bit into her bottom lip, and her nails dug painfully into my skin. She looked a little bit excited and slightly curious, as if all of this between us was new and unexplored.

I traced a zigzag line up the sensitive skin on the inside of her leg, watching as goose bumps lifted across her skin. Her muscles tensed, but when I got to the apex of her thigh, I could tell her body was already warm and welcoming. The secret, sensitive center between her legs was wet and quivering at the slightest contact. Her skin was smooth and silky, but the place I was sinking my searching fingers into was even more so.

We both let out a low moan at the contact. Presley's head fell backward and knocked against the mirror. I wanted to ask her if she was okay, but I had my mouth sealed over her rosy nipple and wasn't about to be deterred from driving her slowly out of her mind with pleasure.

Her body responded immediately to my touch, quivering and shaking around each stroke. I felt heat and moisture build. I felt the way her body tightened and heard the way her breath caught. One of her hands ended up in my hair, and she pulled each time I slid my thumb along her damp folds in search of that spot I knew would make her forget her name.

Since she was already bowed back, I licked my way down her breastbone, arrowing straight across her stomach, stopping briefly to tease the tiny indent of her belly button, before moving my mouth to the place where my fingers were playing. I had to get on my knees to get where I was going, not something I did for just anyone. But, if there was anyone deserving to have the world kneel before her, it was Presley Baskin. She'd been through so much and faced it all stoically and solitarily. She might have been the toughest woman I'd come across, and she didn't even have a clue as to her own power.

She was special. And I was the lucky bastard who got to show her just how special she was.

My fingers and mouth moving in tandem, I touched and tasted, stroked and sucked. I did my best to take her apart, her body responding beautifully to every caress and sensation. I could hear her panting above me. I felt her holding on to my head like she would fly away if she loosened her grip. I heard my name said in a bunch of different ways, but my favorite was when she screamed it in surprise as she finally came apart on my tongue. Her body released in a rush, and I wanted to savor every drop.

She was still quivering and quaking when I pulled away. I wiped my mouth on the back of my hand and leaned forward so I could place a biting kiss on the inside of her creamy thigh. It was a place that no one but me should see, and I got off on the idea of her wearing my mark in such a secret, sensitive place.

I got to my feet and put my hands on the edge of the vanity near her hips. Her eyes were at half-mast, and she almost looked drunk. I wanted to pat myself on the back for putting that dreamy, satisfied expression on her face.

"I'm gonna turn the shower off. Why don't you go lay back down for a little bit, and when you get up, you can start the day all over with a better outlook."

I reached out and brushed a stray strand of hair away from her face as her brows puckered. She looked at me, gaze full of questions, but instead of letting her ask them, I dropped a hard kiss on her mouth and said, "I told you, I *need* you to let me take care of you."

I was starting to see that there were going to be times when I needed her to take care of me, and times when we needed to take care of each other if we were going to keep going down this road. "I've never needed anything like that before. It's as much a first for me, as relying on someone else is for you."

I wanted to believe we had plenty of time ahead of us, so there was no need to rush learning how to be together. She'd had quite a scare not too long ago and didn't need to process the dramatic shift in our relationship on top of everything else she was dealing with right now.

Presley looked slightly shellshocked, so I picked her up and carried her back to her bedroom wedding night style. She was getting deep under my skin, and it surprised me more and more how comfortable I was starting to get having her there.

CHAPTER 12

❧

PRESLEY

Kody sighed heavily and dropped the side of her fist on the kitchen table sitting between us. She was obviously frustrated, and still looked under the weather. I was more worried about her than about myself at the moment. If I'd known she was going to drop by, I would've had time to prepare, and I would have had time to make sure I got rid of Shot before she showed up. But Kody did everything on her own timetable and marched to the beat of her own drummer, so of course she came by to check on me when I was least ready to face her. I tried to stammer some kind of excuse as to why Shot was at my apartment so early in the morning, but Kody simply waved the flustered words away and made herself at home in my sparsely stocked kitchen as Shot slipped out the front door with a promise, or maybe it was a threat, to call me later.

"I've known her since high school. Firing her feels like the right thing to do considering she put you in such a dangerous situation, but I also get that she was terrified of something bad happening to her kids. I don't know what I would do in a similar situation."

She sighed and leaned forward until her forehead was touching the table. "Your former friend is diabolical. She can find anyone's weakness and exploit it so freaking easy. Case told me the trucker who was supposed to abduct you was being blackmailed by a woman he picked up while he was hauling cargo outside of Houston. It seems he's been hauling more than goods across the border for some time. The woman had proof of his illegal activity and blackmailed him into coming after you. It's like she sees everyone as pieces on a chessboard and not as real-life humans who may or may not face the consequences of their actions. She's really and truly evil."

Some of the words were muffled since she was bent over, but I could tell she sounded tired, and some of her usual fire was missing. Without thinking much about it, or overthinking the gesture as I usually would, I reached out a hand and placed it gently on the back of Kody's head. I patted her like one would a small child and asked quietly, "Is everything okay with you? I know there's a lot coming at all of us from different directions right now, but you've seemed off the last couple of times I've seen you. I'm slightly worried about you."

I was actually very worried about her but didn't want to overstep.

Kody's head suddenly lifted, her wildly curly hair swirling around her head like a lion's mane. Her eyes locked onto mine as she grasped the hand I let fall at her quick movement.

"Can I tell you something?" Her voice hitched a little,

almost as if she was torn between being excited about something and equally terrified of it.

I nodded solemnly. "Of course. You can tell me anything." And she usually did, without asking for permission, which made this whole conversation a little odd. This entire morning was going in a way I never would have expected or been able to predict. Which I guess was par for the course in my life now.

"You can't tell anyone else. Not Case. Not Crew. Definitely not Aspen or Della." She sighed. "I don't want anyone to know."

I blinked in surprise and turned the hand she was clutching like a lifeline around so she could grip it firmly. "I won't talk to anyone, Kody. But it seems weird you don't want anyone in the family to know what's going on with you."

She sighed again and squeezed her eyes shut. "It's not that I don't want them to know. It's more that I need to find the right time to tell everyone." She gulped loudly and her eyes flicked open. They were shiny with unshed tears and she looked about as nervous as I'd ever seen her. Her fingers locked on mine tightly enough that I had to suppress a flinch of pain. "I'm pregnant."

Aspen's words about there being something to celebrate down the road rang through my head. I returned the death grip on my hand and said, "Congratulations. That's so exciting. I bet Hill is thrilled."

Kody paled and tugged her hand free. "I haven't exactly told him yet, either."

I blinked at her and slumped back in my seat. "Why not?" Anyone who had spent more than a minute in Hill and Kody's company could tell the quiet, intense Texas Ranger was head over heels for the youngest Lawton. The kind of love that moved mountains and shifted rivers. The man had loved her for a lifetime and would love her beyond. It didn't make sense that Kody would keep something so huge and special from him.

Kody put her hands on her cheeks and shook her head vigorously. "For one he's been out of town on an assignment. He's always off here or there. Do you have any idea what's going to happen if I tell him we're having a kid? He's going to drop everything in his life and focus only on me and the baby. I love him, but there is such a thing as too much attention and affection." She lowered her gaze to the top of the table and muttered, "And if I tell him, it's real. It means I'm really going to be a mother. I'm going to be responsible for another human for the rest of my life. I have no idea how to do that. I'm...scared."

I got up from my seat across from her and walked to where she was trembling in her seat. I wrapped my arms around her shoulders and gave her a hug, resting my cheek on the top of her unruly hair.

"It's okay to be scared. Having a baby is a big deal, and it is a lot of responsibility. I'd be more concerned if you were taking the pregnancy in stride." It sounded as if, like most things in her chaotic life, the baby wasn't planned and had thrown her for a loop. Luckily she had a lot of people in her life to support her and show her the way. She already had her village to help her raise her child. Well, she would have them once she told her family what was going on.

Almost as if she could read my thoughts, she tearfully continued, "It doesn't seem fair. All Aspen ever wanted was to be a mom. She's so good with Hayes, and her and Case make such good parents. And Della and Crew are getting married. They both have stable, successful careers. I don't know if they want kids, but they're both in a place where they could offer a baby a great life. Hill and I barely reunited.

We're just starting to learn how to live together, how to love one another, and now there's a baby in the mix. It seems like some kind of cosmic joke." She gulped loudly and moved her hand so she was holding on to my forearm. "I feel like Aspen might hate me when she finds out. She's done more to bring our family together and help heal us than anyone. I can't bear the idea of hurting her."

I smoothed a hand down her arm and shushed her. "Aspen won't hate you. She's going to be so happy for you. She might be a little sad for herself, but that has nothing to do with you."

Aspen had mentioned her struggles with fertility in an offhand manner more than once. She spoke of the complications and heartache she experienced before getting together with Case and inheriting Hayes as her almost-grown son in the process. She always sounded slightly sad when she talked about the past, but the fertility issues were only part of it. Her marriage before her relationship with Case had also been incredibly rocky and complex. There was lingering disappointment that was simply just a part of who Aspen was, the same way the loss of her first love was such a huge part of who Kody was, and the way the unrelenting need to handle things on my own was so much of who I was. It was both the triumphs and the failures, the wins and losses, that shaped who we were.

Kody sniffed a little, so I let her go and went into the kitchenette to find her something to wipe her face. It was the most she'd let her guard down with me since we'd met, and honestly, it was kind of reassuring to know Kody had the same kind of fears and uncertainties as any other woman. For the longest time, she seemed so much more sure of herself than anyone I'd met. I was confident in my career, and in the knowledge I'd accumulated over the course of my studies and work, but that was the only place where I was one hundred percent certain of myself. Kody seemed to own *everything* in her life, good or bad. She made no apologies, and I thought that was so refreshing and was slightly envious. I'd never had that kind of freedom.

I reclaimed my seat across from her and reached for my abandoned coffee. "I'm going to keep this conversation between the two of us, but I have to tell you, the people who care the most about you, see things you might not be aware of them seeing. If you don't want to tell your brothers and the girls, that's one thing. However, you need to tell Hill. This is something the two of you are in together from the very start." I lifted my eyebrows pointedly. After all, she wouldn't be in her current condition if her relationship with Hill hadn't progressed as quickly as it had. "Trust him to give you what you need and to be your partner in everything. If he oversteps, let him know, but you also need to listen when he tells you what he needs."

She groaned dramatically and smacked her palms down on the table. "Ugh. You're so reasonable. It's annoying. Have you ever done anything rash or reckless in your life?"

She pouted a little bit as I blushed. "Umm, well…" There was no stopping the vivid images of everything I'd done with Shot in my bathroom the previous night. All of that definitely counted as rash and reckless.

Catching sight of the guilty color in my face, Kody clapped her hands together and laughed, tossing her head back. "Oh yeah. I forgot Shot answered your door this morning." Her eyebrows winged upward and a crooked grin twisted her lips. "Do you have any idea what you're doing with him? He's not some nice, polite college graduate. He's not a guy who owns a suit and tie. He's never come across a rule he wasn't willing to break, and he lives every single day knowing there's a good chance he's going to end up in a jail cell or a shallow grave by the end of it." She cocked her head to the side and asked, "Is he really someone you want to get tangled up with?"

I huffed out a breath and averted my eyes. "I'm not so sure I have a choice. No matter how hard I try, or what kind of warning I give myself, I can't seem to stay away from him." I blinked rapidly, remembering she used to have a much different relationship with Shot than she did now. "Oh. I'm sorry. I didn't think before I said that."

Kody laughed. She put a hand on her belly and used the other to wipe away a few tears that squeezed out of her eyes. "You don't think I'm jealous that you're hooking up with him, do you?"

I frowned. "I honestly don't know what to think. You called me in to save him in the middle of the night and he's very protective of you. I never stopped to work my way through what all of that may mean when I started to have very confusing feelings toward him."

It was Kody's turn to reach out a hand and comfort me. Her gaze went soft and sincere as she told me, "Shot and I are friends. We've always been friends. He was there when I needed help with the bar. He was there when I was lost and lonely and needed someone to lean on. We both knew it was never going to be anything more than a very close friendship with an occasional benefit from the start. The benefits ended up being less important to both of us than the friendship. He means the world to me, but I always understood that he is a dangerous man who is fully capable of doing really bad things." She smiled a little as she added, "He's also a very good guy who can and will do great things for others—it just depends on the day. He's not who I would've imagined you falling for."

I lifted my shoulders and let them fall in a helpless shrug. "Truthfully, I've never fallen for anyone before. I can't even say for certain that's what happening. I didn't think he was my type." I frowned. "I still don't." But there was no denying that I'd been fully invested and engaged in what happened between us the previous night. I one hundred percent wanted him, and I couldn't shake the feeling that being intimate with him once would never be enough.

No one other than him had ever stayed in my mind long after they left the room. No other man made me moan and ache when touching me the way he did. There had never been anyone in my orbit who made it easy to forget all the reasons they were so wrong for me, and instead forced me to look at all the reasons why I couldn't stay away. No one who was seemingly right for me had me as confused and confounded as Shot had me.

Kody's pretty features turned into a frown as she stared at me with evident concern on her freckled face. "How have you never fallen for anyone before? You never had a crush on a classmate? You never had to suffer through an unrequited love?" She leaned forward, gaze intense and probing. "I'm going to sound conceited, since we look so much alike, but you're unbelievably beautiful, and you're smart. Even if you weren't interested, I can't believe you didn't have the opposite sex chasing you everywhere you went."

I lifted my eyes to the ceiling, memories of endless lonely and empty nights flitting through my mind.

It might seem odd to her, but there was a very logical reason why I'd been such a late bloomer.

"In high school, I skipped several grades. So I was younger than everyone in all of my classes. No one really seemed to know what to do with me. I was like an alien in their midst. I was too quiet and too serious to make friends. Plus, my mom was sick. There wasn't any money to participate in normal school activities, and any free time I had was spent taking care of her. Dating was out of the question. College was a little better. I dated some, but I was clueless and clumsy with it, since I was still younger than most of the guys I went out with."

I shook my head and sighed. "I never realized it back then, but anyone who was interested in me, or anyone I was even slightly attracted to, Ashby made it her mission to run interference between us. I would go on a date with a guy, then find out she slept with him. If I mentioned I liked someone, she immediately knew a reason why he would never be interested in me, but then I'd find out later she was seeing him behind my back. It honestly didn't matter to me—I was focused on getting through school as quickly as possible so I could start working because my mom's medical bills were out of control. But I hated feeling like I failed at something everyone else around me did with such ease."

I shifted my gaze back to Kody's and frowned in a way that I was sure was almost a mirror image to the one on her face. "When I started working for the ME's office I met a detective. He was the first man I was really, truly interested in. He was smart, ambitious, and his father was battling pancreatic cancer, so I thought we had a lot in common."

Kody practically climbed on top of the table, she leaned so far forward as I spoke. "What happened with him? Did Ashby have an affair with him as well?"

I slowly shook my head. "No. But she did tell me that he was married, and that there was no father with cancer. She told me he was playing me big-time. After everything Ashby was doing to deter me from taking the promotion when it was announced I was the front-runner became clear,

I actually looked the man up to see if he had been another victim of her lies and manipulation. Lying about what he'd done to me would be the least of her crimes, but it was all true. He could tell I was lonely and used my mother's illness as a way to get close to me quickly." I made a disgusted face and told her flatly, "It was the first time in my life I acted dumb over a man and I swore I would never do it again." I sighed again. "Then I met Shot."

Kody got to her feet and walked over to me. She hugged me in a similar manner to how I'd hugged her earlier and whispered, "You didn't have it any easier than we did, did you?"

I let myself melt into the comfort of her hug. "No. It wasn't easy."

However, I knew my mom loved me, and even as sick as she was, she did her best to make sure I never doubted how much. It wasn't until she died that the full scope of what she'd done to make sure I was provided for was revealed. I hadn't grown up under Conrad Lawton's corrupt tyranny like my siblings had, but his misdeeds had found their way into my life regardless.

"You do realize that whatever you have with Shot isn't going to be any kind of walk in the park, right? No matter how casual or serious things are between the two of you, it's going to be complicated." She gave me a look that was hard to decipher. "Case and Crew aren't very fond of him, but they are both growing incredibly fond of you. Maybe just keep that in mind moving forward."

I let out an uneven-sounding laugh. "Now who's being the annoyingly reasonable one?"

She laughed at my flippant comment, and some of the heavy tension from the conversation lifted. "It doesn't happen often, so appreciate it."

I did. And I appreciated her.

Talking with Kody about the things we were afraid of, about the mistakes and memories that lived within us, felt good. Felt cathartic and healing.

It felt like I'd finally found a forever family and maybe even my place within it.

CHAPTER 13

∞

SHOT

To what do I owe the pleasure, gentlemen?"

I asked the question as I leaned against my bike, which was parked on the side of a remote back road. I didn't take my sunglasses off, as both the sheriff and the Texas Ranger made their way toward me.

Case and Hill were dressed casually in jeans, boots, and plain T-shirts. They both wore cowboy hats; Case's was black, Hill's a light gray. It was almost as if their choice in headwear was meant to indicate which was playing good cop and which one was playing bad. Neither had his badge showing, but both wore their service weapons in plain sight, reminding me that, while Case might have called this clandestine meeting, they weren't my friends nor were to be taken lightly.

Hill and Case moved the same, both full of purpose and authority. They held themselves the same, both alert and aware. They reminded me a lot of my brothers and the guys I'd served with. It made sense, since both had been in the military before coming back to Texas and taking up careers in law enforcement. In a different world, the three of us probably would've gotten along just fine. At our core, we had a lot in common, but I wasn't one to walk the straight and narrow. Also, I'd dated Case's little sister, who just happened to be the love of Hill's life, so any bonds of brotherhood between us were bound to be unlikely.

Hill pushed the brim of his hat up and gave me a narrow-eyed look. "Did you come out here alone?"

I shrugged and waved a gloved hand around the barren and deserted landscape. "You see anyone else hanging around, Ranger?"

"Doesn't seem like a smart move. It's empty and isolated. Anything could happen out here." Hill's drawl was slow and smooth, making the threat sound less serious than I knew it was.

I rolled my eyes, even though they were covered, and pushed off the bike. I crossed my arms over my chest and asked, "Really, why did you ask me to meet you out here? I'm busy and have shit to do."

And I didn't like being so far away from Presley. Top threw a fit when I asked him to keep an eye on her while I rode out to meet the boys in blue. He still hadn't wrapped his head around the lengths I was willing to go to for her, and he made it pretty obvious he wasn't totally behind me starting something with her. For Top, the club came first, foremost, and always, much as it had with my father. It was hard for men wired that way to grasp how caring about someone could suddenly take precedence over the brotherhood. In their mind, love, or any faint traces of it, equaled a kind of betrayal.

"We want to talk to you about Presley. We know you've been spending time with her, hanging around her, and keeping an eye on her." Case didn't lift his hat the way Hill did, so I couldn't tell if he was looking at me. He copied my pose with his arms across his chest, and I could see an irritated tic moving in his tanned cheek.

I sighed and moved to push my sunglasses to the top of my head. "You already did the big-brother thing and warned me to stay away. Clearly, it didn't work. Bringing backup isn't going to make a difference." I gave Hill a pointed look.

Case swore and took a step toward me, only to be pulled back by his friend. Hill huffed out an annoyed sound and scowled at me. "You obviously haven't been doing a good enough job protecting her if she was nearly abducted in a room full of people."

Ouch.

Hill was more laid-back and less volatile than Case, but that didn't mean he couldn't be as cruel and ruthless as the sheriff when called for.

I practically growled my response. "That was a mistake that won't be repeated."

I wasn't about to explain I'd been busy getting answers for Presley while she was in danger. That was a can of worms no one needed to open. "I'm not going to let anything else happen to her, so why don't the two of you do your damn jobs and find the lunatic who's trying to hurt her?"

"Do you really think we've been sitting around with our thumbs up our asses?" Now Hill was the one taking a step forward. "I've been all over this damn state, chasing even the smallest lead in search of Ashby Grant. I've been away from home, away from Kody, for weeks on end. Not only am I worried about Presley, but I'm worried about my woman. Kody has grown incredibly attached to her, and if something happens"—Hill shook his head, his expression shifting from anger to stark concern—"I don't know that she'll be able to handle losing someone else she cares so much about."

Kody had lost her mother when she was a teenager. Then her first love committed suicide right before they were supposed to get married. On top of that, Hill had come back into her life because he had been involved in finding out who murdered her father. It was a lot of loss, no matter how you looked at it, and I agreed Kody would take it exceptionally hard if anything tragic—well, more tragic—happened to Presley.

"I still don't understand how whatever it is you're doing, or not doing, has anything to do with me." If they tracked down Ashby Grant they would put her behind bars and run her through the legal system. If I found her, I wanted to put her in the ground where no one would ever find her. Would I? Unlikely. I didn't operate that way, but the desire was there and strong enough that I had to fight against it. That was what really separated me from the two men standing across from me.

Case sighed heavily and finally pushed his hat back so I could see his face. I noticed immediately that he looked tired and stressed out. The kind of tired that went all the way to your bones and ate away at your insides. The kind of tired other people could feel. He was clearly very worried about Presley and the never-ending danger she seemed to be in.

"I hate with every fiber of my being having to admit that our hands are tied. We've done everything we can. We've put as many resources as possible toward the situation, and we still have nothing. Hill and I agree it's time to start thinking outside the box when it comes to keeping Presley safe and finally ending all of this with Grant." He sighed again and I could actually see how difficult this conversation was for him. "We need your help."

I was confused, which I was sure they could see all over my face. "What kind of help are we talking about, boys?" It couldn't possibly be the kind of help where they also wanted the person who had caused so much hurt to their loved ones in a shallow grave with no questions asked, could it?

Case groaned like he was reading my mind. "Nothing illegal. We want you to stick even closer to Presley. Make it obvious you're in some kind of relationship with her. Be loud about it. Make sure there is no mistake that the two of you have something going on. Even better if you can make it seem like she's head over heels in love with you." He lifted a hand and scratched at the salt-and-pepper stubble on his chin. "A few days ago Presley told Kody that Ashby seems to be particularly triggered by the men in Presley's life. She's previously gone out of her way to make sure any relationship Presley tries to start or gets involved in goes up in flames. Hill and I talked it over, and we agree that if you become a constant in Presley's life, it's the best chance we have to draw Ashby out into the open. Plus, if you stick close to her, there's less chance of something like what happened at the bar again."

Hill chimed in. "Presley has been dangling herself out there as bait from the start and it hasn't done any good. Ashby wants to hurt her, to punish her. When she doesn't have something Ashby wants, she serves no purpose. If Presley has you, boom! Ashby suddenly has a reason to resume her plans."

"How do you explain the trucker trying to take her out of the bar, then?" I understood where they were going with this whole plan, but the recent abduction attempt didn't make much sense within that framework.

"I think it was a power move. A reminder she's still here and she's watching. It was also a really great way to throw the family into chaos." Case snatched his hat off his head and plowed a frustrated hand through his hair. "It scared the piss out of Presley, but it made Kody, Aspen, and Della feel like they failed her. It also pissed me and Crew off and brought Hill back home. She's playing with all of us, and Presley is right in the center of the gameboard. There are too many variables. She could go after one of us, one of the family, but there are more of us and the impact is less than if Presley's attached to one specific person. Ashby left Presley's mother alone for the most part until Presley got the promotion over her. But, historically, she's *always* intervened with her love interests. Our best bet to end this is for Presley to be blatantly and over the top in love with someone. And the only believable 'someone' at the moment is you."

I turned his words over in my head, the dots connecting slowly but surely. "I've been hanging around Presley a lot lately. Nothing unusual has happened." I'd already made my interest obvious, which was why Case had warned me away.

"I think the game changer is making it clear Presley is into you. According to Kody, she's mostly indifferent to the men who are interested in her, but she seems to like you more than just a little bit." Case frowned even harder and muttered, "God only knows why."

I snorted and shifted my gaze between the two men. "So you want me to be the bait instead of her? And you want me to manipulate her feelings toward me for her own good?" I shook my head and clicked my tongue. "You both realize if she finds out about this, if any of the women in your lives find out, we're all dead men, right?"

Hill tossed his hands up in frustration. He had to know Kody would castrate him if any of this came to light. "What choice do we have, Caldwell? How long is this going to drag on? How long are we supposed to be walking on eggshells waiting for this unhinged woman to hurt someone we love?

We have to do something, and this is the best idea we've got." He grunted and looked irritated as hell. "It's not like you don't already have something started with the doctor anyway. You might not be formally dating now, but you're doing something. We aren't suggesting you pretend to like her, because we wouldn't want to do that to her or you. We're just saying, show the world and Ashby just how much you like her, and more importantly, how much she likes you."

I bit off a string of swear words and looked up at the sky for a second, the sun nearly blinding me. The bright light was enough to get all the spiraling, disordered thoughts in my head in line. "She's going to be really hurt if she finds out she's being used, even if it is for her own good."

I wanted to date her for real. Well, maybe not date-date. I wasn't a dinner-and-movie kind of guy and Presley had already told me she didn't know a good date from a bad one. But I wanted to see her, and only her. I didn't like the idea of playing this kind of game behind her back at all. I also didn't like the thought of making her angry enough that she might walk away from me for good if she found out what I was really up to. She was so hesitant and careful when it came to getting close to someone else, I didn't want her to doubt my feelings were real, and if she knew what Case and Hill were scheming that was exactly what would happen. I already felt like I was chasing after someone who was reluctant to be caught. I knew I was close to catching her and didn't want to give her a reason to slip through my fingers.

"I can deal with her being hurt." Case's voice was hard and unyielding. "I can't deal with her being dead. Can you?"

Realistically, the longer Ashby was left unfound and un-checked, the higher the probability someone I cared about, even if it wasn't Presley, would be taken away. The club dabbled in a few different gambling ventures both legal and not, so I knew odds and when they weren't in my favor. I hated that Case had a point, and I was begrudgingly impressed he and Hill had come up with a plan that was just on the right side of devious and dangerous.

"All right. I'm game." What other choice did I have? It wasn't like I could step aside and let her be interested in another man. Even if it was just for show. "But I can't make her fall for me. I can't force her to feel any particular way about me." I wanted her to want me the way I wanted her. But love was a different ball game. We were still very different people, and she didn't have any idea what my life was actually like, and I wasn't sure I had the first clue about hers when it wasn't in danger. There was a long way to go before we could start throwing around words like love and forever. Not to mention neither of us really had any experience when it came to having something serious, something you would kill to protect.

Hill shrugged as if Presley's feelings were irrelevant. "All you need to do is make it look like she's stupidly in love with you. Whether she actually is or not doesn't matter in the big picture."

Of course, it didn't matter to him, but to me that seemed like a huge sticking point. I really wanted her to actually like me. The idea of her falling head over heels for me made the inside of my chest warm, and it had all kinds of soft, tender feelings I'd never experienced before sparking to life. My relationship with Presley was almost innocent and pure compared to most of my others. I loathed the idea of anything tainting it.

"Fine. I'll do what needs to be done." I paused for a second, before offering up my own caveat. "I'm telling you now if this crazy woman comes after me or my club, I'm dealing with it my way. If she comes anywhere near Presley while I'm around, I'm dealing with the threat however I see fit. I will not wait for the heroes in her life to ride in on their white horses to save the day."

Hill automatically moved to argue. Surprisingly, Case intervened. He nodded his dark head and met my serious gaze with his own. "We asked you to get involved. We knew the risks."

I was ready to call this meeting done, but I stopped from turning toward my bike when Case continued. "However, if I catch you blatantly breaking the law with no regard for innocent civilians, I will take you down, Palmer."

I flinched at the use of my given name. I didn't hear it often, and I didn't like the way Case said it, as if he was trying to remind me there was a normal man buried somewhere inside the biker. "Duly noted, Sheriff."

I swung a leg over the bike and slid my sunglasses back down over my eyes. Hill walked away without a backward glance, but I could see the tension in every line of his body. Case put his hat back on his head and moved slightly closer to me as I rocked the bike off its kickstand.

"Heard from a buddy in the Austin PD that an anonymous whistleblower dropped an envelope of evidence showing Ashby and Presley's mother's doctor more than likely involved in malpractice which resulted in her death. When he went to talk to the doctor, the man was a mess and had ten broken fingers. He readily admitted to everything, but wouldn't tell my buddy how his hands got so trashed. You wouldn't know anything about any of that would you, Shot?"

I grinned because we were back to Shot as soon as he was suspicious of me. "All I know is a doctor who shouldn't be allowed near the sick and defenseless can no longer do any damage. That might not be your idea of justice, but it is

mine. It's the very least he deserves for his part in breaking
Presley's heart. Her mother was all she had, and he helped
take her away."

Case sighed heavily and turned to walk away. "I don't like
you. I never will. But there are times when I'm damn jealous
of you. It must be nice to have absolutely no one to answer
to. I wonder what kind of man I'd be if I believed I was
untouchable. You have so many damn skills, and you're so
fucking scary. I wonder what you could do if you channeled
all that power into something other than raising hell and
running the club."

His words were part compliment and part complaint. I
chuckled and cranked the ignition on. The roar of the motor
drowned out my words as I told Case's retreating back,
"Even if you don't like me, Case, I've always liked you."

It was true.

I'd reluctantly admired the man from the start and knew
if our roles were reversed, the type of man he would be was
one I would still look up to and respect. He was also skilled
and scary, and a natural leader and advocate for those who
couldn't fight for themselves.

He was wrong about me being untouchable, though.

Not too long ago, an intriguing, leggy, redheaded medical
examiner brought me to my knees without even trying.

CHAPTER 14

∞

PRESLEY

Thanks for coming with me today." I looked at Shot out of the corner of my eye. He'd been quiet throughout the day, hardly interjecting or offering an opinion as we jumped from house to house.

I'd spent the day caught between trying to figure out why he'd insisted on coming with me as I searched for a new place to live, and being secretly thrilled to spend the entire day in his company. When I told him that I was going house hunting with Kody, he'd immediately interjected that it wasn't safe for the two of us to be running around, touring empty houses alone. The attack at the bar was still fresh in everyone's mind, so it was hard to deny that he had a point. He told me he would free up a day to go with me instead, and while Kody hadn't liked the change in plans, she didn't argue too much. Apparently Hill was home for a stretch and she'd finally decided to tell him about the baby.

Unfortunately, I hadn't viewed a single property I liked.

I felt like Goldilocks. All the single-family homes seemed

too big for one person, and the idea of the upkeep was daunting. All the town houses and condos seemed too small and sterile. I couldn't seem to find a happy medium, or a place that screamed "forever home." All in all, I was frustrated and emotionally drained.

My aggravation must've been evident because Shot commented on it when we got back to my car after viewing the final house for the day. When he first showed up at my apartment on his motorcycle, I balked at the idea of getting on the back of his bike. Luckily, he didn't ask me to ride with him and instead asked for my car keys so he could chauffeur me around. Since I would be flipping through listings and scrolling through directions on my phone, I didn't resist in handing them over.

"I'm glad you didn't like any of those houses today. I thought seeing what you were looking for in a permanent place to live would tell me a little bit more about you. It was interesting to see how all the ultramodern and minimalistic designs totally turned you off. They were too cold and empty. Honestly, I had you pegged as a new-build kinda woman."

I tiredly shook my head and repressed a shiver of delight that he was trying to learn more about me. His rough charm was hard to resist when he decided to use it. I brushed a loose piece of hair away from my cheek.

"I'm not sure what I want, but I do know I don't want a place that feels anything like a morgue when you walk in." I cocked my head to the side, thinking about how warm and welcoming Aspen and Case's remodeled Craftsman was. It wasn't a huge house, but it felt big enough to hold the Lawton family and then some. It also had the perfect blend of both Aspen and Case in all the decorating choices. It was a little goth and a little country-western. Two styles that shouldn't mesh well but did. Just like the couple who lived there. "I like Case and Aspen's place. I'm not really handy or crafty, but maybe I need to look at something a little older that I can update and make my own."

Shot chuckled and looked at me out of the corner of his eye. "All the men in your family know how to swing a hammer. If you want to fix a place up, you won't be doing it on your own." His eyebrows winged upward. "And I can always ask the guys in the club to help out, if you don't mind your place being overrun with bikers."

Oddly enough, the idea didn't bother me at all. Before Shot burst into my life, the thought of a house full of scary, leather-wearing strangers was my actual nightmare, but now it didn't seem so bad. Shot and his boys took care of one another. They relied on one another, just like the Lawtons did. It wasn't a traditional type of family, but the bonds they shared were unbreakable, and I liked that. I was starting to think I wanted to form some bonds of my own.

"If I take on a huge project like that, I'll be open to taking all the help I can get." I watched him quietly before asking, "What kind of place do *you* see calling home? I know you and some of the other guys in the club all stay out at the ranch, but some of the members have to be married and have kids. Do you ever picture yourself living in a normal house and having a family?"

He stilled a little and his hands tightened on the steering wheel. I bit down on my lower lip, wondering if I'd crossed a line I didn't know had been drawn in the sand. We were getting to know each other, probably slower than most couples did, since we were both amateurs when it came to starting a relationship. I wondered briefly if I was pushing for too much, too soon. I hated that I couldn't get control of the uncertainty that crept in when I was unsure of myself and my place in the lives of those I was starting to care so much about.

Luckily Shot put my doubts to rest with a surprisingly raw and thoughtful response. "I don't really think it'll be a place I'll call home. I think it'll be a person. Someone I want to see at the end of the day. Someone I want to come back to when the club inevitably gets into trouble. I think home will be the person who gives me a place to go when I need a minute to breathe and not be the president of the Sons of Sorrow. Any roof over my head, any place to sleep, is fine as long as I know I can wake up next to the person who matters most to me."

I gulped because I didn't want to assume he was talking about me, but it kind of felt like he was speaking directly to my heart.

"Kind of like you, no one was the right fit, so I kept looking. I think I stumbled onto a fixer-upper as well." He flashed me a grin, his dark eyes glittering with dangerous promises. "Good thing I'm ready to put in the work to make sure the person I have in mind is going to be my forever home as well."

I couldn't form a coherent thought on the rest of the way to my apartment. He'd stunned me to silence and snatched all rational thought from my mind. It would be so easy to start spinning fairy tales around his words, but I was still scared of believing what he was telling me. Our lifestyles were so different, I couldn't come up with a logical way they would ever seamlessly mesh. We'd been spending more time together, and I was terrified he would get bored of me after a few weeks. But he wasn't letting me put distance between us anymore. In addition to insisting on coming with me today, he was sending clear signals that he wasn't planning on leaving me on my own tonight.

I didn't say anything when he followed me up the stairs to my apartment a little while later. I figured he was going to see me inside and make sure nothing had been tampered with while I was gone for the day. He was taking the whole protection thing incredibly seriously, but when I mentioned he might be going overboard he reminded me of what happened at the bar, which immediately silenced me.

The inside of my apartment was dark and quiet. I was going for the light switch and dropping my purse on the catch-all in the hallway, when suddenly I felt Shot move behind me. I opened my mouth to ask what he was doing and tried to turn so I could see. But my movement stilled when a strong arm wrapped around my shoulders and a heavy hand landed on my mouth. The chill of metal rings decorating the fingers of that hand sent a shiver racing through my body. I dug my fingers into the forearm locked across my chest and kicked at the shins pressing into the back of my legs.

I was intimately familiar with how those thick, rough fingers covered in heavy rings felt pressed against my skin. When Shot didn't let me go as soon as I started to struggle, I shifted tactics and went totally limp in his hold.

It was easy to forget that he'd been a highly trained soldier before becoming an outlaw biker. Anyone else would've dropped me to the floor. Shot tightened his hold and lowered his head so he could whisper in my ear, "You need to leave the lights on when you go out and you should get better locks for your door. Anyone can break through the ones you currently have."

Instead of nodding, I jammed my elbow back as hard as I could, hitting him in the gut and forcing out a whoosh of air. When he let me go, spinning me around so I was facing him, I pushed him with all my might, glaring at him as I pointed a finger in his handsome face.

"Not funny." I really was far from amused.

Shot rubbed what I knew were his rock-hard abs through the cotton of his T-shirt. "Wasn't meant to be funny. I wanted you to see how easy it would be for anyone to grab you if you don't take precautions. I'm worried about you."

I scowled at him. "I don't need you to intimidate me."

He nodded, dark hair flopping across his forehead and falling into his eyes. "Your instincts are solid. Your flight-and-fight responses seem to be pretty equally balanced. If one doesn't work, you fall back on the other without hesitation. Those self-defense classes paid off." He tapped his stomach again and gave me a grin. "You could do some serious damage if you really needed to."

Frustrated at how he went about proving his point, I dragged my hands through the front of my hair and tugged. Everything about him was over the top. There wasn't a subtle bone in the man's big, built body. It was hard to keep up with him. He'd gone from quiet and observant while we were house hunting to an aggressive combatant in the blink of an eye.

But, there was no arguing that he got results. "Hill told Kody that they're going to open an official investigation into Dr. Kemper and that he won't be able to practice medicine ever again." I met his penetrating look with a grateful one of my own. "Thank you for that."

"Didn't do it out of the kindness of my heart. Don't forget you owe me one." He winked at me, and his grin shifted to something along the lines of being downright carnal. "I can't wait to collect my own favor in return."

I shifted restlessly. I'd never had a man show such overt interest in me sexually before. Or rather, I'd never paid any attention when they did. Shot made the simmering chemistry and magnetic pull between the two of us impossible to ignore. Deciding a change of subject was in order before I got in over my head, I mumbled, "Kody also mentioned Dr. Kemper was pretty roughed up. How come you aren't worried about him saying anything to the police about your involvement?"

Shot shrugged and followed me as I walked toward the tiny kitchen. I wasn't hungry, or thirsty, but I needed something to do with my hands before they blindly reached for the man dressed in all black, radiating badass energy as he stalked me with a predatory prowl.

"The good doctor has a lot he'd like to keep hidden. His wife was taking him to the cleaners in the divorce, and he has a long-term side chick he's been keeping in luxury in Austin. Both those factors are costing him a fortune. He's been playing hardball with the wife, but she's suspected that he's been hiding money so she can't access it during the split. She was right. He has a bunch of his assets in an offshore account. Far more than he reported in the divorce." Shot sounded disgusted, which I found a little surprising. I wouldn't have thought infidelity would be a big deal for a guy who admitted to never having a serious relationship in his lifetime. "We hijacked his accounts. Told him if he tried to tell anyone about the club's involvement, we were turning all the assets over to the wife. Also told him he could have the money back once Ashby Grant is in police custody. As long as he cooperates with the investigation, he can have it back."

He had access to his own fully equipped surgical suite as well as a surgeon on call. It didn't surprise me one bit to hear he also had access to someone who could hack into a banking system.

Shot lifted his eyebrows upward. "After I tell the wife all about the secret accounts. She deserves a payday for dealing with his arrogant ass for so long."

He was devious, and shockingly clever. I guess he had to be in order to stay out of prison and to keep his club and its members out of trouble.

"We should've grabbed dinner." I was planning on telling him I would make us something to eat, but the words were cut off when he spun me around with a hand on my arm and by the pressure of his lips landing on mine.

I gasped at the unexpected kiss, and my hands lifted of their own volition to his broad shoulders. He walked me backward, his mouth devouring mine with each step. My back hit a wall, rattling a mirror and a cheap print hanging there.

Shot's palm slid along my side, thumb brushing over my rib cage. His knee pressed between my legs, letting him lean into me, so all our hard and soft parts were perfectly aligned. My breasts pressed against his firm chest, the warmth from his body making my nipples perk up and tighten. I pulled my mouth free when one of his hands gripped a handful of my backside in a suggestive manner.

"Today was technically our second date, Presley." His almost midnight-colored eyes were normally unreadable, but at the moment his intent was very clear. "You told me I could kiss you the next time."

"You're right, I did say that." I searched around for words that didn't make me sound like a lovestruck idiot.

Shot smiled and reached up so he could smooth my hair back from my face. I let my head knock against the wall as my heart started to race with his gentle treatment.

"Do you trust me, Presley?" It was possibly the most sincere question he'd asked since I'd met him.

He was as surprised by my rawly honest "I do" as I was.

We hadn't known each other for very long, but he'd yet to let me down when I needed him, or needed something from him. It was more than I could say for the others who'd passed through my life.

The admission sent Shot into a flurry of activity.

He bent down and tugged my strappy sandals off my feet. When he stood back up, his busy hands brought my plain T-shirt up and over my head. I blinked in surprise when so much of my skin was suddenly exposed. He flicked open the clasp of my bra with no effort at all and watched with appreciative eyes as the silky fabric slithered down my arms and off my breasts. Not one to be left out of anything, Shot dragged his ever-present leather vest off his shoulders, and reached a hand behind his neck so he could pull his T-shirt off over his head. I'd never seen a man use that move in real life, and I instantly knew why it was so popular in TV and movies. It was hot. So hot. However, nowhere near as hot as the sculpted, tattooed body the move revealed. Every inch of Shot's torso was carved with sharp lines and defined muscles. There was more skin with ink on it than was bare. It was a lot to take in, and while I was distracted with my gawking, I missed Shot going to the fastening on my jeans. In seconds he had me fully naked against the wall. The solid surface helped ground my overexcited system in reality and afforded him the leverage he needed to slide a hand under my ass so he could hoist me up.

After I instinctively wrapped my legs around his lean waist, he guided my arms up around his neck, dark eyes watching me closely for any signs of resistance. I didn't have any and if I did, it would've instantly melted away when he kissed me again. The way he kissed made me forget who I was, forget all the normal hang-ups and hesitations I had. It forced me to focus on how he made me feel.

Slowly.

Softly.

Deeply.

He kissed me the way you kissed someone you wanted to kiss again and again. It was the kind of kiss you gave someone you never wanted to forget.

He dragged the tip of his nose across my cheek and stopped when his now-damp lips touched my ear. "You better hold on, Pres."

Again, the name that only he used, something special we shared. He was always the one pulling me closer when I was so used to being pushed away.

I curled my arms around his neck even more tightly and shifted the kiss to something deeper and dirtier. Lots of tongue and plenty of eagerness. He responded by sneaking a hand in between our very close bodies so he could caress my breasts and roll his thumb over the sensitive points of my nipples. When we both desperately needed a second to catch our breath, he moved his mouth to my ear. His teeth nipped at the lobe, and he used his tongue to trace the delicate outline of the shell. When he dropped a tiny kiss on the hidden spot behind my ear, my entire body shuddered. No one before him had ever spent the time to search out all those secret, responsive places on my body. Even I was stunned by how strongly I reacted to the simple peck. He chuckled against my skin and repeated the motion.

My legs tightened reflexively around his waist, and my back hit the wall again. I could feel my insides starting to quiver and clench. My thighs trembled, and I knew if he reached between my legs he would find the area already wet and wanting. I arched my back impatiently when he applied an almost painful pressure to the nipple he was playing with at the same time his teeth locked on the side of my neck. It was a lot of sensation, most of which I'd never experienced before. It all went to my head very quickly.

"Take your pants off." I'd never been this aggressive or open about what I wanted, and I had to admit it felt pretty great.

Shot chuckled against the side of my neck, and the vibration sent sparks of desire shooting through my blood. I raked my fingers through the soft hair on the back of his head and wiggled impatiently in his unbreakable hold. The hand he had caught between our heaving chests moved slowly and deliberately across my skin. It felt like he was touching me everywhere, even though his fingers were clearly on a path to where our hips were pressed together.

A moment later the sound of his belt buckle jingling and his zipper lowering echoed in the otherwise quiet apartment, and I felt the back of his knuckles drag deliberately through the silken folds between my spread thighs. My body jolted as if electrified, and all my nerve endings started to sing with pleasure.

"So soft. So wet. I love the way you respond to me." The husky words did as much to turn up the heat as the way he touched me between my legs.

He shifted his weight and his hold on me so he could use a hand to dig through the wallet attached to his dark jeans by some kind of chain. When his jeans dropped to the floor around his ankles, there was a huge rattle as all the metal hit the ground. The sound was followed by him quickly discarding a pair of black boxer-briefs.

He watched me without blinking as he ripped open the small foil square he'd pulled from his wallet, still waiting for me to resist or pull back. I wasn't going to, but it was nice to know the option was there, regardless of how deep into things we were. He said he'd mind my boundaries as long as they were healthy and in my best interest, and he seemed to be staying true to those words.

As he rolled the latex down the length of his erection, the backs of his fingers brushed against very eager and enthusiastic places. My breath caught when I felt the very tip of his cock press against my opening. He used his hand to guide himself inward, pausing to press the tip against the little bud of my clit. I gasped at the sensation and watched as satisfaction lit up Shot's chiseled face. He looked even more darkly handsome than usual. The carnal slant to his strong features was something that made my heart beat erratically.

I exhaled long and slow when he finally stopped playing with me and pressed all the way inside my body. I was like putty in his hands. I melted around him. Molded to him. My body hungrily pulled him in and clenched excitedly around his long, hard length. We both groaned in pleasure, and I could no longer keep my eyes open. It all felt like a dirty, sexy dream.

I was probably choking the life out of him with how tightly I was clinging to him, from top to bottom, but he told me to hold on, so that was what I was doing.

I moaned his name when he started to move, the motion smooth and practiced. The glide and retreat made my head spin and my body pulse happily around his powerful thrusts. He was so strong. Every part of him that was pressed against me flexed beautifully. I could feel his muscles tense and strain against my skin. It was so, so much better than with any of the polished, soft men I'd been with before him. I thought he wasn't my type, but I was starting to think I had no idea what my type was. He was so much better than anyone before. He grunted against the curve of my shoulder where his forehead was resting. He muttered something that sounded like, "So good," but I was too caught up in my own experience to appreciate the compliment.

His fingers pressed into my flesh where he was holding

me, and I knew I was going to have bruises in the morning. It didn't matter. Everywhere else felt too good to focus on the parts that stung. I felt the edge of his teeth against my collarbone and pulled him closer as his steady rhythm started to falter.

My body clenched in pleasure, everything inside going very slick and hot. Shot swore at my involuntary reaction and shifted so he could wrap the fingers of one hand around my jaw. He forced my head up and, with a growl, asked me to open my eyes. He held my face still, his nearly black eyes burning intensely into mine. He was close to the edge, I could see it in the strain and concentration on his face and hear it in the way his breathing hitched and skipped.

"What do you need, Presley? Tell me." The words were a rough rasp that brought goose bumps on my skin.

I blinked at him and loosened a hand so I could wrap it around his wrist. His pulse thundered under my fingertips.

"I need you." It was true. He didn't need to do much more than focus his full attention on me, and I was ready to fly apart.

"Shit," he swore under his breath right before dropping his hand from my face and sealing his mouth over mine. His tongue moved in and out of my mouth in the same rhythm as his body and I could no longer think or see straight. "What are you doing to me, woman?"

The question was enough to push me to the breaking point. I felt my body lock down on Shot's cock and squeeze. He swore again, his hips rocking wildly against mine. The temperature seemed to skyrocket, and time felt like it was standing still. Everything in the world was centered on the two of us and where we were joined.

I felt his cock flex and throb inside of me, and a moment later he let out a groan of satisfaction that was music to my ears.

I was not a woman who had sex against the wall with a man whose entire body was covered in swirling, spiraling ink. I was not a woman who lost her head over a bad boy with all kinds of sexy swagger. I was not a woman who floated on a cloud of satisfaction because she'd brought said bad boy to the point his knees were shaking and he had to set her down before he dropped her.

Only, I was starting to wonder if I *was* that woman and not who I'd believed I was before Shot and the Lawtons turned my world upside down.

It was the best education a girl could ask for.

CHAPTER 15

❦

SHOT

Do you know how many people I've had to examine after a motorcycle crash?" Presley looked at my Harley apprehensively. "Too many. They've always been some of the worst cases to come across my table."

She took the helmet I handed her and hugged it to her chest instead of putting it on her head. She looked doubtful and unsure, much like she'd looked an hour ago when she'd been on her knees in front of me in her cramped bathroom. This time I'd been the one leaning against the vanity, afraid the whole time that I was going to rip the thing out of the wall as she stumbled her way through a clumsy blowjob. Who knew that hesitation and inexperience were such a damn turn-on? Every wary touch, every cautious flick of her tongue, had me feeling like the top of my head was going to blow off. It was so honest. So much more real than all the practiced and slick moves of the women who knew their way around giving head. She told me it wasn't the first time, but it was the first time she'd enjoyed the experience, which made me feel ten feet tall. There was something about her inherent innocence that flipped my switch in such an unexpected and exciting way.

She really needed to find a new place to live. The apartment was garbage, totally unsafe, and the bathroom didn't have enough room to do half the things I wanted to do with her. She needed a walk-in shower, one with enough room for two. I wanted to take her up against a tiled wall while the water cascaded all around us.

Making sure she found a place that was in a safe and secure neighborhood was only one of the reasons I'd tagged along with her during her house hunt the day before. The other was so people around town would know I was taking the time I spent with Presley seriously. I wasn't the type to spend a whole day doing something like looking at suburban houses, but I did it for her, which was bound to make a statement.

I knocked on the helmet in her hands with my knuckles and winged an eyebrow up at her mutinous expression. "Put this on. Loveless is tiny. We aren't going cruising on the highway or racing across the state. We're just riding down to the diner to grab a late breakfast because we both burned a butt-load of calories last night."

I really was hungry, but it was also a good opportunity to make a bit of a show of being together the way Hill and Case had suggested. I didn't press her yesterday when she obviously didn't want to get on the back of the bike, but things were different now that I'd taken her to bed. The club had been set up outside of Loveless for years, and in all that time, I'd never had a woman on the back of my bike. I'd also never put in the effort to take one on a date, regardless of how low-key the encounter might have been. I might've been a handful of firsts for her, but she was also a shitload of firsts for me.

When Presley didn't jump to follow my order, or smile at my slightly suggestive words, I plucked the helmet out of her hands and plopped it on top of her glossy hair myself. I attached the strap under her chin and bopped her on the end of the nose with my finger.

"Gotta get used to it sooner or later." I bent down and kissed her nose on the same place I'd tapped her. If we were going to be together, regardless of how real or not it was, she needed to get comfortable being on my bike. The big machine was pretty much an extension of who I was, and one of my most prized possessions. It was the only thing I took away from my childhood, and the only thing waiting for me when I got home from each deployment.

I watched her visibly gather her courage and set her jaw in a determined line. She nodded briefly before placing a pair of mirrored sunglasses over her worried green eyes.

I climbed on the bike first and instructed her how to get on behind me. She gingerly placed her hands on my shoulders and tossed a long leg over the leather seat. I was surprised at the way the simple motion made my gut clench. I wasn't expecting to like the way her slight weight felt pressed up against my back as much as I did. I was a solo rider. Always had been. But there was something nice and undeniably sexy about having a lush, warm female body locked against mine.

I heard her gasp when I turned the engine over, and I grunted when she squeezed me tightly enough to push the air out of my lungs as the bike moved forward. I reminded her to move with me and to hold on tight.

It seemed I was always telling her not to let me go in one way or another.

When her life wasn't in danger and the woman who was responsible for all her hurt and heartache was no longer a factor, we were going to have to sit down and have a serious discussion about those words and what they really meant.

The ride to the diner only took five minutes. Regardless, Presley's legs were shaking when I helped her off the bike. She leaned against me until she got her equilibrium back, which made me chuckle. I ran a reassuring hand up and down her spine as she popped the helmet off and shook her strawberry-tinted hair back into shape.

"So?"

She wrinkled her nose. "It wasn't too bad. I guess I can see the appeal." She pointed at the helmet I rested on the seat. "You should wear one of those. I've seen what happens to riders who don't. It isn't pretty."

I threw an arm around her shoulders and guided her toward the front door of the diner. "I wear one when we ride anywhere out of town and if we ride into a state that has a mandatory helmet law." No way was I giving the cops an easy reason to pull me over and give me a ticket. "My dad had me on a bike almost before I could walk. I'm more comfortable on two wheels than on four." As much as I resented my old man and most of my stolen childhood, there were a few things I was thankful he'd given me. My love of motorcycles was at the top of the list.

Presley pushed her sunglasses to the top of her head as we entered the diner. It was one of only a handful of full-service restaurants within a fifty-mile radius, and it was always pretty full of regulars, even when it wasn't prime hours. Which made it a perfect place to flaunt my budding romance and get the gossips going. The sooner Ashby Grant made her move, the better. I wanted a chance to see if what Presley and I had could work without one of our lives hanging in the balance. I'd never had what most would consider a normal relationship before, so I was going to have to learn the basics right alongside her.

My favorite waitress, Darlie, broke into a big grin when she saw me walk in. That grin quickly faltered when she saw I had my arm looped around Presley. Darlie was cute and fun. I'd spent some time with her on and off when I first got to town. I realized too late she looked at me like I hung the moon and was going to be her ticket to the good life in this small town. I wasn't into anything more than a good time and a few stolen hours in the dark, so I'd cut things off. She still smiled whenever she saw me come into the diner, and she made it obvious she was waiting for me to change my mind.

"Hey, Shot. You and the boys haven't been by to see us in a while. How have you been?" Darlie skimmed her gaze over Presley and cocked her head to the side as she sized up the pretty redhead next to me. "Who's your new friend? You look really familiar, but I don't think we've met."

I should've known Presley was going to hate being put on the spot like this. I was instantly irritated at Case and Hill for convincing me to put her on display for everyone and their mother. I could feel her squirming uncomfortably along my side.

"She's close to the Lawtons." It seemed like Darlie might be the last person in Loveless who hadn't heard about Conrad Lawton's infidelity and his illegitimate child.

"Oh. That's right. I remember hearing that Kody was all up in arms over their old man having a bastard who he left his entire estate to." It became clear too late Darlie knew exactly who Presley was and was just pretending so she could be catty and mean. "You look like Kody, but she's much prettier."

Presley sucked in an audible breath and I felt her stiffen next to me. My instinct was to jump in and defend her, but Presley quickly reminded me she'd grown up being the outcast, the one blacklisted from social circles and not invited to sit with the cool kids.

She copied the waitress's head tilt and blinked her long lashes with exaggerated innocence. "I'll be sure to tell Kody you think so, though I doubt she's going to take it as a compliment. Are you going to show us to a table or should we just seat ourselves?"

It was the perfect response. Everyone in town knew the Lawtons were tight and ready to throw hands if any one of them came under attack. Presley, none too subtly, just reminded Darlie that while she might not share their last name, she was part of the family and not someone Darlie wanted to pick a fight with.

Darlie sniffed in indignation and whirled around to grab a few menus. We followed her to a table by the window where she practically threw the menus down as she bit out, "I'll send Felicia over to wait on you guys." She gave me a look and muttered, "You can do so much better," before she stomped away.

I looked at Presley, an apology on the tip of my tongue, but she was buried behind the laminated menu. I sighed and tapped my knuckles on the table to get her attention. "Sorry about that."

A snort came from behind the menu. Irritated she was hiding from me, I reached up and pulled the big barrier down, only to be pinned in place by her emerald glare.

I lifted a shoulder and let it fall. "What do you want me to say besides sorry? It's not like I lived like a monk before we crashed into one another."

She made a face, her nose scrunching in an adorable

way. "Knowing it and having it shoved in my face are two
different things. It's better to just hang out in my apartment
if we're going to have an unpleasant encounter with one of
your former flames every time we step out the door."

I rolled my eyes. "We can go to Austin on our next date
and run into *your* exes, if that'll make you feel better."

I was trying to make her laugh, but her gaze got slightly
sad and her mouth didn't shift from the hard, straight line it
was set in.

"The difference is my exes wouldn't care if they saw I'd
moved on, and yours obviously do." She looked up when an
older woman with salt-and-pepper hair stopped by the side
of the table and asked what we wanted to drink. I ordered a
black coffee; she ordered sweet tea.

When her eyes shifted back to mine they were filled
with all the confusion and regret I'd done my damnedest
to eradicate last night. "I'm still not entirely sure what you
see in me."

I grunted and leaned forward. I caught one of her nervous
hands in mine and rubbed my thumb over the back of it.

"I see all the things you don't see. I see how strong you
are. I see how resilient you are. I see how brave you are. I see
how sexy you are. All the things you've always overlooked,
I see them clear as day." She watched me with wide eyes as
I lifted the hand in mine to my lips and dropped a quick kiss
on it. "And I never dated Darlie, so she isn't technically my
ex. Neither is Kody. They are just women I spent some time
with at one point or another. We weren't together. There was
no breakup." I made sure she could see how serious I was
when I told her, "With you, we are definitely doing more
than spending time together, and if you want to get rid of
me, you're going to have to say the words. I'm not walking
away without a backward glance like I usually do. I don't

know how to date any more than you do, but I'm making the effort. That should show you I'm not doing it out of any obligation because you saved my life. I'm doing it because I want to."

I meant every word I was saying, but it also served a secret purpose. I knew Felicia was hovering close by waiting for a good time to drop our drinks and take our order. The woman was a huge gossip and wouldn't wait even a second before spreading my conversation with Presley to anyone who would listen. Ashby Grant was bound to get the news Presley had a man in her life if she was keeping tabs on anyone in Loveless.

"And while I am eternally grateful you showed up that night when Kody called you in a panic, I have never, not once, felt obligated to repay you with my dick."

Presley's eyes bugged out and I heard a shocked gasp from somewhere over my shoulder. Felicia was getting more than an earful and had apparently had enough. Our drinks were plopped down in front of us, some of the coffee sloshing over the rim of the mug and hitting the table. She hurriedly asked what we wanted to order. I got a burger and Presley ordered a club sandwich. It was honestly the closest thing to a real date I'd ever been on, which made the underlying subterfuge behind it twist in my gut.

Presley played with the straw in her drink as she switched the conversation to somewhat safer ground.

"The girl who sat us said she hadn't seen you and the boys in a while. Do you and the club members spend a lot of time in Loveless? Your clubhouse is pretty far out in hill country."

"We come to town when we need to. I don't know how much of the ranch you saw that night, but we pretty much have everything we need out on the property. It's better if we stay off the sheriff's radar. Case was just a deputy when we set up this chapter of the club, but he's never been overly fond of us or our proximity to his town."

"How did you end up in Loveless in the first place? And where are you from originally? You don't have any kind of discernible accent."

I chuckled at that. "I was born and raised in Denver. That's where the Sons of Sorrow were founded. My dad was stationed at Fort Carson when he was in the service and fell in love with the state." I snorted at old, bitter memories as they started to rise up from the very dark and deep pit inside my heart where I kept them locked away. "His bike. His club. His brothers. And Colorado. Those were pretty much the only things my father ever gave a damn about."

She made a sympathetic sound. "Is that how you ended up in Texas? Were you stationed here?"

I shook my head and reached for the coffee. "Nope. I had an uncle—or rather one of the club members who stepped up and helped raise me, since my dad wasn't interested—and he was from here. When I enlisted, he left the club and bought the ranch where our clubhouse is. He grew up in Loveless and wanted to come back home."

He hadn't told me he was sick and living on borrowed time. He also hadn't told me he was leaving me the ranch in his will. What he had told me was that being a Son, and the son of one of the founding members of the Sons of Sorrow, meant I was never going to be able to walk away from my legacy. I hated the way my father lived, but I didn't hate being part of a club and having a group of men who I knew would unquestionably have my back. He left instructions to set up my own chapter and coolly reminded me that when my dad was gone, I would be up for the vote to sit at the head of the table for the entire club.

"When he passed away I got the ranch and all the property. I was out of the military by then and had no intention of going back to Denver, so really Loveless was the only place I had to go."

Top didn't have a home to return to, either, and by then I'd been collecting misfits and outcasts who didn't fit into any mold or box. We weren't meant to fit in. We were made to stand out. I was a pro at being blacklisted by polite society.

She gave me a crooked grin. "It's weird that in a town called Loveless, people seem to be tripping over the people they're meant to spend the rest of their lives with. When I first heard the name of the town, I expected something very different."

Honestly, so had I.

I hadn't expected to find a place that finally felt like home. I hadn't expected to find a place and people I was eager to return to whenever I left. I hadn't expected to find friends like Kody, and enemies I respected the hell out of like Case. And I definitely hadn't expected to find a woman who was going to make me realize that while I might live in a place called Loveless, I didn't actually have to live a life that was loveless.

CHAPTER 16

❦

PRESLEY

I was exhausted.

My hiatus from work was the longest period of time I'd gone without being in the trenches. While I hadn't left under the best of circumstances, the break ended up being a nice way to hit the reset button. I loved my job. I believed it was important. But I had a tendency to forget how much it could take out of me emotionally. Working with the dead didn't have the same kind of pressures that came with trying to heal and save the living, but there were unique drawbacks and downfalls when you worked in a morgue that somehow had slipped my mind while I was dealing with the rest of my life crumbling around me.

Before my mother had passed away, it was a welcome distraction to be caught up in other people's worst-case scenarios. What I dealt with at my job was a good reminder to be thankful for what I had, for every single moment I still had my mother around. When I left work for the day before my hiatus, I'd always had something dealing with my mother waiting for me, so it was easier to flip the switch from professional to personal mode. Now that she was gone, I was finding it difficult to drop the harsh realities of my career at the door. Even with all the crazy currently going on in my life, some things lingered and affected me long after the case I was working on was closed.

One of the big things that I'd forgotten about my job was the strong smell of disinfectants and chemicals, as well as other things no one wanted to think about, that seemed to cling to me no matter how hard I scrubbed after a shift. It probably wasn't noticeable to anyone not familiar with what a morgue smelled like, but to me, it was overpowering and felt like it was embedded in my skin and wrapped around each of my hair follicles. I usually showered once before I left work, and then again as soon as I got home. Shot complained about the janky shower in my apartment every time he stayed the night, and I was starting to agree with him that when I found a new house, I needed to look into building some kind of luxurious master bath. It'd be nice to have a spa-like experience after an exceptionally long day at work.

Because now I wasn't just juggling the pressures and pitfalls of my job, but also of navigating a new relationship. Shot was becoming a regular fixture in my life, and while our version of dating tended to be nights in at my apartment, or the occasional trip to the diner or Kody's bar rather than romantic dinners and flowers, it was still definitely dating. For the first time I was trying to leave work behind when I left for the day. A challenge I wasn't doing so great at. Shot never seemed to bring his biker business to my door and I was attempting to do the same, but it felt like an impossible task.

These days when I left work I didn't make the drive back

to my apartment unescorted. I tried to tell Shot it was overkill to have one of his biker buddies wait for me, since I never knew when I was going to get off work for the day. However, despite my protests, each and every day there was a man on a motorcycle wearing one of those vests Shot always had on, lurking somewhere near my car. I was starting to be able to recognize a couple of them. I'd tried to apologize a few times for them having to babysit me since their president was overly cautious, but they all waved me off and told me it was no problem. I secretly felt they were worried I would tell Shot if they were anything other than gruffly polite to me, but I kept that speculation to myself.

Most days, Shot would appear at the door shortly after I got home. I didn't need to tell him I was safe and sound, because his brothers did it for me. On the days he didn't show up, he always called or sent a text to let me know someone was keeping an eye on me through the night. He never gave an explanation as to what he was up to or where he was at. At first, his vagueness didn't bother me because I was too busy settling back into the routine of being at work and juggling all the new responsibilities I would have as the chief ME. It started to grate on my nerves a little when I realized he literally knew every move I made almost every second of the day, and I couldn't even begin to guess where he disappeared to.

Could we actually be considered as being together if I didn't know what he was up to half the time? I knew that neither of us knew how to date and we were learning together, but some things felt like they should have been obvious, like each knowing where the other was the majority of the time. I was trying to be patient and understanding, but the truth was the difference in our lifestyles was growing more glaring the closer we became, and I couldn't stop worrying the bridge crossing the divide was going to crumble at any moment.

Telling myself I was just overly tired and thinking too much when there were more pressing matters at hand and bigger picture items still at loose ends, I pushed into my apartment and practically stripped at the door. I let my purse fall to the floor along with my keys and left a trail of clothes on my way to the bathroom. I cranked the shower on as hot as it would go and climbed under the stream once it was warm. It stung a little, but the burn was a nice distraction, as it was meant to be.

Fifteen minutes later, when I pulled the flowery shower curtain back, I let out a shriek when I caught sight of a large figure dressed head to toe in black leaning against the bathroom sink. Shot had his heavily tattooed arms crossed over his chest and an intense scowl on his darkly handsome face. I noticed he had my abandoned cell phone in one hand, and the screen showed several missed calls from him. I put a palm to my chest over my racing heart and reached for one of the fluffy towels hanging on the rickety towel bar attached to the wall.

"You scared me to death." My voice was still husky from fear. I covered myself with the towel and pushed my soaked hair away from my face. I was too tired to kick his ass appropriately this go-around, but there was still a spark of anger behind the fear.

I didn't like how easily he invaded my privacy, or how blasé he was about showing up out of nowhere when he knew I was worried Ashby might do the same thing. Irritation as I thought about how inconsiderate he was being toward my feelings and current state of mind started to claw its way under my skin.

Shot held up my phone and wagged it in my face. His

voice was an angry growl, which I normally liked a lot, but not today. "You scared me to death as well. Do you have any idea what went through my mind when I couldn't get ahold of you? Do you want to know all the crazy things that ran through my mind?"

I snatched my phone away from him and returned his glare. On a normal day, I'd have been freaking out that he was fully dressed for battle and I was not, but right now I was too heated to care.

I pointed my phone at his chest and snapped, "That's how it is for me all the time, Shot. I don't know where you are. I don't know if you're dead or in jail. I don't know if you're breaking the law or saving someone's life. You come and go as you please and expect me to be okay with it, and yet if I step sideways you have an entire legion of bikers reporting back to you. Do you think I don't worry? Do you think I'm not here wondering and imagining awful situations you might be in?"

His expression softened slightly. He made a move to reach for me, but I brushed past him and marched toward the kitchen. The march wasn't as dramatic as I had hoped, since I was dripping everywhere and barefoot, but it made me feel a little bit better. Tonight I needed a drink if I was going to deal with the badass biker who seemed to know how to push buttons I didn't even know I had.

Shot followed, his footsteps heavier and louder than mine. I didn't ask if he wanted a drink, just poured him a matching gin on the rocks and wordlessly pushed it his way. He looked at the glass, then back at me. He cocked his dark head to the side, eyebrows furrowing as he asked, "You want to tell me what's got you so worked up tonight?"

I sipped the liquor and scoffed. "I just did."

Shot swore under his breath and rolled his broad shoulders.

"Come on, Pres. Tell me what's going on. I get that you worry about me, which you should. That's what people do when they're together. But this outburst isn't like you."

I gripped the cold glass tighter in my hand and whispered, "You wouldn't understand." So few people did. When you spend your days with the dead, most already found it hard to relate, and no one ever wanted to have the reality and inevitability of their own eventual demise shoved into their face.

Shot moved closer and plucked the drink from my hands. He set it down on the counter and put his hands on my bare shoulders, forcing me to look directly at him. "Talk to me. You don't know if I'll understand or not until you try me. Remember, I've spent time in the worst places in the world. I've witnessed the worst humanity has to offer. Nothing you tell me, nothing you share with me, is going to shock me or send me running." A wry grin touched the corner of his mouth. "Tell me what's got you worked up, besides me, and once you get that off your chest we can talk about all the reasons you're so pissed at me right now."

I huffed a little. "All the legitimate reasons I'm pissed at you. I don't like that you broke into my house and scared me."

He just dipped his chin down in agreement and watched me as I tugged at my wet hair in aggravation. It took me a second to marshal my thoughts into an order that could express why I was so on edge. "I can't say much because most of the work I do involves open investigations. My day at the office never goes by without coming across some pretty horrific examples of how people can die." I gulped hard and pulled on my hair even harder, my fingers slipping through the slippery strands. "The days when there are kids involved are harder than others." My breath caught a bit and I felt tears press at the back of my eyes. "It's something I've never managed to grow numb to and this week, there were multiple cases that came through involving very young children. An intern quit over one, and a seasoned forensic pathologist needed to take a break in the middle of an autopsy while dealing with another. I was out of work for several months, so I guess I let myself forget what a bad day felt like in my field, and just how hard it is to leave this kind of work at the office when it's time to come home."

Shot took a step that brought him closer to me. He caught the back of my head in one of his big hands and pulled me forward until my forehead was resting on the center of his chest. I felt him press a kiss on the top of my head as he rubbed my back in light circles.

"It's never easy when kids are involved. That was my least favorite part of being in the Marines as well. I think it's admirable that you haven't numbed yourself to those feelings. What you do, the things you see, you could be a cold, hard person and you're not. You still care. You still hurt, and that makes you very special."

His words were like a cool balm on the parts of my heart that burned at the injustice and unfairness of a life lost far too soon. I'd never wanted to burden my mother with the weight of my worries, since she had her own to tackle on a daily basis. Ashby had always been much like Shot described, cold and hard. She often told me I needed to toughen up when a case got to me, when I felt broken at what I'd seen and experienced. So, I'd suffered alone and kept all those emotions to myself. It was amazing how nice it was to unload those feelings on someone who wasn't going to judge or tell me to get over it. There was a lightness in my heart I rarely felt.

Shot grabbed a handful of my hair and pulled my head back. I tilted my chin up so I could meet his gaze. He rested a warm palm on one of my cheeks and used his thumb to caress my jawline.

"When you have a bad day at work, I want you to tell me what you can. I respect that there are parts of what you do that you can't share with me for legal reasons, but you don't need to keep all of that bottled up. If you gotta cry, you cry. If you need to scream, go ahead and scream. I'm here, but you gotta give me the same leeway. What I do"—he shook his head ever so slightly—"and where I go, I can't always talk to you about those things, sometimes for legal reasons, sometimes for your own safety. It's not because I don't want to, but because it's not only me who's affected if I do. I don't do things I'm ashamed of or regret, but that doesn't mean the rest of the world sees it the same way." There was a rebellious glint in his eyes that I found inexplicably attractive. "I promise to give you as much information as I can, and I swear I will always check in with you when I'm able. If I end up dead I will make sure one of my guys lets you know. Same if I end up in jail. The latter is more likely than the first, but you know better than anyone that nothing in life is certain. All we can do is take each day as it comes."

I stared at him for a long time. This relationship was balanced on a precipice, and it seemed like any minute things could fall either way. I wasn't sure I was made of tough enough stuff to maintain that delicate balance being with him was going to require.

But I wanted to try...as long as there were some ground rules we agreed to follow.

"What you do and what I do, they might collide in the worst way down the road. If that happens"—I pleaded with my eyes for him to understand—"my job comes first, even if it affects you and the club adversely."

I was surprised when he let out a little laugh. "Top pretty

much gave me the same warning. How about we cross that bridge when we get to it? If I think I see a collision coming I'll try to head it off at the pass, and if I can't, I'm willing to accept the consequences." He gave me a little wink, trying to lighten the mood. "Just like I'm willing to face your wrath for breaking into your place because I'm worried about you and can't think straight."

I sighed. He was trying to be sweet but was still missing the point. "But I'm going to have to deal with those consequences, too. Do you realize what it will do to me if I'm the one who hurts you or one of your members? How am I supposed to live with that? With the guilt and the loss?"

Didn't he understand how hard that would be for me?

Shot bent his head and pressed his lips against mine. It was a hard kiss, a reassuring kiss. A kiss that meant business.

"We can worry about all the possibilities that we can't control, or we can focus on the actualities we have complete say over. If all you do is worry about what *might* happen, instead of embracing the moment we're actually in right now, you're going to miss out on some pretty great experiences."

Shot couldn't know he'd pretty much laid out my biggest regret when it came to my childhood. All day, every day, I waited and watched, worrying about what was going to happen with my mother. My entire existence was built around what-ifs. What if she died today? What if I didn't get to say goodbye? What if she'd never been sick in the first place? What if my life was different? What if *I* was different? Always wondering. Always waiting. And where had it gotten either of us?

Nowhere.

He kissed me again and I was appropriately distracted. It was so much better to get lost in him than it was to wander in the past where things couldn't be changed.

I wrapped my arms around his neck and lifted up on my toes to return the kiss. Within seconds my towel was on the ground and Shot had his hands all over my naked skin. I thought I would get used to how it felt to have his hands and mouth on my body. I honestly believed the electric spark that fired to life under my skin everywhere his fingertips trailed would fade away after a few intimate moments. Holy hell, was I wrong.

Every time he touched me, every time he made love to me, it was more intense, bigger, and better than the time before. Maybe it was because I was more comfortable with myself the more familiar we became with one another, but it was more likely that Shot was just that potent, just that skilled, that he had something new to bring to the table each and every time we got together.

There were very few flat surfaces in my apartment that had gone unused since Shot started being a regular visitor. It was by far the most intense and physical relationship I'd ever been in. It was highly flattering how he seemed unable to keep his hands off me, but the reverse was also true. He was hot. He was incredibly sexy. And for the first time in my life, I was actively invested in experiencing all that someone else had to offer and making that other person feel as good as they made me feel.

When Shot pulled away so we could breathe, he touched his forehead to mine and told me in a very quiet voice, "I'm sorry I overreacted when you didn't answer your phone. Until Ashby is behind bars, I can't promise I'll behave rationally. I lose my mind a little when I think you might be in danger."

It was actually kind of sweet, and I'd never had anyone who cared that much about me before, aside from my mother—and it wasn't like she'd ever been in any kind of condition to rush to my rescue should I need it. Who would've ever thought I was going to end up with my very own hero...or rather, my very own antihero? Who would've ever believed I would need someone willing to save the day?

Not me.

I leaned forward so I could nuzzle the tip of my nose against his. Without question, he had so much more experience in all aspects than I did, but he always seemed to like when I took the initiative, no matter how clumsy or wholesome the gesture came across.

"I forgive you. Now take me to bed."

CHAPTER 17

❦

SHOT

I kissed Presley the entire way to her bedroom. My clothes joined hers on the hallway floor, leaving a scattered trail to the back of her apartment. I considered it a win that she was now comfortable enough with me that she didn't seem fazed at all being naked outside of the bathroom or the bedroom. She still had moments of shyness I found utterly endearing and sweet, but I liked that she was getting bolder and more obvious when it came to her wants and needs. Watching her come into her own was beautiful, and I fully believed one day she was going to see herself the way others did instead of through the eyes of a scared, ostracized child who grew into a reserved, cautious woman. Not only was she like a butterfly breaking free of a cocoon, she was also learning how to spread those big, beautiful wings so she could fly.

Her hands skimmed over my skin, her nails scraping lightly over the designs inked on my ribs and across my stomach. Every hurried step brought my straining cock into contact with her soft skin. It was already so hard it hurt in a good way, and the brief contact had the slit slippery with excited wetness. I didn't bother to turn on the lights in her bedroom. I'd spent plenty of time in the room lately, so I could find my way without being able to see everything clearly. I also knew my way around her body by feel and by taste. I could find the soft spot behind her ear that drove her crazy even if I was blindfolded. I could feel the way her nipples tightened and the way her body shivered in the darkness. I could hear the way her breathing hitched and then came out in an excited rush, and I knew she was excited without being able to see her eyes or the rosy flush covering her pale skin.

When we reached her bed our kisses slowed, and it was more like we were breathing each other in as our lips touched. I ran a hand down her hair and across her back. I put the other on her backside and pulled her flush against me. There was no hiding how my body reacted to her, or her gasp when she felt the hot length of my erection trapped between our bare bodies. Her hands curled around my biceps and her lips landed on the edge of my jaw. She kissed her way to my ear, and I swore quietly when her tongue flicked out to trace along the outer shell. My ears weren't as sensitive as hers, but it still felt nice. I liked it when she played with the silver hoops dangling from the lobe. I liked when she showed her sweet side, and she seemed to appreciate all the things about me that were different from all the other men who had briefly been in her life.

I groaned when she slid a hand between us and wrapped it around the rigid flesh pressing eagerly against her stomach. She gave my cock a playful little squeeze before dragging her thumb through the moisture leaking from the tip and spreading it around in a smooth glide. She stroked her hand up and down, making the muscles in my stomach clench in pleasure and forcing me to lock my knees when they became slightly watery. I pulled back just enough so she could move her hand up and down unhindered, and closed my eyes so I could enjoy the sensation. Her hold was delicate and light, a feather-like touch I felt all the way to my bones. I enjoyed the way she handled me like she was afraid she might hurt me, or that I would break if she was too rough. No one treated me like I was fragile, not in my whole life, until she came along. It was a precious experience, so I didn't tell her I could handle so much more. It was fun letting her find her own way and figure things out. I was happy to be her sexual learning curve.

I groaned when she tightened her hand and used her thumb to trace along the throbbing vein that ran along the underside of my cock. Now, that spot was extra sensitive, and I liked it when she did that, a lot. I bent my head so I could find her mouth. In the dark, I caught her chin first and kissed it until she giggled. It was such a carefree sound, considering the mess she'd been when I broke into her bathroom earlier. I would never classify myself as any kind of hero, but I felt like I saved the damn world when I could make her forget about her bad day and focus on something else.

I growled against her lips when her questing fingers found their way between my legs and skated over the supersensitive orbs tucked away down there. My balls were already pulled tight with desire, and I could feel them pulse with pleasure when her fingertips danced across the tender surface. When she was done playing and I was on the brink of losing my mind, I gave her an almost punishing kiss and maneuvered her so she fell backward onto her bed. She landed with a gasp and another giggle.

Instead of following her down to the mattress, I moved to her mirrored nightstand so I could dig protection out of the drawer. Once I was suited up and ready to go I moved back to the bed. To my surprise, in the shadows filtering through the darkened space, I could just make out that Presley was touching herself with her long, pale fingers. I instantly regretted not turning on the light because that was a show I didn't want to miss a second of. I heard her let out a breathy sigh and felt my body respond. Anticipation clenched tight at the base of my spine, and heat pounded through my cock.

Shifting so I could smooth a hand along the outside of her toned thigh, I caught hold of her hip and guided her to flip over so she was on her stomach. She made an alarmed sound and turned to look at me questioningly over her shoulder. I tugged her hips up so she was on her hands and knees in front of me, and I nearly lost it at the overtly sexy sight she made.

Gruffly I told her, "Keep touching yourself." It was hard to get words out when all the blood in my body felt like it had shot to my dick.

She made a little sound of embarrassment but did as I ordered. She braced herself on one hand and let her head fall forward so that her face was hidden by her long, reddish hair. I put my hand on the elegant line of her spine and dragged it down to the small of her back. I repeated the motion until I felt some of the tension leave her body. Soon, the slick sound of her fingers touching all the delicate, hidden parts of her body whispered through the room.

Using my thumb to press the base of my erection down, I lined myself up with her heated and damp opening. My fingers dug into the curve of her hips as I pressed myself into her body. She moved her fingers so she was touching the tiny bud of pleasure hidden within her velvety folds. We both moaned long and loud once I was fully seated inside of her. The backs of her fingers brushed erotically along my cock as I started to thrust.

I closed my eyes and swore when I felt her body clench around mine, surrounding me in liquid heat and warmth. We fit together like we were made to do this with one another. Inside of her was quickly becoming my favorite place to be. When Presley started to press back against me, when she started to move in tandem to my thrusts, I quickly lost any kind of rhythm and started pounding into her in a totally uncivilized way. It was a good thing she was vocal about how much she enjoyed the increasingly rough handling; otherwise, I would've worried it was all too much for her to do anything about.

The sound of our bodies colliding was incredibly satisfying. The faster I moved, the more breathless and frantic she became. It wasn't long before I was engulfed in the heated flood of her release. She gasped my name and fell forward, her forehead hitting the mattress as her body convulsed and throbbed languidly around mine. I kept moving, that coiled tension sitting low in my spine, slowly spreading outward as gratification lit my blood on fire. Once the last ounce of satisfaction and completion was drained from my body, I collapsed in a nearly boneless heap on top of her. She turned her head so I could drop a kiss on her lips, but the angle was awkward and I didn't have full control of my limbs back yet.

It took a second to gather the strength required to roll off of her and onto my back. I blinked up at the dark ceiling and wondered if this was really it for me. If she was the one I would never get tired of. If she was the woman who I would never be able to get enough of.

The more time I spent with her, the more it felt like she might be.

I got up and made my way into her small bathroom so I could clean up. I gathered our discarded clothes from all over the floor and went back to her bedroom. I had things to do tonight that hadn't included fighting and making up with Presley, but I was glad for the interruption. When I got back to her bedroom, she was already under the covers and appeared to be fast asleep. She did look tired when she came out of the shower, and I didn't doubt going back to her stressful job was adding more stress to her already tension-filled days. I got dressed as quietly as I could and put a hand on the mattress so I could lean over her and press a kiss to her forehead. She made a soft sound and her rust-colored eyelashes fluttered, but her eyes didn't open and she didn't wake up.

I closed the door behind me when I left her room. I also found a Sharpie in her junk drawer and a crinkled envelope, so I could leave her a quick note. I apologized for having to leave and told her I didn't want to wake her up. It wasn't the first time I'd had to bail in the middle of the night, and it wouldn't be the last. Luckily, she seemed to be understanding of the situation and understood I didn't keep banker's hours.

When I hit the parking lot, Digger, the young prospect who had just gotten out of the Army and moved to Texas, gave me a nod and sat up straighter on the vintage bike he was lounging on. So far most of the brothers had been cool enough about keeping an eye on Presley when I was unable to. I'd managed to give the task to prospective members and newer guys so I didn't ruffle too many feathers. I wouldn't entrust Presley's safety to anyone I didn't believe fully capable.

"I have to head back to the clubhouse." Top had taken a call concerning a businessman missing in Colombia, and whether or not we were making a trip into cocaine country, which was crawling with guerrilla soldiers. His family was desperate to get him back, his business rival was ready to counteroffer to make sure he stayed gone. Taking either job was up for a vote. I needed to be there to moderate the discussion and to weigh the pros and cons of accepting either offer. "I'll make sure you have a replacement here by the time she has to leave for work in the morning. If anything seems even slightly off, I don't care what it is, you check it out. The locks on her apartment are garbage. If you need to get inside, do what you have to do."

I'd offered to change them out for her, but Presley kept telling me she would take care of it herself when she had time. I would've done it without her permission and for my own peace of mind, but I did my best to observe those boundaries she was so fond of when it came to something simple.

The kid nodded and assured me he knew the drill. I patted him on the shoulder and climbed on my bike. The clubhouse was a solid hour outside of Loveless, so the sun was going to be coming up by the time I finally made it to bed. Not a situation I was unused to, but I was getting older, and pulling an all-nighter didn't hold the same kind of appeal it used to.

I was just getting into the backcountry where the hills started rolling and dipping, requiring more concentration and effort as I rode when I came across a stranded motorist. At first, I didn't think anything of it. This area was remote, and it wasn't too uncommon to find a car broken down and abandoned by the driver. Only this car wasn't abandoned, which immediately had every instinct I possessed on high alert.

The hood of the small, red two-door was open and a cloud of white smoke was billowing upward toward the night sky. There was a young woman leaning against the side of the car, looking completely distraught. She was waving her arms frantically in my direction, and I had a feeling if I didn't stop she was going to run out in the middle of the road and try and force me.

Swearing under my breath, I pulled my bike to the shoulder of the road, the weight of the weapon I was never without heavy against the small of my back as bits and pieces of this particular scenario started to click into place. I rested the bike on its kickstand and climbed off. The woman hurried over to me, red hair flying behind her and green eyes wide and pleading.

I'd seen enough pictures of Ashby Grant to know what she really looked like. She was a stunning woman, blond and blue-eyed, and built in all the right places. It was no guess how she managed to get what she wanted from men. This woman didn't look anything like the pictures. No, this woman was supposed to look like the centerfold version of Presley. All the best parts of Presley were overdone and made bigger and brighter. This woman was meant to stop traffic and catch the eye. It was as if she was tailor-made to fit my exact type in a way that was impossible to ignore. I had to hand it to Presley's former friend, she definitely knew how to hide in plain sight.

My fingers itched to reach for the gun tucked into my waistband, but I'd made a promise to Case and Hill that I would play this game by the rules they set out. I was just the bait, not the mousetrap that was supposed to clamp down on the vermin's neck. However, with the reminder of all this woman had put Presley through swirling through my mind, I was struggling to keep my expression blank.

"Having some trouble?" Each word felt like it sliced across my tongue. I couldn't recall having the urge to hurt a woman ever before, but for this one, I really wanted to make an exception.

"It just started smoking. I have no idea where I am and the battery on my phone died. I'm so lucky you came by. Can you help me?" Overly done eyelashes fluttered in my direction as she chewed provocatively on her lower lip.

I lifted an eyebrow at her and did my best not to roll my eyes. Her act was highly exaggerated. I wondered if men were really so driven by what was between their legs they couldn't see that they were being played.

"I can take a look at it." The smoke was white, so it was a good guess that she'd pulled the radiator hose when she heard my bike coming.

"Oh, the car is a rental. I can just leave it here. Can't you give me a ride into town? I have a motel room waiting." The eyelashes flickered beseechingly, and I had to shove my hands into the pockets of my jeans so she couldn't see them clench into fists. The boys in blue were going to owe me so big for this farce.

"Nope. I'm not headed toward town. I can call Triple-A or the cops for you. I know the sheriff pretty well. I'm sure he'd send a deputy out to give you a lift. Or I can take you to my clubhouse." And keep her there until Case and Hill showed up to arrest her—that is, if the members didn't take her apart first.

The woman balked, clearly aghast I hadn't jumped on the overt invitation to join her in her motel room.

"I can't go to a motorcycle club in the middle of the night. Do you think I'm stupid?" She smoothed a hand over her skintight shirt and licked her lower lip. "You should come with me instead."

She wasn't stupid. She knew enough not to walk into a situation she wasn't going to be able to walk out of. The clubhouse was pretty much impenetrable and inescapable.

"No thanks." I barked the word and let out a loud yawn. "Like I said, I can look at it for you or call someone if you don't want to come to the club. That's about it."

She huffed out an irritated breath and crossed her arms over her ample and nearly exposed chest. "Fine. Please take a look at it. It's late and scary all the way out here."

She was a damn good actress, but even with the colored contacts in her eyes, I could tell her gaze wasn't quite right. Even if I didn't know for a fact she was a murderous psycho, I would've kept my distance from her based on the wild look in her eyes alone.

When I bent over the car I made sure she caught sight of the gun at the small of my back. I kept an eye on her as I worked, making sure she didn't get close enough to touch me in case she was going to try something funny while my hands were occupied. It seemed like Case and Hill were right—she was more interested in seducing me than in hurting me. She chatted endlessly about how glad she was I'd stopped and how lucky she was I could fix the car. She mentioned more than once wanting to get my number so she could thank me properly while she was in town. It galled me to no end that I was going to have to give it to her, and that I couldn't just end this charade right now.

"Do you have a girlfriend? Or a wife? Wait, you call them 'old ladies' when you're in a motorcycle gang, right?" She giggled, and unlike when Presley did it, the sound made my skin crawl.

I clamped the hose back in place and used the screwdriver on my Leatherman to tighten down the bracket to keep it in place. After telling her the car should be good to go, I straightened up and closed the hood, giving the woman who ruined Presley's life a considering look.

"I'm involved with someone, but it's pretty new." I wiped

my hands on my jeans and asked her for her phone. She squealed when she handed it over and clapped as I popped my number into it. "I'm Shot, by the way."

She nodded, taking the phone back and immediately sending me a text message with a heart emoji so I also had her phone number. "Ashley."

I couldn't hold back a snort. "Ashley, huh?" It was as close to *Ashby* as she could get. The obviousness of her entire ploy was grating and insulting.

"If you're really sure you don't want to follow me to the motel tonight, I'll call you later this week. It was nice to meet you, Shot."

I grunted when she threw herself at me for an unnecessary hug. She flounced back to the car, wiggling her fingers in my direction as she went.

As soon as she was out of sight, I called Case, not caring that it was almost dawn.

He swore at me before asking me what I wanted.

"It's started. Ashby just made the first move. You and the Ranger better be ready to end this before I take matters into my own hands."

Case grumbled and I heard him moving around on the other end. "What did she want?"

"She wanted me to go to a motel with her in town."

Case swore again. "Did she leave you a way to contact her?"

"She did."

"Okay. Then you need to reach out and agree to get together with her. Meet her at the motel. Get her to confess. Give me something solid on her so I don't have to drag Presley through a trial and all this can end quietly and quickly."

I groaned and dragged my hand down my face. "What if she just wants to fuck and not talk? After all, it's all about making Presley miserable for her. She's not gonna want to chitchat."

"I'll arrest her either way. We'll wire the room and put a mic on you. But you can't let the girls know what's going on. Presley won't want you in the line of fire, and Kody will blow her top and demand to know why we didn't just pick Ashby up on the spot. This is complicated, and the less people with their hands in the mix, the better."

"Agreeing to meet this woman alone at a motel makes me look bad, Case. If Presley finds out, she's going to be heartbroken, regardless of the intent." The last thing I wanted to do was betray her in any way, but I wanted her safe and Ashby Grant behind bars.

Case yawned loudly in my ear. "Didn't peg you as the type to worry about how you looked, Palmer. Makes me dislike you a little bit less. The good thing about Presley is that she's far more reasonable than Kody. When she knows the truth, and the reasons why you were alone with the woman who tried to ruin her, she'll come around. She cares about you. She's not going to abandon you that easily."

"I hope you're right." If he wasn't, I'd risked it all for nothing and Ashby Grant would get exactly what she wanted, even if she ended up behind bars. "If this goes bad, it's gonna go bad for both of us."

And I knew neither one of us wanted to lose the ground we'd gained when it came to proving to Presley we weren't going to let her down.

CHAPTER 18

∞

PRESLEY

Are you sure you're okay here by yourself if I head home?"

I looked up from the paperwork I was double-checking, knowing full well I was going to triple-check it before sending the findings over to the detective in charge of the case. After all the work Ashby put into tainting my spotless track record, I was hyperaware and extra vigilant, determined that nothing less than perfection would fly in my new position. Until she confessed and admitted that none of the mistakes that had endangered the cases I worked on were made by me, and that she had caused them purposely to cost me the promotion, I was going to feel the unseen shadow of doubt about my abilities hanging over my head. I didn't care that it meant I needed to put in longer hours and be even more diligent than I'd been before. No mistakes were going to slip through the cracks as long as I had anything to say about it.

I looked up at the young intern who appeared to be ready to fall asleep on her feet. She was going to go far in this field. She was detail oriented, calm under pressure, and hadn't bailed when we'd gotten back-to-back cases that were enough to turn even the seasoned professional's stomach. Not wanting her to burn out before she even got started, I nodded and replied, "I'm fine. I won't be much longer."

It was a lie. I was nitpicking the details of the autopsy findings in front of me. I wasn't going anywhere anytime soon, but I didn't want to scare the young woman off unnecessarily. Not everyone who got into this line of work let it take over their entire life the way I had. I was just now learning about balance in all aspects. Mostly because I had people worrying about me and wondering where I was if I disappeared into my work for too long. If Shot didn't call or text to remind me to eat during the day, and if I didn't know he was waiting for me to get off work, there was a solid chance I would have slipped right back into being a severe workaholic, especially with my mother being gone.

And even if I didn't hear from Shot I had Kody checking up on me, reminding me there were people outside the morgue and my office walls who needed me and wanted me around. She'd finally told Hill about the baby and, as expected, he was over the moon. Kody was right in thinking he was going to overreact to the news to the extreme. Hill told her he didn't want to be on the road all the time with the Rangers if they were going to start a family. He wanted to quit his job, but she wanted him to keep it. It was an argument they couldn't seem to find middle ground on, and as a result Kody had ended up spending more and more time searching me out to be a sympathetic ear. We grew closer and closer every day, and I could no longer deny she really felt like the little sister I'd never even known I wanted. Now I couldn't picture my life without her, and my brothers, in it.

I still worked a lot, buried my head in reports and results.

Pored over findings and court cases. Read up on all the new technology and advancements in my beloved field, but now, I also made time to take care of myself throughout the day. Thanks to Shot, I was getting better and better at leaving the dead behind when it was time to go home. I wasn't as consumed as I'd been before. There was balance now, which I hadn't realized I needed.

There was also a delicate harmony in our relationship. Being with Shot was never predictable or boring. I never knew when he was going to show up or what he was going to have planned for us. There was a level of excitement in my life now that I'd never thought I wanted but had to admit was fun. Being forced to learn how to embrace sudden spontaneity wasn't as challenging as I imagined it would be, mostly because I felt safe when I was with him, and I knew whatever adventure he pulled me into, he would make sure the experience wouldn't harm me in any way. It was like I got to run wild for once in my life, but I still had a security blanket protecting me from any damage that might befall me.

The flip side of all that unexpected and unplanned was that whenever Shot came to see me, after a good day or bad, he knew he was walking into a calm, controlled environment and could leave the chaos that was always chasing him behind for a little while. He'd mentioned more than once that he liked that it was quiet when it was just him and me together at night. I could see some of the tension that he always carried with him fade when he settled into my basic and boring routine.

He kept things interesting. I kept them serene and steady. It really felt like we were starting to *need* each other to keep in perfect balance, rather than just wanting to be around one another as we stumbled our way through dating and that first uncertain flush of falling in love.

I waved the intern off after reminding her to make sure nothing was amiss in the workroom before she headed out. No one could come into this part of the building without an ID card, which had to be scanned in order for the doors to open, so there was nothing to lock behind her. There was also an armed guard who patrolled the building and made sure to stop in and check on me every hour or so. Plus, it wasn't unheard of for a uniformed policeman or a detective to pop in unannounced. A night receiving clerk was also working in an office on the other side of the building. I was as secure as could be, tucked away in my office. Not to mention I still had a leather-clad shadow following my every move. I didn't think twice about being alone in a place that would generally give most people the heebie-jeebies.

I was just finishing my second scan of the report and gearing up to start the third when an odd knocking sound caught my attention. I rubbed my tired eyes and looked toward the darkened morgue. All the doors were closed and the interior lights off, so it looked as it was supposed to. There were any number of electronic devices that could be rattling in the room, so I didn't go investigate. But I decided I needed a cup of coffee to help me power through the next couple of hours, so I pushed away from my desk and made my way over to my Keurig. I pushed the start button and paced while I waited, my white lab coat fluttering around my legs. My steps faltered when the knocking sound got louder.

I frowned and walked to the door so I could stick my head out in the hallway and see if anyone was around. It was empty, but the sound persisted. A sharp chill shot up my spine, and a shiver of unease started to make my hands shake.

Patting the pockets of my coat I found my cell and tried to call Shot. I was sure I was just overreacting and the sound was nothing, but no one could blame me for being overly cautious considering the current state of my life. I held the phone to my ear, listening to it ring and ring, surprised Shot didn't immediately answer. I knew he wasn't always going to be available when I called him, but this was the first time he didn't pick up when I really did need him to. Even if he was busy, he usually answered and let me know he would call back as soon as he could. This total silence was a first, and I didn't enjoy it one bit.

I fired off a text letting him know I was creeped out. All I wanted was to hear him say, "Everything is all right." It wasn't until this very moment that I realized exactly how much I'd started to lean on the burly biker, how much I'd started to trust him to have my back and be there for me when I needed him.

Sucking in a breath and holding my phone even tighter in my hand, I took a step into the hallway and followed the loud, tinny sound. I tried to call Shot again and was immediately sent to voice mail. I scowled at the device in my hand and looked around for the armed guard. Every instinct I had was telling me to go back into my office and call for help, but I couldn't seem to keep my feet from moving forward.

Without realizing what I was doing, my fingers pressed another contact on my phone. This time a deep, gruff voice answered immediately when the call went through.

"Presley?" Case's voice sounded both curious and concerned. Kody was usually the Lawton I reached out to, but in this instance, for some reason, Case was the one I wanted if I couldn't have Shot.

"I'm sorry to bother you so late." I kept my voice a low whisper as I tiptoed down the hallway.

"I can barely hear you. Is everything all right?" I could hear him shifting around as he muttered something to Aspen. "Where are you?"

"I'm at my office in Ivy. I'm working late." As I got further down the hallway the sound got louder. It seemed like it was coming from the night clerk's office. "There's a weird sound coming from one of the offices and I don't see the night patrol guy anywhere. I was just a little freaked out and didn't want to go investigate without someone knowing what was going on." I frowned as I paused outside of the other office door. "I called Shot but he didn't answer. I guess I could go outside and grab his buddy who he has watching me and have him check it out, but I'd feel stupid if it turns out to be nothing."

I tentatively reached for the doorknob as Case swore softly in my ear. "I'm assuming the building is pretty secure?"

I nodded, then realized he couldn't see me. "It is. Normally I feel safer here than I do at my apartment."

"How hard would it be to call the night guard to check out the sound instead of you doing it?" There was the sound of clothes rustling as Case asked the perfectly logical question.

"Umm...I'm already in front of the door. I'm going in." I felt like I had to so I could prove to myself that there was nothing to be afraid of. This place was my sanctuary, or it had been before Ashby corrupted it. I was slowly taking it back, and opening the door in front of me was part of that.

"Stay on the phone with me, Presley. No matter what, don't hang up." Case's order was strong and demanding in my ear. Again I nodded, even though he couldn't see me. His raspy drawl was reassuring and so was his presence on the other end of the line.

Taking a deep breath I twisted the knob and pushed the door open.

The startled night clerk looked up from his desk. He let out a little shriek and dropped the jar of pickles he had in his hands. The lid of the jar was dented and deformed from where he'd been pounding on the edge of the metal desk. He tossed his hands up in the air and asked, "What are you doing, Dr. Baskin? I didn't even know you were still here. I thought everyone checked out for the day." He put a hand to his chest as he glared at me. "You scared the life out of me. Why didn't you knock?"

I exhaled slowly and couldn't stop the nearly hysterical laugh that bubbled up my throat. "I'm sorry. I heard the banging and wondered what on Earth it was. I didn't see the night guard anywhere, so I figured I'd go and investigate myself. I apologize for intruding."

Case's low laugh in my ear calmed the rest of my frazzled nerves. I apologized again and told the clerk I would be leaving within the next hour or so. I knew there was no way I was going to be able to concentrate enough to finish what I started. The files would be there in the morning when my mind wasn't spinning and my heart rate had returned to normal.

"Case. Thank you for answering my call. That was ridiculous. I'm really sorry for wasting your time." On the way back to my office I passed the night guard and gave him a polite nod of acknowledgment. He asked if everything was all right, and I assured him everything was business as usual. "I'm gonna call it a night and head home. Go back to bed and apologize to Aspen for me as well. I'm sure my call woke her, too."

I was embarrassed, as much as I was relieved.

Case grunted again. "You call. I don't care what time it is, or what the reason is. You call and I will answer." He chuckled. "And Aspen is used to the phone ringing in the middle of the night. I'm the sheriff. I get called out for everything from loose livestock to shots fired, all hours of the day. And she's an attorney. Her clients call whenever they need her as well. If we're available for strangers, you damn well better believe we're available for family."

His words sent warm fuzzies flying through my stomach and made my heart feel feather-light.

"I'm still getting used to having people in my life I can rely on. I have to say, it's a very nice feeling." I'd gotten off to a rocky start with the Lawtons, but now, I honestly didn't know what I would do without them.

"You sure you feel comfortable going home alone? I can send a deputy out to Ivy to escort you—or if you want to wait, I can drive up there and follow you home." Case was really good at the big-brother thing. Even though I was new at being a sister, I could tell it was a role he was born to play.

"I'll be fine. As I said, one of Shot's club members follows me to and from work every day. Regardless of what time I leave or come in, someone is there." But it would've been nice if Shot was the one waiting when I walked out the door. Seeing him instantly made me feel better and made all the scary things I was facing feel less threatening.

"Okay. Well, send a text when you get back to Loveless. I won't be able to go back to sleep otherwise." I promised to send a text and told him good night.

By the time I hung up I was back in my office and ready to be done. I was suddenly tired on top of being slightly annoyed I still hadn't heard from Shot.

I shut my office down, making sure to leave myself notes for review tomorrow, and threw out my wasted coffee. I probably should've reheated it and drunk it on the way home, since my eyes felt heavy and I couldn't stop yawning, but then I'd be wired and awake when all I wanted to do was sleep as soon as my head hit the pillow.

Making sure, I had my keys with the mace canister attached in one hand, and my phone in the other, I let myself out of the building and out into the parking lot. I faltered a step when I didn't immediately see a motorcycle parked near my car. I frowned into the darkness, steps quickening as I hurried to where I was parked. The tiny hairs on the back of my neck lifted, and for the first time in a while, I felt alone and vulnerable.

I was practically running when I got to my car. I could hear how harsh my breathing was, how loud my racing heart sounded as it thundered between my ears. I wished I'd taken Case up on his offer to come and follow me home, or at least that I'd stayed on the line with him until I was safely inside my car with the doors locked. I couldn't believe that Shot not only was unreachable, but he'd left me unprotected without any warning. I had no idea what was going on with him right now, but I was starting to worry about him as much as I was worrying about my own well-being.

Panting. Sweating. Shivering. And I clumsily tripped over myself as I struggled to yank open the car door, so I didn't notice the person watching me fall apart with considering and concerned eyes.

"Pres."

I screamed so loud it hurt my ears and could probably be heard miles away.

I threw my keys wildly across the top of my car, hitting Shot in the shoulder.

"What in the hell?" He bent to pick up the fallen keys, then looked at me with wide eyes. "What's your problem?"

I was going to strangle him.

Clutching the top of my car door I snapped, "What's my problem? Are you kidding me right now? You scared the hell out of me! Where did you even come from? Why didn't you answer my call earlier? Do you know how worried I was? Where's your motorcycle?" The questions poured out, one after another. I felt like I was about to go crazy.

"I had business with the club when you called earlier. I couldn't answer. I saw your text that something freaked you out so I got here as soon as I could. There's no way into the building, so I figured I'd wait for you out here to make sure you were all right. I sent you a message telling you I'd be waiting. Did you not see it?"

Aggravated and still breathing hard, I looked down at my phone and saw the notification light blinking. Sure enough, he messaged me while I was on the phone with Case and I hadn't noticed.

"Son of a bitch," I whispered and closed my eyes as if I could block out this entirely ridiculous scene. I was embarrassed and a little ashamed at my overreaction.

"My bike is parked next to this van. I guess you couldn't see it, or me." He sighed heavily and pounded his fist on the roof of my car. "I didn't mean to scare you. You had to know I wasn't going to leave you alone and unprotected. What have I been telling you since the beginning, Presley? I'm not going to let anything else happen to you."

It would've been better if he'd sounded frustrated or annoyed. But he sounded disappointed that I doubted him, which made my heart hurt and made me feel about two feet tall.

I cleared my throat and nervously moved some of my hair away from my face. "I'm sorry. My nerves were shot. I wasn't thinking clearly."

He frowned and slid my keys back in my direction across the roof of the car. "I don't know what I have to do to get you to believe I will put you first no matter what."

I sniffed a little. "I don't think that's true, but I appreciate you saying it. I'd appreciate it even more if you answered your phone when I'm trying to get ahold of you. The last time I didn't pick up your call, you broke into my apartment and scared me to death. Don't you think I'd react the same to not being able to get ahold of you when I really need to? You can't be both the center of my universe and a black hole when it's convenient for you. I'm sorry I over-reacted, but you've been known to take things to an extreme as well."

He swore and I could see the frustration clearly on his face. But once again, like I was the night he appeared out of nowhere in my bathroom, I was frustrated that he didn't seem to be able to grasp why I was particularly sensitive at the moment, and why my emotions were all over the place.

I grabbed my keys and told him flatly, "I'm heading home. I'm tired, and I have to be back early in the morning."

He made a sound low in his chest. "I'll follow you."

I tilted my head to the side and considered him silently for a long moment. I guess this was our first real fight. It didn't feel good at all, and I suddenly had a whole new level of sympathy for the turmoil Kody was going through in her relationship. I knew being with someone, and being there for them, wasn't exactly an easy feat, but I realized I was kind of clueless as to how hard it could actually be. No one had mattered enough to me before to have my emotions so fired up. "I won't fight you following me home." I was still on edge and good and freaked out after all. "But I want to be alone tonight."

I needed a minute to catch my breath.

"Presley." Just my name, but the way he said it sounded so sad. I never planned on hurting him. I was truthfully still stunned that someone like me even had that kind of power with someone like him.

"I need a night, Shot." I made sure he could hear the exhaustion in my tone.

It took a moment, though he eventually nodded in agreement. I should have felt like I'd won this round, but for some reason I had the distinct impression we'd both lost.

CHAPTER 19

∞

SHOT

Presley's one night had turned into several.

The stars had aligned to keep us from sitting down and talking things out. She'd gotten called in to oversee a triple homicide case coming out of Austin, and I got tied up in club business, which pulled me away from Loveless for a few days. I came back feeling more tired than I ever had in my life, and I realized how healing Presley's serenity in my life had become. I was planning on camping out in her living room until we patched things up, but before I could even get my footing back from the last ride, Case called and told me it was time to put our plan to get Ashby to confess in motion. He had the surveillance set up and wanted to take advantage of the fact Presley was busy and less likely to stumble into the middle of the setup.

So I called the woman I hated most in the world and pulled the trigger on ending the threat hanging over Presley's head once and for all.

Only things hadn't gone right from the start.

It took several calls to finally get Ashby to agree to meet. It felt like she was playing with me, but I was worried she realized she was walking into a trap. And while we'd made arrangements to keep Presley out of the scene when Ashby and I finally did meet, there was no plan in place should another woman who would instantly interfere walk into the middle of things. It felt like karmic retribution for all the shitty things I'd ever done when I caught sight of Kody pulling into the parking lot of the diner across the street from a motel, hours and hours before she was even normally awake.

I turned my head away from the redhead who was openly flirting with me as I stalled from taking her into a motel room, toward the furious blonde who was marching toward me with murder in her eyes. A chill shot up my spine as my name rang out through the parking lot.

"Shot Caldwell, I'm going to kill you!"

There was no stopping her as she marched toward me. I was sure if Kody took a second to think rationally she would recognize the redhead as Ashby Grant. Everyone in Presley's life had been briefed on what the woman looked like, and even with the drastic cosmetic changes, she was still fairly recognizable. Only when Kody was angry, she acted first and thought things through much later.

My head jerked to the side as her palm smacked across my cheek, drawing a shocked and clearly delighted sound from the woman across from me. I was sure both Hill and Case were getting a good laugh from where they were monitoring the situation in a nearby room. The microphone they'd attached to one of the rivets that dotted my cut was meant to pick up the smallest sound and was designed to grab anything incriminating Ashby might say. They were planning on taking the woman into custody today regardless, but everyone was holding out hope I could get her on tape admitting that she murdered Presley's mother as well as Conrad Lawton. It wasn't the way I would go about things if this was fully club business, but I felt like my hands were tied. If I dealt with things the way I wanted, the problem of taking Ashby out of Presley's life forever would be solved, but there was no doubt Presley would then risk losing me as well. There was no way I wouldn't be the prime suspect if the awful woman disappeared suddenly, so for the time being I was pretending to be law-abiding. However, Kody's sudden appearance might flush the whole manufactured scenario down the drain.

I rubbed my stinging cheek and met Kody's glare with one of my own.

She looked at the redhead, angry smoke practically coming out of her ears. I didn't need Kody's drama on top of trying to keep my own emotions in check. I stopped Kody from lunging at the woman by my side, just barely, and bit back a litany of swear words.

"Knock it off, Kody." I barked the words in a warning tone but they didn't do any good. I was annoyed by the interruption but even more irritated that Kody didn't know me well enough to know I wouldn't be talking to a woman who wasn't Presley in front of a motel, in broad daylight, without a damn good reason. Kind of the way I was irritated that Presley thought I would leave her alone and scared without responding the night we'd had that ugly fight outside her work. I couldn't be in two places at once, and I was starting to realize how hard it was going to be to prioritize someone else as much as I prioritized my club.

Kody looked like she wanted to hit me again but she restrained herself. Instead, she puffed out an aggravated sound and crossed her arms over her chest. She tapped the toe of her orange cowboy boot on the asphalt in front of her and glared daggers at the redhead, who seemed pleased by the interruption even though she was doing her best to look scared instead of triumphant.

"I can't believe you. Do you have any idea what would happen if Presley saw you right now?" She shook her head and made a disgusted face. "I was the only one in the family willing to support the two of you being together, because I know you. At least I thought I did. Now"—she gave me a look that made me feel about two inches tall—"I feel like all of us Lawtons should band together and protect Presley from you...from this." She waved a hand in the direction of the fake redhead, who was now clutching my arm.

I swore long and loud. I felt firmly stuck between what I needed to do and what I wanted to do. I couldn't tell Kody all of this was for Presley's own good, that I was trying to bring her some much-needed closure. And I had no doubt the narrative Kody was going to take back to the woman I was trying to protect would paint me in a terrible light. I could have kicked myself for not sitting Presley down and telling her our plan just in case things got twisted like this. I thought I had a handle on fixing all of this without her involvement, but just like my loss as to how to smooth things over from the other night, it seemed like I didn't know anything when it came to falling in love.

"You're reading too much into this, Kody." I tried to keep the fact I was disgusted hidden. It stung that she was so quick to jump to conclusions and that she was so ready to take those misinformed assumptions back to Presley. They were incredibly close now. I wasn't so sure if Kody painted me in a bad light, there would be a way to talk myself out of this mess.

I'd never had a relationship with a woman I was frantic

to protect before and I had to say I didn't like how helpless it made me feel. I wanted to hit something...or someone. Namely the gleeful predator who was still clinging to me. I'd never lifted a hand to a woman, but then again, I'd never been so close to a woman who killed without qualms before.

"Well, this has been loads of fun, but I have other commitments today, so can we get back to what we were doing before we were so rudely interrupted?" Ashby said. Those fake green eyes glittered triumphantly as Kody snarled and took a step forward. This little confrontation played right into Ashby's hands. Word of me spending time with another woman was bound to get back to Presley even quicker than she'd expected. She was practically quivering with anticipation. Because of Kody's outburst, it was obvious to her how deeply invested Presley was in me and our relationship, making this apparent act of betrayal all the more potent and painful.

Kody bit off a slew of ugly words as she turned on her heel and marched away. It was bad luck and bad timing all around.

I knew it was a calculated move on Ashby's part to only agree to meet me at the motel during the day. There was only one motel anywhere near Loveless, and everyone who went anywhere in the small town had to pass by it to get where they were going. My motorcycle was pretty unmistakable, and so were this woman's bright hair and overtly sexy outfit. She wanted someone to see us meeting in the parking lot, and I had no doubt she had someone lurking nearby to take photos of me walking into that motel room so she could send proof of my infidelity to Presley. I knew she wanted to seduce me, but I hadn't figured out if she was also planning to get rid of me. Aside from getting me to sleep with her, having Presley blame herself for my demise was undoubtedly the best way Ashby could destroy her for good. If Presley believed I lost my life because I'd fallen for her, there would be no coming back from that. She already had so much guilt when it came to people she cared about being in danger because of Ashby.

This woman wasn't just crazy, she was evil. She'd proved it multiple times.

I tried to keep the scowl off my face and even put my features into something that appeared more anticipatory as I guided the redhead toward the wired room. I doubted I was successful. My insides were churning, and every single part of me that craved vengeance for the woman I very well might be in love with howled in outrage at being ignored.

"Who was that woman? Was that your new girlfriend?" Obviously she knew that it was not, but asking was a good way to get information, and if I was stupid I would be spilling exactly why Kody was so worked up and thus give Ashby a new target to take aim at.

"Former girlfriend. We stayed friends, so she's always all up in my business. Apparently, she doesn't think it's a good idea to screw up my new relationship by spending time with you."

"Interesting. It sounded slightly more personal than that." There was a calculating gleam in her eyes, and once again I wondered how anyone who got anywhere near this woman couldn't make out that she was a predator of the highest order. No wonder she'd practically eaten Presley alive.

"I've got my own shit to deal with. I don't take on others. I also have things to do today, so let's get this show on the road. You said you wanted to thank me for helping you out with your car and that you were just passing through town.

I have limited free time, so if you wanna pay me back, it's now or never."

I was pretty sure Kody was already on the phone with Presley telling her what an unfaithful asshole I was. And if Case wasn't the one behind this whole wayward plot, I had no doubt he and Crew would both be racing in my direction ready to kick my ass once they heard about this shitshow.

"You're in a hurry. That's so sexy." The words were purred in a sultry voice as her fingernails trailed over the tattoos on my forearm.

My skin crawled in response. "I don't waste time when it comes to taking care of business."

"Ahhh, I found myself a real-life bad boy to play with. How fun." She grinned as she opened the door. "I bet your girlfriend has no idea what to do with you, which is why you called me. How sad for her. She must be pathetic."

More like I had no clue what to do with my pretty doctor. I wanted to give her as much as she'd given me since we started spending time together, and the best way to do that was by finally getting rid of the awful woman standing next to me. But even in doing that, I'd still managed to mess up, and I knew it was going to hurt the one person I promised to keep anything from happening to.

"You seem pretty interested in the other women in my life." I knew why, but it was obnoxious regardless. The worse she talked about Presley, the harder it was to bite my tongue. "This is only a one-shot deal."

"It doesn't have to be a one-time thing. My plans might be flexible. I kind of like you, bad boy biker. I think we could have some fun together." She grabbed the front of my vest and pulled herself up so she could touch her lips to mine. "It's been a long time since I've had someone interesting to play with."

My stomach rolled and I had to bite the tip of my tongue to keep myself from telling her to go straight to hell. She had a special spot reserved just for her, I was sure of it.

"Where did you say you were from again? And what brings you to Loveless?" They were asinine questions, but I wanted to keep her mouth occupied so she would keep it off of mine. She suddenly seemed like she had more arms than an octopus and the suction of a Hoover. It might've been the first time I worked so hard at avoiding the advances of such an attractive woman, but all I could see was her black heart and evil eyes. And that she wasn't Presley.

I didn't want to kiss someone who wasn't Presley, which made it even more clear that I was no longer falling in love with her—I'd fallen, all the way. Nothing could've prepared me for the landing, either. It was a startling revelation that couldn't have come at a worse time.

To my surprise, Ashby—or Ashley, as she kept referring to herself—vaguely answered the dumb questions I threw out to buy time.

"I'm from close by. I used to work in a town between here and Austin, so I'm familiar with the area. I came back to visit a friend." She slid her hands over my shoulders and under the leather of my cut. I fought to hide a wince as she did her best to work the well-worn leather off my body. "I haven't seen her in a while and I'm long overdue for a visit."

"Oh yeah? Who's the friend? Everyone in this town knows everyone else. I bet I'm familiar with whoever it is." If I could get her to admit on tape she was here for Presley, that was the first step in getting some kind of confession to all of her misdeeds.

I let her take the leather vest off and stood still as she slid her hands up and under the cotton of my plain, black T-shirt. There was a limit to how far I was willing to let her go no matter what she was going to say or not say, and she was getting close to my breaking point. Everywhere her hands touched my skin felt dirty. There was a nasty taste in my mouth, and an unsettling vibration humming underneath my skin. I wanted to put my hands around her throat and squeeze. Again, I'd never be inclined toward violence when it came to women, but she really was the exception.

"Oh, she's just a friend I went to school with. We worked together for a bit as well. She isn't a very nice person, though. She has a bad habit of taking things that don't belong to her and thinking she's better than everyone else. I haven't seen her for some time. I thought it would be a good idea to check and see if she's changed. I'd like to think she's learned some hard lessons lately." A sour look crossed her face even as she tugged my T-shirt off over my head. Some of the pretense she artfully wore slipped just a little. If I hadn't been paying attention, I would've missed it. Under her perfectly normal mask was a layer of maliciousness that gave even me the creeps. I'd seen a lot in my life, but this woman's warped sense of reality was truly alarming.

I cleared my throat and grabbed her shoulders in a punishing grip when she touched her lips to the intricate tattoo of a bullet hole that rested right over my heart.

"Doesn't sound like you're actually friends at all."

The woman pouted and stepped away from me so she could slither out of her nearly indecently short skirt and skintight top. She was wearing a matching set of lingerie that was so ridiculously wasted on me it was almost funny. It didn't matter what the package was wrapped in, I knew the stuff on the inside was rotten to the core.

"We were best friends. I loved her, but she kept hurting me over and over again. Eventually, I had no choice but to hurt her back." Sharp fingernails dug into my skin and angry lips attacked mine. It was like being caught in a whirling tornado of seduction and anger.

Prying myself free and struggling to catch my breath and keep my cool, I forcibly pushed the nearly naked woman back onto the messy bed behind her. I lifted an eyebrow and asked, "How did you hurt her back?"

The woman smirked at me and crooked her finger in a "come closer" gesture. I ignored the command and instead put my hands on my hips and regarded her with a bored expression. I let out a very real yawn because I was tired and, even more so, tired of all this. Being the good guy was so not my bag. It took far more patience than I was blessed with.

The woman frowned at my apparent disinterest and sat up on the edge of the bed. "She took something that was rightfully mine, so I took something that was hers. Only I got in trouble for making things even, and nothing bad happened to her. Nothing bad ever happens to her. I came back to see her because I deserve an apology. I deserve a lot of things." She reached for the buckle on my belt just as there was a knock at the door.

We both turned to look in surprise. For once her shocked expression didn't seem fake. This wasn't part of the plan. Mine or hers. I'd barely got her talking. We weren't anywhere close to a confession.

Assuming it was Kody, back to chew my ass out, I walked to the door and yanked it open.

And was pinned in place by a pair of accusing green eyes. Only, they weren't Kody's.

I knew things looked bad.

I was naked from the waist up in a motel room with another scantily clad woman. There were discarded clothes all over the floor and I was sure I had lipstick smeared across my now slack mouth.

Unlike Kody, who raged and exploded without thought, Presley simply looked at me like she could see into my very soul…and couldn't find anything there worth loving anymore.

CHAPTER 20

✺

PRESLEY

I knew I needed to apologize to Shot.

I knew that I'd shut him out, both figuratively and literally, burying myself in work instead of dealing with my complicated and confusing emotions. It was all just a misunderstanding, but there were deep-seated issues lurking under the surface of it all. I cared about Shot more than I'd planned on caring about anyone after losing my mother. I trusted him. I relied on him. But I was realizing that as long as we were together I would never come first in his life, and I wasn't sure how I felt about that. I told him he couldn't be the center of my world, so did it make any sense that I was starting to want to be the center of his?

I had to give him credit, though. While I was hiding from everything that felt like it was going wrong, he'd made the effort to make sure I was doing okay. He texted me good morning and good night every single day, and still reminded me to eat and take a break while I was at work. He told me he was going out of town with the club, but I still had a scary biker escort to and from work every single day. He was giving me the space I asked for and respecting the boundaries I told him I would protect with everything I had, which made me feel terrible. He was supposed to be as clueless about relationships as me. But he seemed so much better at all of it than I was.

I called Kody a few days after the dustup and asked her to meet with me. I needed someone to talk to. Someone who would give it to me straight. She'd already warned being with Shot would never be easy, but I needed someone to assure me if I decided to put the work in to be with him, it would be worth it. I also needed to hear that I was worth it. That eventually I'd hold as much importance in Shot's world as his club and members did. Really, I needed Kody to talk me off the edge.

When Kody answered, she was clearly groggy and almost incoherent. I forgot that she tended to get off work super late and had probably just lain down to go to bed. She mumbled her way through a few sentences before I cut her off and apologized for calling so early and out of the blue. I told her I would call her back at a more reasonable hour and went back to pacing my apartment and trying to figure out how to mend the fence I'd purposely kicked down in a panic over my unchecked emotions.

My phone rang as I was finishing up getting ready for the day. I was pinning the top part of my hair back and away from my face when she ordered me to meet her at the local diner for a quick breakfast. She still sounded tired, and a little bit cranky, so I didn't dare argue with her. I rushed through the rest of my routine because I only had a few free hours to spare before leaving for work.

I was jogging toward the entrance of the diner when I caught sight of Kody angrily pacing back and forth in front of the doors. She seemed to be talking to herself under her breath, and it was easy enough to tell she was not pleased with something, or someone.

My first thought was that she was mad at me for waking her up and then running late, but as soon as her eyes landed on me, she went pale and all her anger turned to something that looked a lot like sympathy.

"Sorry I'm late. My mind is a little all over the place today." I gasped in surprise when she pulled me close and locked her arms around me in a rib-cracking hug. "Oof. Is everything okay?" For a brief moment, I was worried that something bad might've happened with the baby or to Hill while he was on assignment. Kody was always touchy and expressive, but this was a lot, even for her.

Kody squeezed me even tighter, making me squeak in protest. I peeled myself out of her suffocating grip and put my hands on her shoulders.

"What's gotten into you this morning?"

Like a switch had been flipped all her anger was back full force. Her freckled face turned a bright pink, and her green eyes blazed with an intensity that was almost scary. I'd seen her look this way before. She'd had a similar expression when she confronted me about Conrad leaving everything he owned to me in his will. At the time we didn't know Ashby had been behind that fiasco as well. She was trying to drive a wedge between me and my new siblings before they'd even thought to welcome me to the family. Kody was the one who confronted me, and we almost came to blows. I'd been frightened of her then; now I was terrified to find out exactly where her fury was directed. She only let a handful of people get close to her, and this level of heat and aggravation meant someone important had set her off.

"You're not serious about Shot, are you? Please tell me

you were calling me this morning to tell me that the two of you broke up because you realized how different you are and it'll never work out between the two of you." She grabbed my hands and was practically begging me to confirm her furious rush of words.

I felt my eyebrows shoot up to nearly my hairline as she clutched my fingers in a painful grip. "Well, no. I did call because Shot and I got into a little squabble recently and I wanted your advice on how to best go about apologizing. I'm not the best at communicating when it comes to my feelings or understanding someone else's. I'm better about being honest with how I'm feeling with him, but talking to him this time is too important to just wing it and hope for the best."

She frowned and dropped my hands so she could shove hers through her unruly curls. She grabbed handfuls of her wild hair, her frustration and anger palpable. "I really am going to kill him. Or I'm going to have Hill do it for me. I'm sure he knows how to get away with murder."

Completely confused over the tone and direction of this conversation, I tossed my hands up in the air and demanded, "Can you tell me what in the hell is going on? You're stressing me out." And my nerves were already stretched painfully thin.

Heaving a sigh so deep it sounded like it came from the very depths of her soul, she looked directly at me and told me in a flat tone, "Shot just went into a motel room with some random redheaded woman. I confronted him and he didn't even deny that he was up to something sketchy. I mean, I know he used to be a player and never really took anyone he was involved with too seriously, but I would've put money on the fact that you were different. He seemed...smitten with you. He was so much softer and gentler with you than

I've ever seen him. I can't believe he would do this. I thought I knew him better than that." She looked like she might cry, while I suddenly felt like I was made of ice. "I'm so sorry, Presley. I already plan on having Case and Crew kick his ass for you. And if Case can find a reason to lock him up, I'm all for it. You deserve to be treated so much better than this."

Cold.

Everything inside of me was suddenly frozen.

I'd been told I was frigid on more than one occasion. But this was the first time the words actually fit. I was winter. My emotions a blizzard whipping through me as arctic winds blasted through my heart.

"Which room did he go into?" My voice cracked and broke. The words were barely audible. I felt numb, and getting my body to respond to the signal from my screaming brain was difficult.

Kody blinked in obvious surprise. "You want to confront him?"

I wasn't a violent or confrontational person. That was partly how I ended up such an easy target for Ashby in the first place. However, I wanted to see the proof that Shot betrayed me with my own two eyes. I had no clue what I would say to him if Kody's accusations were truthful. I was holding on to a shred of hope that she'd just misread the situation. As much work and effort as Shot had put into trying to convince me he was serious about being with me, it didn't make sense that he would throw everything away after one silly argument. He was reckless and dangerous, but he wasn't careless or thoughtless. In fact, he was probably the most compassionate man I'd ever come across. He definitely understood me better than anyone else ever had, so he had to know what finding him with another woman would do to me.

He couldn't be that cruel...could he?

I had to shake Kody to get her to stop ranting about the bodily harm she was going to inflict on Shot, and to get her to focus long enough to give me the room number. It was another battle when I told her I wanted to go alone. I appreciated her support and the unending sisterhood she was displaying. She'd known Shot longer, had been much closer to him than she was with me, but all of that aside, she was one hundred percent on my side and ready to do battle for me, no questions asked.

I loved her from the bottom of my heart. Not since I lost my mother had I been so certain of how I felt about another person, but I knew I adored Kody in a way only one sister could feel for another. She was part of me and I was obviously a huge part of her. Finding the space for her had happened when I wasn't even looking, and I was so glad she claimed it.

I was shaking from head to toe as I got closer to the motel room door. My head demanded to know if Shot had crossed a line there was no coming back from, but my heart was scared to death of the answer. I couldn't believe he'd gone from standing guard over me on a regular basis to hooking up with someone else all within the span of a couple of days. It made no sense, and I'd learned there wasn't much Shot didn't do without a rock-solid reason.

I could clearly hear voices on the other side of the door.

One male. One female.

That little sliver of hope I was desperately holding on to started to ice over and crystalize like all the rest of my insides.

Lifting my hand, my fingers curled into a fist and hung in the air for a long moment as I wavered over whether I could face what was on the other side of that door or not. After a brief pep talk, where I reminded myself I had survived losing my mother, finding out my father was a terrible person, learning I had a whole new family, and almost going to jail for murder because of my best friend, I let my fist fall. I pounded on the door, imagining it was a vital part of Shot's anatomy instead.

The voices on the inside of the room went quiet and a moment later the barrier was jerked open.

He looked shocked.

Not guilty.

Not sad.

Not afraid.

Not remorseful.

Just stunned to see me standing there, almost as if he'd been expecting someone else.

He didn't have his leather vest on, or a shirt. He had lipstick smeared across his mouth, and there was a strong floral scent wafting off his bare skin. There was an obviously female body standing behind him and clothes were scattered all over the floor. It was a case of a picture being worth a thousand words, and all of them were incredibly damning.

He didn't say anything and neither did I.

I wasn't sure if there was anything left to say and I knew I couldn't find the words even if there was. It felt like he'd reached inside and my chest squeezed my heart. I couldn't get a solid breath out, and I knew the only reason I wasn't sobbing and hysterical was because I was frozen on the inside. I'd never been so cold. And I'd never felt as betrayed.

My best friend tried to frame me for murder and threatened to kill me. A man I viewed as a mentor had looked the other way while my mother was murdered. My long-lost father had wanted nothing to do with me and turned out to be a terrible man. And yet, none of that hurt the way seeing Shot half naked with another woman did.

I guessed there was no use denying it any longer. I had to be in love with him. There was no other way to explain the way I felt like I was being stripped down and broken apart on the inside.

My mind was working a mile a minute because it still didn't compute that he'd switch gears so fast. He was a guy who was all about loyalty and honor, even if he made up his own rules and lived his life his own wild way. But the pain inside my heart was too loud, drowning out any whisper of logic that was trying to be heard.

I turned away and blindly started walking away from the scene that would be forever burned into my brain. I lifted a shaking hand to wipe away a stray tear, thinking I needed to let the office know I wouldn't be in to oversee any of the ongoing work on my current cases for the day. I would be a liability in my current condition. I knew I wasn't going to be able to focus on anything other than how things had gone so wrong with Shot.

My head jerked up as I heard a shout. It came from across the way, where Kody was standing in front of the diner.

Too late I realized she was shouting a warning.

Between one blink and the next, a man moved from between two cars parked in front of the motel and was standing directly in front of me, almost as if he'd been waiting for me to appear.

I gasped in shock at his sudden appearance and at his actual appearance. It looked like half of his face had been melted off. The right side was a mass of healing and scarred skin as if he'd recently been in a horrible fire. He honestly could've passed for someone wearing a Halloween mask well out of season. I'd seen some pretty bad things in my line of work, but he was enough to shock and surprise.

I lifted a hand and started to apologize for nearly bumping into him when I caught sight of the gun in his hand. A hand which was also horrifically scarred and mangled. It made me nervous the way his hand shook.

He didn't speak. I had no idea if it was because he couldn't or because he wouldn't. Not that anyone would've been able to hear him over the screaming. It took a second to realize the sound was coming from me as he pointed the menacing-looking pistol directly at my face. If he pulled the trigger there would be no survival.

There would be nothing.

Facing an armed assailant was about the only thing that had the power to distract me from my imploding love life. My mind was suddenly racing while trying to put the pieces of what was happening together: like who he was and why he was there, and, most important, why did he have a gun pointed at me? Then I heard my name called loudly in the middle of this bizarre nightmare. I turned my head to look at Shot, because there was no ignoring the panic in his voice.

The man with the scars also took his intense focus off of me and moved the gun slightly.

A second later the disfigured man pulled the trigger and I screamed so loudly I was certain my lungs were going to pop. I swore I felt the breeze created by the bullet as it whipped past my face. The sound was absolutely deafening, but the explosion of pain I expected wasn't nearly as severe... for a moment. I was lifting my hands to uselessly ward off what was happening when I suddenly had no control over my body. I was letting out a breath of relief that the gun that had gone off in my face hadn't killed me, when a blaze of agony suddenly burst across my entire back, knocking me swiftly to the ground. I fell gracelessly in a heap, the metallic scent of my own blood tingling in my nose almost instantly. My cheek hit the asphalt and I knew the impact should hurt, but I didn't feel anything. Couldn't feel anything.

As I struggled to breathe, everything seemed too loud, too bright, too much. My vision started to waver and get blurry around the edges. I barely saw the boots of the scarred man, standing in front of me as another pair raced into the corner of my vision.

I wanted to ask for help. I wanted to push to my feet. I wanted to plug my ears because the noise happening somewhere above my head was incredibly loud. I also wanted a warm blanket because I was freezing and shivering uncontrollably. I thought I was cold when Shot opened that motel room door, but I had no idea just how cold a person could be when their life started to leak out of them.

There were more agonizingly loud pops and voices yelling over my prone form. I felt shaking hands touch my hair and stroke over my face. The touch was followed by a woman's voice shouting my name over and over. I tried to focus on her, but my body wouldn't obey anything I told it to do. I managed to get my eyes open for a brief second and saw Kody bent over me. She was crying and looked hysterical. Even though my mind was foggy, I wondered where Shot was. The tiny piece of my heart that wasn't crushed still wanted him when things were going really wrong.

I wanted to look around and make sure he was okay, since it sounded like there were bullets flying everywhere. I desperately needed to know he wasn't also lying on the asphalt, covered in blood and being sucked under by an indescribable pain the way I was.

I was so tired. And so cold. It sounded like a high-budget action movie happening around me, there were more and more gunshots. More voices screaming all kinds of obscenities and calling my name. Suddenly there were sirens. But it was too hard to keep track of it all. I hurt so badly I just wanted everything to go away.

I couldn't keep my eyes open, no matter how hard I tried. I felt like a very heavy weight was tied around my consciousness pulling it down into a deep, dark hole. There didn't seem to be an end to the free fall. I was sinking fast. The blackness got bigger and more vast until it eventually took me over and everything both inside and outside of me went deathly quiet and scary still.

My very last thought before I couldn't think, or feel, or hear anything else, was that I really hoped Shot was okay.

CHAPTER 21

∞

SHOT

You find anyone who knew Jed Coleman made it out of that fire alive. And when you do—" I curled my hand into a fist and exhaled a deep breath "—you make them pay." I looked at Top's somber face and waited for him to nod in understanding. "Anyone involved in keeping the fact Jed was still alive and his whereabouts from us is going down. No exceptions."

I was issuing death warrants for anyone who had a hand in putting Presley in the hospital.

Top nodded and dragged a hand down his face. He looked haggard, like he'd aged ten years in one day. He was tired of seeing me get shot, and I couldn't blame him.

When I saw Presley go down it felt like time stopped.

Nothing mattered but getting to her and making sure she was still alive.

I didn't care about Top taking out Coleman.

I hardly noticed that Ashby had exited the motel room behind me as I chased after Presley. I didn't register she also had a weapon and was taking aim from behind me. I didn't acknowledge that Case and Hill had jumped into the fray with weapons drawn. All I could see was Presley and the blood spreading across her back before I, too, was knocked to the ground and blacked out. I wasn't aware I'd gotten winged by the bullet Coleman fired until after they'd loaded Presley into the back of an ambulance and rushed away from the scene.

The shootout that took place in the motel parking lot was going to leave a mark on all of Loveless for a long time. And ultimately, Top was the one who finally put an end to Jed Coleman's quest for revenge. The protective detail I'd had on Presley had called Top the minute she showed in the parking lot of the diner. My guys knew she was supposed to be at work and out of the way while I tried to bring down her nemesis. Top and a couple of the other members had shown up seconds after Jed Coleman took his shot. I was eternally grateful he'd been aiming at me instead of Presley. I was also lucky Top had pulled the trigger before Coleman got another round off.

No one involved when the bullets started flying made it out unscathed, but some of us had wounds that were worse than others.

"You sure you're okay to bail on your hospital stay? You don't look so good." Top scowled at me as I struggled to get into the clothes I'd asked him to bring me. "You were practically in a coma a couple of hours ago. You know you've got a severe concussion. You're gonna fall off your bike if you try and ride up to Austin right now."

He wasn't wrong.

But Presley was barely clinging to life in a hospital an hour away, and that was where I needed to be. That was the only place I *wanted* to be. She had been life-flighted to

Austin at the same time I'd been rushed to the local Loveless emergency room for treatment. Of course, I'd fought being taken in, but ultimately lost the battle when Top told me it wouldn't help Presley any if I bled to death.

The bullet Jed fired at me had missed its intended mark. I'd turned at the sound of Ashby Grant shooting at Presley from behind me, so the bullet meant to hit me right between my eyes had winged the side of my head instead. It'd skimmed my temple and taken off the top of my ear. I was lucky, all things considered, but the impact was enough to knock me out and rattle my brain pretty significantly. The doctors were worried about my brain swelling and wanted me to stay in the hospital a few days for monitoring. Not happening. I had to be where Presley was.

It would haunt me for the rest of my days that Ashby's aim had been so much better.

Presley had taken a bullet in the back. I didn't know how extensive the damage was, but before I passed out I knew there was a lot of blood. Too much blood. And she hadn't been moving. I'd been unable to get many more details, but I planned on being filled in on my way to the hospital in Austin.

My ride was due here any minute.

I put a hand on the rail of the hospital bed as the act of sitting up made the room start to spin around me. Top swore and called me a stubborn bastard just as Case Lawton appeared in the doorway of the room.

"You ready to go?" The gruff question was met with bristling hostility from my VP.

"What are you doing here?" Top's drawl was extra heavy when he was angry.

Case gave the other man a look and inclined his chin in my direction. "Taking him up to Austin, since he can barely stand. If Presley pulls through she's going to want to see him. If she doesn't..." Case's deep voice trailed off and I noticed his normally tanned complexion turned very pale. "We'll all need to be there to say goodbye."

I growled involuntarily at the thought of her not making it. That wasn't a possibility I was willing to consider. She was strong. She was a fighter. She wasn't going to leave me. I didn't care if I had to make a deal with the devil, or if I had to start praying to the highest order. She was going to be okay, she had to be.

"Why are you taking him? All you've done is warn him to stay away from her." Top turned to me. "Are you sure this isn't some bullshit setup, Shot?" He scowled at the sheriff. "I don't trust this guy."

Case snorted in Top's direction as I rubbed my forehead, which was wrapped up like a mummy's. My head was killing me and my vision wasn't so great. I also felt like I might throw up any second, but none of that was stopping me from getting to Presley.

"I'm taking him because I owe him. He wouldn't have been in that motel room with that sociopath if it wasn't for me. Presley wouldn't have been hurt if it wasn't for my plan. I was the one who urged him to keep quiet about what we had going on with Grant. I'm the bad guy here, not Shot. Despite how smart she is, my sister seems to be in love with him, so anything that's going to help her turn a corner right now, I'm willing to do. If she makes it, I won't get between her and your president again."

Case was the one who stopped Ashby after she shot Presley.

As soon as he and Hill heard what was going down with Presley over the live feed, they'd rushed out of the room where they were monitoring things. Only bullets started flying, so Hill's focus had been on keeping Kody safe as soon as he caught sight of her. This left Case to face off with the woman who'd tormented his family and murdered his father in cold blood.

Top told me the sheriff had handled the situation in a far more professional and rational manner than either of us would have. According to him, Case gave Ashby the opportunity to surrender. It was clear her long reign of terror was over. There was nowhere else for her to run, and no one left for her to harm. Instead of surrendering quietly, she'd taken aim at Case, leaving him no choice but to take her out. Top had noticed the movement of her gun at the same time the sheriff had and also got a shot off. Case's shot wasn't lethal. My VP's was.

It was all over…except Presley's life was still hanging in the balance.

"Let's go." I wasn't sure how much longer I was going to be able to remain upright, and all the energy I had I would need to reserve for begging Presley to forgive me once I knew she was going to be okay.

Top frowned and turned so he could point a finger at Case. "If you let something happen to him on your watch, you'll have the entire club ready to rip you and your town apart, Sheriff."

Case made a sound that was somewhere between a growl and a grunt. "Anyone ever tell you threatening a law enforcement officer isn't a good idea?"

Top smirked. "All the time." He switched his gaze back to mine and gave a curt nod, letting me know he would handle business while I waited to hear if the woman who had my heart was going to break it or take it with her. "When you get back, shit will be taken care of. Do what you need to do the next few days and don't worry about the club."

I nodded and the room immediately started to spin. I needed to hear those words before I followed Case out of the hospital. I needed the assurance that something would go the way it was supposed to, because nothing else had.

I needed to brace myself against the wall, then reluctantly hold on to Case once we left the hospital. My steps were unsteady, and my head felt like it was going to split into two. The nausea was growing and I ached all over. I'd definitely seen better days, but at least I was awake and aware. I wouldn't complain about any of the discomforts until I knew Presley was going to pull through and see another day.

"Tell me how she's really doing." I wanted the order to be impossible for the other man to ignore, but even I could hear how weak and wobbly my voice sounded.

Case sighed and reached up to pull his Stetson off. He threw the hat toward the back of his county-issued SUV and turned to look at me with tired eyes. He looked as haggard as I felt.

"Not good. Believe it or not, you guys are going to have matching scars. The same bullet that hit you when Coleman fired, skimmed the side of her head in an almost identical spot as yours. But, for her, that's the most minor of injuries sustained. The bullet Grant fired lacerated one of her kidneys and nicked her liver. She lost a ton of blood and went into shock. She was in surgery for hours and barely pulled through." He swore quietly and curled his fingers around the steering wheel, clenching it so tightly that his knuckles turned white. "We were all pretty optimistic that a corner was turned, but then her surgeon told us that her remaining kidney is showing early signs of chronic kidney disease. Not totally unexpected considering what her mother went through, but it means she needs a transplant. The sooner the better."

"Jesus." The throbbing in my head intensified and my

rolling stomach lurched dangerously. I closed my eyes and rubbed my chest where I swore I could feel my heart shattering into a million painful pieces. "She can't catch a break, can she?"

Case grunted his agreement. "The entire family got tested to see if any of us are a match. Well, all of us except Kody." He made a sound. "Did you know that she's pregnant?"

I shook my head and felt my expression shift to slightly shocked.

"You can't be a donor if you're expecting. I thought she was going to faint when she had to explain to us why she couldn't get tested. It sucks that such happy news had to come out during a life-or-death situation. Hill didn't look happy about the timing at all. I'm sure they wanted to share that with the family on their own time in their own way, but it is what it is. One of us who did get tested will gladly donate if at all possible. Since we're all only half siblings the probability of being a match is less likely. I left to come and get you before we got the results back, and I haven't heard from anyone, so they must still be waiting."

"What if one of you isn't a match? What happens then?"

Case shook his head, steely eyes locked on the road ahead of us. "We look for a donor outside of the family. We look until we find someone who can save her."

"And if that fails, she goes on the national waitlist and probably loses her life before a donor becomes available." I bitterly bit out the worst-case scenario. I wasn't going to let that happen. "The Sons of Sorrow have chapters all over the U.S. There are thousands and thousands of members. If I need to go to my old man and force him to make every single patched-in member get tested for a match, I'll do it." It was honestly the least my old man could do for me.

Case blew out a breath. "Hopefully it won't come to that. The sooner we have a solution, the better. She's hanging in there, but just barely."

I put a hand on my stomach and closed my eyes so I could rest my bandaged head against the window.

"Case, how did you stop yourself from putting a bullet right between that woman's eyes? After everything she's put the people you love through, how did you restrain yourself?" I was honestly curious. How could anyone have that much integrity? That much self-control.

He chuckled but it wasn't a happy, joyous sound. "Do you think I didn't want to kill her? That's all I wanted to do. But my job isn't about revenge, it's about justice. I wanted her to have to answer for everything she did. I wanted the world to see who she really was. I wanted my sister's name cleared and justice for her mother."

"That is one major way we are very different, Sheriff. I just wanted her gone."

Another painful-sounding laugh came from the driver's seat.

"We aren't as different as you'd like to believe, Palmer." I winced at his use of my real name. "You were alone with Grant several times. I know what you're capable of. She could've gone missing, never to be seen again, despite all the work we put into drawing her out into the open. You knew it was important for Presley to clear her name. You knew she needed closure on her mother's murder. You were willing to give her that, instead of just taking Grant out. That's what justice ultimately looks like."

I snorted. "Look where justice got Presley. Revenge would've meant she wasn't fighting for her life right now."

Case sighed and I heard his fingers tapping on the steering wheel. "I actually owe you an apology. I hate that Presley walked in on you with that woman. I think there are a lot of things wrong with how you live your life and go about your business, but I know you aren't a disloyal man. I know my sister can trust you. I also know you would never purposely hurt her the way she was hurt today. I think we were short-sighted, and maybe keeping things from her for her own good wasn't the right call. When she wakes up, when she's ready to listen, I swear I'll clear everything up between the two of you. Trust me to fix this."

I groaned a little as a sharp, stabbing pain lanced through my head. "Right now all I care about is her waking up. The rest can wait." But I did appreciate what he said. It was almost a compliment.

We lapsed into a heavy silence, worry and helplessness thick in the air around us. It was a battle not to pass out or throw up the entire ride, so I stayed as still as possible and tried not to let my imagination run wild. I couldn't fathom losing her. I couldn't picture my life moving forward without her. Even though we hadn't quite figured out how to fit together seamlessly, I knew if I lost her, there would be a gaping hole in my heart that would never heal.

I must've dozed off, which was incredibly dangerous considering I had a complex concussion. When I peeled my eyes open as Case shook my shoulder, I realized we'd traded the sleepy streets of Loveless for the much more hectic pace of Austin. I practically had to crawl out of the car. My head was swimming, and any little movement I made felt like someone was poking my brain with an icepick. Also, the army of stitches holding my temple together had started to itch and tingle. I knew painkillers were off the table because of the head injury, so I was just going to have to tough it out.

Again, I needed to use Case as a crutch until I found a wall to lean against. It was a long, painful walk to the ICU.

Once we hit the waiting room the tension was so thick and heavy it was suffocating. Hill was on his feet pacing back and forth like a caged tiger. Della and Aspen were huddled around Kody like a protective shield. Crew was slumped on the floor with his back to the wall, looking every bit as anxious as his little sister. It was easy to see she was the most distraught of the bunch. When she caught sight of me, she got to her feet and rushed over to me. I braced myself for another smack across my face, even though my head was half concealed in white bandages.

Instead, she hit me with the force of a linebacker and wrapped her arms around my waist as she sobbed. I gently put a hand on the back of her head and whispered that everything would be all right.

She lifted her tear-stained face to look at me, and the sorrow in those familiar green eyes hit me in the gut like a punch.

"I'm sorry, Shot. I never think before I act. I should've known you wouldn't cheat on Presley. That's not who you are. She would've never been in that parking lot if it wasn't for me." Her sobs shook her whole body. I patted her uselessly on the back and sent Hill a pleading look to help me out.

"It was all a mess, Kody. It was bound to go badly from the start. I should have just been honest with Presley about what we were planning. I was trying to protect her, and instead I led her right into the line of fire. Let's keep the blame where it belongs, on the bad guys who don't care about anyone."

She nodded lightly and rubbed her damp cheeks furiously. I gratefully handed her off to the Texas Ranger when he reached for her. I was looking for a place to sit down before I fell over when a woman in a pair of scrubs suddenly entered the small space where we were gathered.

She offered a kind smile, her eyes skirting over the assembled family and me.

"We rushed the tests through and got a positive result with one probable donor." She cast a glance at each of the men, pausing when she got to the rodeo star who was pushing to his feet. "Crew Lawton?"

The dark-haired cowboy nodded as Della got to her feet and made her way over to her soon-to-be husband. They locked hands and shared an intense look. "I'm Crew Lawton."

The doctor nodded and gave him a lopsided smile. "I know. My husband is actually a big fan. He was an amateur rider when he was younger, so he follows the rodeo circuit pretty closely. You are almost a perfect match. There are more tests that need to be done, and you all need to consider that there is a much higher risk of the body rejecting the transplant when it is a male-to-female donor situation, but as of now, you are the best bet we have. If we expand the search, the chances of finding someone else with as many matching antigens is highly unlikely." Her smile turned soft and kind. "This is a big decision and highly risky on your part. Not to mention it may directly affect your career. Please think things over very carefully before you decide what you want to do. We've got Ms. Baskin as stable as possible for the moment."

The doctor spoke some more about dialysis and what they could do to keep Presley stable while they waited on the transplant.

When she finished, Crew didn't even hesitate to step forward and rasp, "I'm doing it. I don't care about the risks. If I'm a match, I'm doing it. I'm not going to let my sister die if there's something I can do about it."

Della immediately burst into tears and threw her arms around his neck. Aspen and Kody followed suit, and soon he was wrapped up in a group hug, surrounded by sobbing women. Both Case and Hill had tears in their eyes as well. It was actually kind of beautiful to see.

Presley had mentioned that Crew was the one slowest to welcome her to the family, that he was the one who still kept his distance. It looked like all those walls had dropped now.

Family was family in a crisis, and the Lawtons always stepped the hell up.

If my head hadn't been broken I more than likely would've had wet eyes right alongside them.

The doctor mentioned she would send a specialist in to speak with Crew and get the ball rolling. She also warned that the process had just started, and nothing was going to happen overnight. She indicated that not only was Presley going to need everyone to stay strong and healthy, but now, so was Crew.

When she went to walk past me, I reached out and caught her arm. She took one look at my bruised and battered face, and clicked her tongue. "You aren't supposed to be out of bed, are you?"

I grimaced and muttered a quiet no. She shook her head at me and asked, "Are you the boyfriend?"

I dropped my chin in acknowledgment since I was pretty sure nodding would actually kill me. "I am. How did you know?"

She hooked a thumb in the direction of the rest of the family gathered in the room. "They told me you were coming. They also said you were going to be the game changer. Ms. Baskin needs to fight. They told me you'd be the one to remind her she's a fighter."

I gulped, hard. Emotion clogged my throat, and those tears I was so sure I couldn't produce burned at the back of my eyes.

"Can I see her?" Even if she said no, I was going to make it happen. It would take an army to keep me away from her.

"Yes. But just for a few minutes. She has a very serious concussion as well. She hasn't woken up yet, but we're hopeful it will be soon. She's got a whole legion of different specialists in and out of the room at the moment, so just try and keep out of the way."

I nodded and immediately regretted it. However, I didn't complain. I just silently followed the doctor to Presley's room, nearly collapsing when I saw her in the hospital bed.

She had tubes and wires all over the place.

Her head was wrapped up in a manner similar to mine.

Her skin was a sickly grayish color, and the pretty red in her hair looked dull and flat.

She was so still and quiet. I hated it.

Now I was crying without a doubt. For the first time in a long time, there was no stopping the flood of emotion leaking out of my eyes. My heart hurt even worse than my head.

I stumbled to her side, picking up one of her hands like it was made of glass, so I didn't disturb all the medical equipment taped to the back of it. I ran my thumb over the faint thrum of her pulse and closed my eyes so I could ask whatever heavenly body I hadn't pissed off or forsaken to grant me a miracle.

I reached out and ran my index finger over the arch of one eyebrow that was exposed. She felt cold, and I swore I would do whatever I had to do to keep her with me.

If I had to pick her or the club, in that instant, I knew it would be her, hands down. I could do what my father had never been able to do and put family first. I just hoped it would be enough to convince her to stay with me.

I brought her fingers up to my face and put them against my cheek.

"You still owe me a favor, Presley. You can't leave a debt like that hanging." My voice cracked, and my entire chest felt like it was being crushed under an immense amount of pressure. "Please wake up. Please don't leave me. I'm asking you to pull through this because I'm pretty sure you love me, and I'm damn sure I'm in love with you." I closed my eyes and whispered, "Open your eyes so we can teach each other how to be in love."

She stayed still and remained cold to the touch, but I swore I saw her eyelids flutter.

The response wasn't much, but it was enough to give me hope, and I was going to hold on to that with everything I had.

CHAPTER 22

∞

PRESLEY

I knew I was alive because everything hurt.

Head to toe I felt like I was engulfed in flames of agony.

It was pretty jarring to go from nothing, an absolute void, to being awake and feverishly wishing for the darkness to come back so I could get a reprieve from the pain. While I was out, there hadn't been any kind of epiphany moment. No disembodied voices pulling me back. No vision of my mother telling me my time wasn't up. It should've been disconcerting, but it hadn't been. It'd been peaceful, and I missed the moments where I didn't feel like I was tangled up in a torment that wouldn't end.

There was a swarm of doctors and nurses fluttering around every time I opened my eyes. I was pretty sure Shot was there as well. I could smell the hint of leather in the room. It was comforting, but I was in no shape to have a conversation with him, or anyone. I was sure Kody had been standing by to hold my hand and to answer the doctors' questions on my behalf when it was too hard to open my eyes. I had a vague recollection of seeing her worried face hovering over me, and I distinctly recalled her whispering that Ashby would no longer be a problem for any of us, leading my sluggish thoughts to figure my former friend was the one who shot me, not the man with all the scars. But mostly, I couldn't focus on anything other than taking my next breath through the fog of painkillers and constant discomfort. When they said the struggle was real, this was what they had to mean by it.

I knew I'd undergone not one but two major surgeries. One resulting from the bullet I'd taken in the back when Ashby shot me, the other a kidney transplant I'd needed to save my life. I also knew the reason I'd been unconscious for more than a week was because I'd been winged by a bullet flying past my head and ended up with a concussion. In order to prevent edema from getting any worse, the doctors had decided a medically induced coma while they tried to keep me alive was my best bet if I wanted a full recovery. It was a lot to take in, and I was glad Kody had taken on the role of speaking for me and to me when I was unable to communicate.

It was also all so overwhelming there was no time or space to invest my limited energy in wondering and worrying about why Shot was in that motel room with Ashby. Now that I knew who the other woman was, the sense of betrayal and abandonment had all but dissipated. Even with my brain rattled and my body barely hanging on, I knew he wouldn't have been in that room with her without a solid reason.

It was several days later when I could finally keep my eyes open for more than a few minutes at a time and felt like I could move my limbs without wanting to throw up from the pain motion caused. There was still a fleet of medical personnel in and out of my room, but today there was also a very handsome man with dark hair and a concerned expression on his face parked next to my bed. I knew Crew was the one who donated the kidney that saved my life, but seeing the athletic and typically hearty man move slowly and carefully really drove home that he'd risked his life and career for me.

Faced with his sacrifice, I wanted to sob, felt the way my body fought to shake and quiver. However, I was still totally battered, so all I was capable of was silent tears and a whispered, "Thank you."

Crew had been the least welcoming. He was the one who still had suspicions about my intent toward my new family. And yet he'd saved my life because at the end of the day, we were family.

The charming rodeo rider gave me a lopsided grin and put a hand to his side where I knew we would eventually have a pair of matching surgical scars.

"It's rare to really get a second chance. I got one, so I know how special it is. Make sure you don't waste yours, Presley. Let's be sure we live well and take care of each other going forward. Family first from here on out." When he grinned at me I heard a nurse sigh, and if I'd been able to, I would've returned his smile.

I barely got the words "Family first" out to agree with him, when it all got too much. I closed my eyes to get my composure back under control and must've fallen asleep. When I opened them again, my other brother was in the room, and I could tell from a crack in the blinds over the window that it was starting to get dark.

Case looked ten times worse than Crew did, even though the younger one had just been through major surgery. His usual scruff was reaching actual beard stage, and his already silvery and black hair looked like there was more white threaded throughout. His eyes appeared tired, and there was no missing the dark circles underneath. His face looked slightly gaunt, and the deep grooves that fanned out from the corners of his eyes seemed even more pronounced than usual. Case was always ruggedly handsome and never really looked his age, but sitting slumped in an uncomfortable-looking chair next to my hospital bed, he looked every year he'd had to weather and win.

I must have made a sound alerting him to the fact I was now awake. Watching him, it was apparent he hadn't slept much and was stumbling over his own feet. He stopped at the side of my bed, and I was surprised enough to jolt slightly when he reached out and put one of his big, scarred hands over mine, being careful of the tubes and wires connected to the back. His touch was warm, but there was no mistaking the faint tremor in his fingers. Case was usually so stoic and so good at keeping himself contained. We were similar that way, so I knew that tiny quake was an indication there was an actual landslide of feelings happening inside the man.

"I sent Shot home." His words were extra raspy and his bright blue eyes shone with regret. "He's been by your side since the beginning. He isn't eating. I don't think he's slept more than a few hours. His club was threatening to storm the hospital if they didn't get proof of life, so I made him leave. It wasn't easy." Case sighed and softly squeezed his hand around mine. "He'll be back."

I blinked in surprise, because it hadn't crossed my mind to wonder if Shot had stayed by my side or not. I knew he'd been in the room while I was unconscious, because like always, that scent of leather and sunshine lingered behind him wherever he went. I didn't understand why Case was so adamant I didn't doubt the man I knew he'd warned away from me.

Case pulled his hand away from mine and curled it around

the rail of the hospital bed. His knuckles turned white as he clenched his fingers around the surface.

"I owe both of you an apology. I was the one who asked Shot to draw Ashby Grant out into the open. I was the one who urged him to keep the plan a secret from you. He wasn't with her because he wanted to be. He didn't have a choice." Case shook his head and sighed heavily once more. "If it had been up to Shot, Ashby would've disappeared from all our lives for good with no one being the wiser. He played by my rules because I convinced him it was better for you. I told him it would be best if she confessed to being involved in your mother's murder and if she confessed to screwing with your cases to cost you the promotion. I was the one who wanted you out of the way so my plan could work. So I'm the one who left you unaware Ashby was back and close enough to harm you. I fucked up. It wasn't Shot."

He sounded so remorseful and looked so devastated, my heart broke for him.

He was blaming himself for everything that had happened. I knew those feelings intimately. I'd drowned in blame when Ashby murdered our father because she wanted to hurt me. I let the guilt bury me when she burned their childhood home to the ground in an effort to further divide us. So while his plan had been flawed, the only person who was responsible for me being in my current state was my former friend.

It took a lot of effort and all the energy I had to reach up and put one of my hands over his. The tension in him was so tight that it felt like he might shatter at the slightest touch.

"Don't blame anyone...but Ashby, and that man." I awkwardly tried to pat his hand. "If Shot went along with your plan, he must've seen some truth in what you were saying. He doesn't blindly follow anyone. I was in the wrong place at the right time. It couldn't be helped."

It was a lot of words at once after I hadn't said anything in days. My throat was dry, and getting my tongue to work the way it should took some work. But it was important that Case didn't carry around the weight of what Ashby did any longer.

"Things went awry, but if I hadn't needed surgery, who knows when I would have found out disease was eating away at my kidneys. I felt fine but I was slowly dying. Getting shot might've saved my life. Things worked out the way they were supposed to, Case. You did what you did to protect me. I've never had a big brother before, but it seems like that's what you're supposed to do. I'm not mad at you and I'm not mad at Shot." Almost dying put things in perspective.

If you cared about someone, loved them, and knew they felt the same way about you, instead of running away or assuming the worst, you owed it to them to give them the benefit of the doubt. I knew Shot. Knew him better than I ever thought I would. Sure, it hurt to see him with another woman in a compromising position, but I should've known there was more to the story. I let my heart overrule my head and in hindsight regretted it. I was supposed to be smart, but then again, love made fools out of everyone.

"Things will work out with Shot if they are supposed to as well." And if they didn't, I'd be okay because I had him and Crew and Kody. No matter what I was facing in the future, I was no longer alone. I no longer had to stand by myself when the world was coming down around me.

Case cleared his throat aggressively and blinked his eyes rapidly. I knew he was fighting to keep back tears, and I was completely touched. I was also totally wiped out. My eyes drifted closed and my hand slipped away from his.

"You're probably tired. Go back to sleep. I'm gonna hang out until the doctor pops in to check on you and get an update on how you're doing. Now that you're awake, we hope we can take you home soon."

I dipped my chin just a little to agree, however I was asleep before I could lift it back up. Case might've seen and spoken with my doctor, but I slept through her coming and going. I didn't wake again until the faint light of dawn was coming through that crack in the blinds. This time when I peeled my eyes open, my gaze immediately landed on the slumped-over figure sleeping in the uncomfortable chair next to my bed.

Shot looked just as bad as Case had. He had the same gaunt appearance and his normally smooth jawline was peppered with dark stubble. He had dark shadows all over his face, and there was a frown between his heavy brows even though he seemed to be dead asleep. He had a thick, white bandage on the side of his head near his temple, and ugly dark bruises all over that side of his face. His hair was a mess, looking as if he'd combed it with his fingers. What was maybe most shocking about his appearance, he wasn't wearing the leather vest with all the patches that seemed to be as much a part of him as his tattoos were. Thus far, I'd only ever seen him without it when we were in bed.

He must've felt my eyes on him, because a few moments later his big body shifted in the chair and those inky eyes of his popped open. When our gazes locked, he audibly swallowed and slowly got to his feet.

"Case said he made you go home." I tried to keep my voice light, but I still didn't sound like myself and talking still took some work.

A lopsided grin crossed his face but immediately fell away. "Case isn't the boss of me. No one gets to tell me to stay away from you."

He blinked at me as he reached out a tattooed hand so that he could smooth some of my hair away from my face.

I was sure it was filthy and gross, but Shot didn't seem to mind. "I love you, Presley." He closed his eyes quickly and when he opened them back up I could see his heart shining out of the dark depths. "I almost lost the chance to tell you that I love you. I'm not going to let that happen again." He lowered his head, his voice a rough rasp as he assured me of what I already knew. "I've never said those words to another woman. To anyone, really. You have to know how special you are to me."

I wanted to tell him that I loved him as well, but I couldn't get my mouth to cooperate. Maybe the words were too heavy, too important. I coughed a little and motioned that I needed something to drink. He came back after a minute with a cup of ice chips and delicately helped me munch on a few until I could speak.

I caught his hand and held it to my cheek. He was so warm and for the first time since I'd hit the asphalt outside of the motel, my insides started to warm up.

"I love you, too, Shot. I wasn't sure what I was feeling, but you were the last person I thought about when I nearly died, and you were the first person I thought about when I knew I was going to live. I've never been in love before, so I was confused and careless with it, but I know now." I blinked up at him as emotion stormed through his typically unreadable eyes. "I want to be with you, no matter what." Even if it meant knowing there were times his club was going to come first. "Why don't you have your leather vest on?"

He started and looked down at himself. Surprise crossed his face in a flash as he shifted his weight uncomfortably. "I must've rushed out of the clubhouse and forgot it." He looked absolutely bewildered. "This is probably the first time since I started my own chapter that I haven't had it on." He gave a wry grin. "Top's gonna give me hell when I get back."

I tilted my head ever so slightly since too much movement still hurt. "You look different without it on."

One of his eyebrows arched upward. "I look like Palmer Caldwell instead of Shot."

I gasped a little and squeezed his hand as I realized I had never bothered to ask him what his real name was. To me, he'd always been Shot. That was who I'd fallen in love with. That was who I wanted to spend the rest of my life, or at least the rest of our love, with.

"Palmer?"

He chuckled and nodded. "Yeah. The only person who calls me that is Case. My real name goes on the paperwork when he's arrested me. He does it to remind me there's a man behind the motorcycle club president. It's a reminder I need sometimes." He looked down at me, his eyes suddenly serious and intent. "If you need me to be Palmer in order to be with you, I can. I'll do whatever it takes not to lose you, Pres. When you went down, when I saw you covered in blood that day—" he swallowed hard and turned his hand over so he was holding mine "—I knew I couldn't live without you. I can't say that about the club. If I ever left, or they forced me out, it would suck and I would miss it and the members, but I wouldn't feel like my life was over. Watching you nearly die—" he shook his head "—I know I can't give you up."

It was sweet sentiment, and I knew he meant it in the moment. I also knew that down the road if I made him walk away from something that was so much of what made him who he was, he would resent me and eventually feel like he had lost himself. We were both going to have to sacrifice in order to be together, but that didn't mean walking away from who we were.

"I like being with Shot. I understand him. I rely on him. I love him. But I won't say no to spending time with Palmer." I gave him wobbly smile and told him, "I want to know everything about you, and I want you to know everything about me."

"Nothing I learn is going to change my mind about being with you. Like I told you before, I'm always going to put you first." He leaned down so he could touch his lips to my forehead. "Don't see that changing anytime."

I closed my eyes and basked in his assurance and presence. "That's sweet, but still unrealistic. I didn't get that part of our disagreement wrong. My work is important. Sometimes I get so engrossed in the cases I'm working on I forget about the outside world. I have a family now, and occasionally they will have to come first, too. None of that means I'll love you less; it just means when those things happen I have to work twice as hard to show you how much you mean to me. It's all about balance. I overreacted that day because I was scared and frustrated at being out of control of my emotions. Loving someone means you're opening the door to inevitably being hurt by them, and I thought I could avoid that if I forced some space between us." When he looked like he wanted to argue I rushed to assure him, "I know it won't work now. I felt awful after our fight and I feel terrible for not giving you a chance to explain what was going on at the motel before everything went to hell. I won't make that mistake again. If we put each other first when we can, and understand in the times we can't, I think that's how we make things work between us. That's how we show that we really love and understand one another."

Shot was quiet for a long moment, and when he spoke his voice was full of raw sincerity. "We're both new to this love thing, so we're both bound to misstep here and there. We got time to figure it out, which I am so damn grateful for." He cleared his throat and dragged a hand down his face. "No more catching bullets. My heart can't take it."

I reached for his hand and closed my eyes as he laced our fingers together. I still hurt all over, but the spot in my chest where my heart was happily throbbing felt better than ever.

"Same to you. I'll consider it a personal favor if you stop getting shot as well."

"If I do that favor for you, you'll owe me one." There was a hint of humor in his tone, but I didn't know how much longer I could keep my eyes open. Pain was starting to filter in through the drugs again, and sleeping through it seemed easier than trying to put on a brave face so he, and whoever else popped up at my bedside, wouldn't worry.

"I owe you everything, Shot. I'll make good for the rest of my life."

EPILOGUE

∽

PRESLEY

Six months later

Y ou look good, Pres. Are you sure you aren't looking to get
yourself into some trouble tonight?" Shot's tone was teasing,
but the look in his dark eyes was serious.

I looked at his reflection as he came up behind me in
the mirror. He was always so ridiculously good-looking.
Even with the stark white scar that now decorated his
temple and made his hairline slightly uneven on one side.
Even with the rough stubble shadowing his jaw because
he'd been on the road with the club for the last few days
and apparently shaving hadn't been a priority. Even with
the flakes of drywall dust and flecks of paint dotting his
T-shirt from where he'd been helping me renovate the bathroom in my new house. Since he was a bathroom snob,
I'd let him run wild with the design and fixtures. He was
leaving his mark on other parts of the house, which I'd
bought shortly after being discharged from the hospital.

Like the way there were now jeans and T-shirts hanging next to my boring, professional work clothes in the newly expanded walk-in closets. And the way the master bathroom was unequivocally his baby and he wasn't going to stop tinkering until it was perfect. He loved that damn bathroom almost as much as he loved me. There was also a shiny new outdoor kitchen off the back of the house that was perfect for big barbecues and gatherings. I was sure the stainless steel grill got used more than my top of the line oven inside the actual house since it was what he preferred to cook on.

We didn't live together, per se. He still spent a good portion of his time out at the clubhouse, but when he didn't have club business to attend to, or when he'd been gone for an extended period of time, he would show up on my doorstep and camp out at my place until he got called away again. All in all, it wasn't too different from the way Hill and Kody's relationship worked, only when Hill was gone Kody knew where he was and that he was trying to save the world. When Shot was gone, all I could do was hope he made it back in one piece and that he hadn't put events in motion that were going to cause the world to burn. Honestly, I'd come to realize it was better if the club was raising hell as far away from Texas as possible. It meant our personal and professional lives were less likely to intersect. Shot mentioned the same thing and told me he was focusing more on the club's international pursuits versus the ones closer to home. So while it was never fun to have him gone, welcoming him home had become one of my most favorite things in the whole world. I'd learned to let all the worries I had take a back seat and to appreciate the time we did have together, because it was impossible to guess when those precious moments might be stolen away from us.

Unconsciously, I lifted a hand to touch the scar that slashed across my own temple. It was nearly identical to his, only mine was a little more jagged and didn't quite reach into my hairline. We'd gone from being so different and seemingly having nothing in common to sharing something permanent and unmissable that was going to tie us together forever. The scars felt more important than a wedding ring and more purposeful than any tattoo. They were a constant reminder of what we'd come so close to losing. They represented a start line and a finish line. They showed us that everything that mattered, everything that should be cherished, began and ended with us. Together we survived. Together we were better than we were apart.

I was no longer alone. I was no longer lonely.

"You know I won't drink anything. I'm just going to spend time with the girls." The kidney transplant had been touch and go for the first few months. For a few tense weeks, it seemed like my body might reject the donation. So once I was in the clear, I made sure to do whatever I could to take care of Crew's generous gift. I wanted to be around for as long as possible, so giving up something frivolous like alcohol was no sacrifice.

Shot snorted and moved farther into the room. He wrapped his arms around my waist and rubbed his chin on my exposed shoulder. His stubble rasped against my skin and left a red mark, which I'm sure was the point. His fingers skimmed along the side of my stomach, reverently tracing the big scar hidden under the slinky fabric of my silver dress. Della insisted we dress up tonight, since the actual wedding had been such an informal affair.

As soon as I was out of the hospital and strong enough to travel, Della and Crew announced that instead of their cute country wedding with all the trappings getting pushed back once again, they were going to Vegas to elope. According to Della, the details no longer mattered—she just wanted to be Crew's wife. The designer dress was left behind, and the groom ended up wearing jeans, boots, and his Stetson after all. The whole family attended, and they even invited Shot. It was fun and romantic, and so oddly fit the couple, but now that some time had passed, Della decided the one part of the traditional wedding she missed out on and wanted to make up for was the bachelorette party.

I think she was just looking for an excuse to get a very pregnant and very cranky Kody out of the house. As some-one who was always in motion, always up to something and involved in everyone else's business, being slowed down by her big belly and uncontrollable fatigue, as well as hounded by persistent nausea, had Kody ready to climb walls and ready to fight everyone. It was probably a good thing she'd convinced Hill not to quit the Rangers. We all wondered if he would've survived if he'd been home for the entire pregnancy. He'd taken leave the last couple of months so he could be there for Kody as her due date got closer and closer, and he'd definitely taken the brunt of her chronic bad mood. There was no doubt Hill loved my sister with every fiber of his being, because I had no doubt any other man would've ducked for cover and called a time-out long ago.

"You can't drink. Kody can't drink. Why don't you guys go somewhere else other than a strip club?" His midnight eyebrows lifted questioningly as I blushed when his hands started slipping and sliding over the silky surface of my dress. The simplest touch from him still had heat crawling up my neck and into my cheeks, even though there was no part of my body he hadn't claimed as his own. I belonged to him, heart, body, and soul, which could be very scary at times. However, he always reminded me that he belonged to me in the same way, and that took some of the fear away.

"The strip club was Kody's idea. I think she assumed Della would balk and then she wouldn't have to go." But Della knew Kody well and called her bluff. So now we were all getting dressed up, heading to dinner, and then going to watch a bunch of oiled-up beefcakes shake their stuff. It wasn't how I pictured spending the next girl's night with everyone, but nowadays I was pretty much game for anything. Now that I'd gotten a second chance to live my life, I wasn't going to do it with any hesitation. I was all about embracing new experiences and adventures. The unknown was no longer my enemy and biggest fear. Shot was the one who taught me that the best way to conquer the things I was most afraid of was by going out and experiencing them for myself. That included my fear of falling in love with him.

Loving Shot didn't hurt nearly as much as facing the possibility I might not even get the chance to try. It was also less terrifying than thinking I might die having never been able to let him know just how much I cared about him. He was the first man I'd let push me out of my comfort zone, and now that I knew what it felt like to run wild with him, I never wanted to go back to my safe and secure little bubble.

Turning in his arms, I put my hands on his shoulders and lifted up on my toes so I could kiss his chin. The stubble tickled my lips. I liked the way it made him look even more rakish. Almost like a modern-day pirate.

"I won't be out too late. Trust me, I know what I have at home will always be better than anything else out there." I grinned. "And I bet Case gave Aspen a curfew."

Of course, I was kidding. There was no couple in existence who had a more balanced and equal relationship than Case and Aspen. However, ever since he popped the question and

put a very big, very sparkly ring on her finger, his posses-
siveness had seemed to ramp up a few notches. It was almost
like he was afraid she was going to remember what a jerk
he'd been before they started dating and change her mind.
Everyone who wasn't the surly sheriff knew that would never
happen, but it was good that Aspen kept Case on his toes.

Aspen hadn't really been eager to remarry after her first
marriage ended in disaster, but she'd become very fond of
and deeply invested in one of the teenagers involved in one
of her more complicated cases and was beyond frustrated
that the court had declined her offer to foster the young man
because she and Case weren't officially married. It was a
common prejudice that women faced in small-town America,
and especially in the South. Knowing they were going to be
together until the end regardless, Case decided it was time
for both of them to take a second chance on marriage. It was
just a bonus that they would be able to help out a kid in need
once they did.

Shot snorted at my comment and let me walk him backward
toward the king-sized bed in the center of the room. There
were so many nice things about being in my own house. A
luxury bathroom and a big bed were just a few. I also liked
that I didn't really have any close-by neighbors, which was
beneficial when I suddenly had a gaggle of bikers over.

The club was his family, and thereby had started to
become an extension of mine.

Shot and I agreed that it was better for me to keep my
distance from the clubhouse unless there was an emergency.
However, I'd had to close more than one bullet wound since
Stitch was getting older and less able as the tasks the club
took on grew more and more varied and dangerous. He was
still the club's first choice to fix them up, but when the
injuries were really serious, like life or death, they knew

they could call me. I couldn't say no, even though I knew I should, which meant I'd earned my stripes as far as the rest of the club members were concerned, even Top. Those who questioned why Shot was with me, or if I was a good fit for his lifestyle, were silenced once they saw how beneficial I could be. And I think Top finally realized that I loved his best friend so I would do my best to protect him, which meant keeping secrets that weren't mine to share, and accepting that what I didn't know couldn't hurt me.

Another thing I liked about having property and a place of my own was that I now had room for a dog. I hadn't committed to bringing one home yet, but it was on my to-do list. I wanted to wait until more of the renovations were done. I was finally settling in somewhere that felt like it wasn't going to go anywhere. I felt like I could finally plant some roots and I was excited to see what was going to grow.

I also had room for family. I could host holiday dinners and weekend barbeques, taking some of the pressure off of Aspen, who was normally the one making room for everyone. I'd never had to cook or plan an event for the family before, but I was excited to take on the task. It made me feel connected to the Lawtons in an all-new way. There was no more keeping them at arm's length and treading carefully. After Crew risked his life and his livelihood for me, I could no longer pretend like I would be okay if they were suddenly yanked away from me. I loved them all and could feel that they loved me. We were all still learning about each other, but it was the best education I'd ever received.

Crew and I had instantly bonded much tighter than we had been prior to the transplant. I literally had a piece of him inside me, keeping me alive. There would never be a big enough way I could show him my gratitude; luckily he was pretty selfless about the whole thing. I often teased him that it was having some of his wildness inside of me that made it possible for me to handle being with Shot. The biker and the rodeo rider were cut from very similar fabric, and now that the two had spent some time together, they got along pretty well. They weren't exactly friends, but they were something close to it, which made the big gatherings less stressful. Case and Hill still watched Shot like a hawk, but there was a level of begrudging respect, and relief that everyone was alive and well, that permeated through any animosity these days.

We were family—a dysfunctional one, but a family nonetheless.

When the backs of Shot's legs hit the side of the bed, I gave him a little push until he fell over onto his back. I brushed some of the white dust out of his black hair and dragged the tip of my finger down the bridge of his nose and across his lips. I traced an outline around his mouth and grinned when his dark eyebrows danced upward. He wasn't the only one who could take initiative, at least not anymore. He taught me how to be bold and to be fear-less. He taught me to see all those things he loved about me on a regular basis, and I did my best to put them into action.

He stacked his tattooed hands behind his head and watched me with unreadable obsidian eyes as I reached for the hem of his T-shirt. I admired the delineated lines of his cut abs and the sharp V on either side of his hips. I took in the designs marked onto his skin, which I had memorized with my mouth and hands. He had added some new ink since I'd been released from the hospital. He had a guardian angel on his ribs and a single heartbeat across the side of his neck. He said it was the same beat that registered when I finally opened my eyes after being unconscious. I appreciated the raised scars on his flesh that reminded me how lucky I was to have him, and I knew I would never squander a single minute of being with him because he could be taken away any second of any day.

"Aren't you going to be late picking up Kody?" The question was asked in a gruff tone as I moved my hands to the buckle of his belt and started working the leather free. I could feel that he was already hard and see the way his muscles had tensed in anticipation.

"She won't mind if I'm a little late." In fact, she would probably appreciate it. "She understands I'm all about seizing the moment."

I was going to seize more than the moment as soon as I got his pants and boxer-briefs off. I tugged at the fabric that was in my way, urging him to lift his hips so I could slide everything down his thighs. His ruddy erection pointed upward, already looking slick across the smooth head. I stuck my tongue out to lick across my suddenly dry lips and heard Shot groan in response. Swallowing back a laugh, I leaned forward so I could drop a kiss on his mouth. He tasted like coffee and cream. Sweet and bitter, which was a perfect representation of him. I kissed him again, this time flicking my tongue against his until both our lips were wet and slippery.

When I pulled back he groaned his complaint, only the sound quickly shifted to a gasp when I started to kiss my way down the center of his body. I dragged my teeth over his Adam's apple and stopped to circle each of his flat nipples with my tongue. I licked my way down his tattooed chest and across the rock-hard plane of his stomach muscles. I let the tip of my tongue dip into the indent of his belly button and tickled the fine hairs of his happy trail with my fingertips. By the time I reached my destination, I could practically feel the way his cock was throbbing and when I circled the hefty length with my hand, I felt it kick in response to the light touch.

Shot swore softly when I lapped at the already damp head. He shifted so he could clutch at my hair when I started to circle my tongue around the leaking slit as I lightly squeezed the wide base. I knew what he liked now, knew that he liked things both soft and hard. The dual sensations always seemed to make him lose his mind. I traced along the heavy vein on the underside of the rigid flesh and grinned at the wet kiss of the tip against my cheek. I always felt so powerful, so desired and loved, when I knew he was responding to me as strongly as I always responded to him.

I took him into my mouth, sliding my mouth down as far as I could without gagging. I found a comfortable rhythm, bobbing my head up and down as his big, strong body writhed underneath my hands and mouth. I sucked until my cheeks hollowed and his entire length was wet and slippery. I could tell he was getting close to completion when he started pulling my hair and when his hips lifted haphazardly from the bed.

It was music to my ears when he moaned my name and I couldn't tell if he was begging me to stop or urging me to keep going. I pulled off of him with a sexy *pop* and got to my feet, so I was standing between his legs. He looked like some kind of ancient warrior, lying there, waiting there to be serviced and satisfied. When he reached for me, I shimmied out of his grasp so I could lift the hem of my dress up and slid my fancy, lacy panties down my legs.

Shot gave me a quizzical look when I climbed on the bed and hovered over him, my legs on either side of his hips. The silver dress slithered across my skin and pooled in a silky puddle around where I was braced over him. There was something undeniably sexy about having him under me, completely naked and exposed, while I was still mostly covered up.

I put a hand on the center of his chest as I reached the other one between our bodies. I let out a little moan when I dragged the tip of his erection through my already wet folds and felt it nudge and press against all the right places.

Shot chuckled and I felt the vibration blast through all of my nerve endings. "If you aren't careful, you're going to have to change your dress before you go." Sex with him could be soft and sweet, but it could also be rough and messy. I liked both variations, as long as he was the one I was with.

"I have another dress." What I didn't have was the patience to worry about ruining this one if I got a little too into the moment. I liked it when things got a little messy and we had to clean everything up afterward.

Shot's big hands locked onto my hips in an almost punishing hold. He lifted me up a little bit, reminding me just how strong and forceful he could be. The material of my dress slid across my skin, which was an unexpectedly erotic kind of caress. The heat and hardness of his hands clashed with the soft, slippery material. The contrasting sensations had my skin feeling like it was on fire as my blood blazed underneath.

He lifted his hips in a powerful upward thrust just as I started to sink down onto his waiting shaft. He instantly went as deep as he possibly could, filling me up and spreading heat throughout my body. I gasped at the sharp pleasure and curled my hands into fists where they rested on his broad chest. I rocked forward and rotated my hips as I sank back down.

Shot's long eyelashes fluttered and his fingers dug even deeper into my hips. His eyes watched my every little expression as I started to ride him in earnest. Spending all that time on the back of his bike once we'd gotten our relationship back on track had proven beneficial. I'd learned to move with him instinctively, with a rhythm that was bound to make us both lose our minds.

One of his hands snaked under my dress and found my own raised scar. He always touched it, traced it, caressed it. I thought it might be his favorite part of my body because that scar meant I was still here. It meant I could fight with him. I could ride with him. And it meant I could love him. He always mentioned he would've loved me forever even if I hadn't pulled through the extensive operations I needed to save my life, but because of the transplant I was here to love him back.

The room filled with the sensual sounds of our heavy breathing, and the sounds of our bodies rocking together. I moaned his name and felt my insides clench tightly around him when his hips suddenly kicked upward. His eyes drifted closed as a rush of heat unfurled inside of me. I felt every throb and pulse of his cock as his body went lax with pleasure and satisfaction. Before I could form a coherent thought, his hand skated across my overly sensitive skin and dipped between my legs. His fingers unerringly found that tiny, hidden spot that was sure to set me off. It only took a slight touch, a tiny little circle, before I followed him over the edge.

I sighed and leaned forward so I could rest my forehead against his. We were both a little sweaty and I'd left lipstick smeared all over him, but we'd never looked or felt better, I was sure of it.

One of Shot's hands lifted and cupped the back of my head. His lips touched mine in the lightest of kisses and he whispered, "Do me a favor. Don't let any of those pretty boys touch you tonight. Don't let them grind on you or get close enough to breathe on you. No one is allowed to put their hands on the woman I love. I might lose my mind if I think about it too much and if I do that..."

I let out a little sound of annoyance. "If you do that then you'll send your boys to break up the party and no one will leave happy."

He chuckled but had the good grace to look sheepish. "Probably."

I shifted so I could drop a kiss on the tip of his nose. "You'll owe me one."

He smoothed his hand up my back and pulled me down so I was wrapped in his arms. "Good thing I have the rest of my life to make good."

He made good every single day. And he made every single day good.

AUTHOR'S NOTE

Hi all!

I hope you enjoyed this wild ride through Loveless. It was a blast, wasn't it?!

I just wanted to take a moment and share some fun little tidbits with you about the Sons of Sorrow and some of the locations alluded to throughout the series.

First of all, as some of you may know, the Sons of Sorrow were introduced in my Marked Men series back in 2013. Shot's dad, Torch, plays a key part in my book *Rome*. It was interesting to learn a little bit more about the man who made Shot who he was. And since the club was based in Colorado, it's loosely based off of the Sons of Silence. I'm pretty sure I have mentioned that before as well.

Second, do you have any idea how hard it is to write a book with a biker and a club, and not have all those bad boys and their hijinks take over the whole book!? It's real hard...LOL. I never planned on writing a motorcycle club book. I love to read them, but I know very little about the actual lifestyle and frankly didn't have time to become a biker babe myself. At its core, *Blacklisted* is a book about two people who are on the outside of life, the world, their families, society…each really finding their niche and place where they thrive, and then finding the person who completes them without forcing them to change. I still wanted this book to be mostly about family and friends, with a lot of romance and a splash of suspense. And I still wanted it to have that cozy and warm small-town feel…the bikers were just a bonus. It was a delicate balance I hope I achieved.

Third, Loveless and Ivy are made up. But they could honestly be any of the tiny towns that sprawl out past Austin toward Lake Travis and between Austin and New Braunfels. And when I'm talking about the bar with the tin roof where the skinheads are, I am totally picturing the Chupacabras' clubhouse in Jonestown on the way to the lake. I think it's shut down now, but it's exactly the kind of sketchy bar/building I described.

Also, I am aware that the timeline from finding out about Presley's illness after she gets shot, to the medical testing is very rushed and not realistic in the slightest. But sometimes a writer has to take liberties with fact to make the fiction flow. It really would've slowed the story and the buildup of such a critical point to have everyone wait around for days and even weeks for the results. So, I sincerely apologize to those who are sticklers for exact details and hope you can understand where I'm coming from on the creative side. Hopefully you're so invested in what's happening on the page, there's no place for boring reality to be a burden! ☺

ACKNOWLEDGMENTS

This is where I shamelessly beg and plead with you to drop a short review of *Blacklisted*. Good, bad, or ugly...any review is so, so helpful to a new release and to the author. Your review is far more likely to attract a new reader than anything I say or do! Please help a gal out. ❤

If you've read any of my books, or if you're new to me and *Blacklisted* is a first, I'm sure you can tell how much I love an opposites-attract story line. There is just something really special and extra interesting about bringing together two people/characters who shouldn't work. Finding the beauty and appreciation in those differences is my favorite. It was also really fun to write two people who don't really relate well. I'm writing this with Valentine's Day right around the corner, and I have to say, I so feel Presley and her resistance to romance and relationships. That's never been my thing, either, and it would take someone really special and dynamic, like Shot, to get me to change my viewpoint. ☺

As always, a huge shoutout to anyone who blogged about, posted about, talked about, and shared *Blacklisted* and the rest of the Loveless series. The heart and soul, and ultimate success, of any book is in your hands. I sincerely appreciate every single person who helps give one of my stories life and love. You da best. ❤

The Loveless series has brought so many new readers into the fold, so I just want to say, "Welcome to the Crowd!" We're chaotic and crazy like the Lawtons, badass like the bikers, and almost all of us have HUGE hearts. Thanks so much for being here and allowing me to chase every dream I've ever had.

A huge thanks to the girl gang that surrounds me and helps me be a better version of myself. I'm a better Jay and a much better writer because of all the women in my life. Shout-out to my new editor, Madeleine. It's not easy to jump into an existing series and to tackle a hero the readers have been dying to know more about, but Madeleine dived in headfirst and fearlessly. She was easy to work with, and she really did make Shot shine. My agent, Stacey, who is a real-life superwoman. My friend/assistant, Jill of all trades, Mel. My publicist, Jessica. And my kickass beta team who still stick around even though they know how ugly and terrible my rough drafts tend to be. Any part of the story you love, they made it 1,000 percent better! Thanks for being rad and super-duper helpful Sarah, Pam, and Alexandra. Honestly, don't know what I would do without you ladies.

Until next time! If you are interested in keeping up with me these are all the places you can find me on the web. I strongly suggest joining my reader group on Facebook and following me on Bookbub. Those are the best places for updates!

Bookbub: bookbub.com/authors/jay-crownover

Website: jaycrownover.com

My store: shop.spreadshirt.com/100036557

FB page: facebook.com/AuthorJayCrownover

Twitter: twitter.com/jaycrownover

Instagram: instagram.com/jay.crownover
Pinterest: pinterest.com/jaycrownover
Spotify and Snapchat: Jay Crownover
I strongly suggest joining my reader group on FB. I hang out in there a lot and you get pretty much unlimited access to me:

facebook.com/groups/crownoverscrowd

If you're enjoying the Loveless, Texas Series,
don't miss the thrilling first novel

Justified

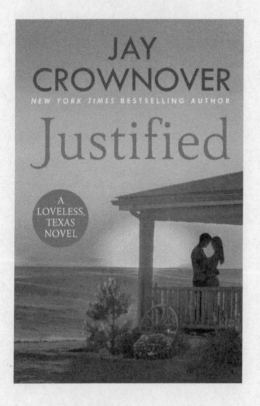

Available now from

HEADLINE
ETERNAL

Return to Loveless, Texas in the exciting second novel

Unforgiven

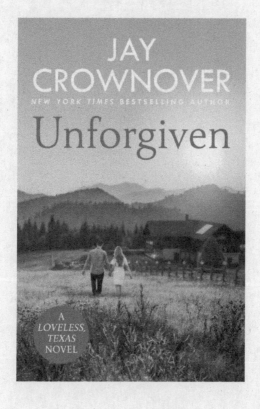

Available now from

HEADLINE
ETERNAL